BAD BOYS DO IT *Better* 3

In Love With an Outlaw

A NOVEL BY

PORSCHA STERLING

I need a gangsta
To love me better
Than all the others do

To always forgive me
Ride or die with me
That's just what gangsters do

- Kehlani

Janelle

"*Y*ou might feel a little pinch."

I closed my eyes, sucked in a sharp breath and tried to think about rainbows or unicorns… anything that could settle my mind. And then, just as I was able to conjure up an image of the perfect rainbow, complete with a leprechaun at the end of it holding a pot of gold, there was a pinch, no a stab, right through my flesh.

"OWWWWW!"

"Punk."

Cutting my eyes at Luke, I frowned, pushing my lips out in disapproval at the teasing grin on his face.

"I'm not a punk! That hurt."

He only smiled. He was doing that more and more often and I loved seeing it.

"Done," the woman above me said, pulling away her instrument of torture. "See, that was it!"

Pursing my lips, I looked down at the small piercing on my navel. The pain had just begun to subside and I could fully appreciate her work. It was cute. The owl belly ring that Luke had picked out for me sat nicely at the top, pressed snuggly against my flat stomach.

"It's beautiful," I whispered.

1

Luke bent down and kissed it gently, erupting a series of butterflies in my stomach. I squeezed my thighs closed and tried to ignore the aching in my middle. We'd been at it all night and I was sore, but my body was still begging for more torture.

"We really came in here for tats but she punked out," Luke informed the woman who was now sitting at my side and I felt my cheeks go hot when she gave me a side eye, accompanied by a mocking smirk. Yeah, I knew what she was thinking. She had a full sleeve of tattoos, piercings all down her ears from top to bottom, in her nose, her lips and God only knew where else. But I was not the type of person who welcomed this type of torture.

"There is still time baby," Luke whispered, leaning close to my ear.

I shuddered when he flicked his tongue out and licked my earlobe. It had been this way since I left my apartment with him the night before. He craved me with no shame and no care of whoever was around. I wasn't used to the public displays of affection, but I enjoyed it all too much to push him away.

"No, I don't think I can right now…you can still get whatever you wanted, but I'll wait."

He shook his head.

"No, I won't get that one until you're ready for yours."

Handing the woman a few bills to cover the payment and tip, he grabbed my hand into his and we walked out of the storefront together, as a couple. For the first time ever, I was his and he was mine, but it was no longer a secret that we cherished together while holed up inside of my small apartment. It was now something we were willing to share with the world, without fear and without wondering if they approved of our love. There was no better feeling than being free.

"You passed the car," I informed him when I noticed that we were walking much farther than we had to come into the store.

"No, I didn't. That's not what we're getting into right now."

Smirking, I cut my eyes in his direction and saw him biting back a smile while trying to keep his attention straight ahead. Unable to resist my probing stare any longer, he turned slightly and glanced at me for only a second. Still, I saw the twinkling in his eyes. He was hiding something, and I knew it was a surprise. I sighed and didn't press further. I'd enjoy the wait.

We stepped into a building right in the middle of Manhattan. A tall skyscraper filled with offices that housed several top-level companies. I instantly felt out of place in my jeans, Converses, and hoody, surrounded by what looked like executives all in suits. Luke, on the other hand, was completely at ease. He'd switched up his style and, though different, it was so sexy to me. The gold grill was gone and he had swapped the jeans for slacks, the Giuseppe sneakers for Giuseppe loafers, and had on a button down with the sleeves pulled up, showing off his sculpted, tattooed arms. The jewelry remained—he wasn't willing to make those kind of changes. He was on his grown man and I was loving every bit of it. And every bit of him.

I wasn't loving the extra attention he was getting. Luke always drew the focus of women in the hood, but now? It didn't matter if it was a black chick from Brooklyn or a white one who was the chair of a Fortune 500 company, he had them all salivating over him. It didn't matter if all they could get was a simple glance in their direction, they were panting for it. And God forbid if he actually waved…

But he was mine. *All* mine.

"Hello, Mr. Murray. Wow, you look…"

A young white woman with blond hair and a slender build walked up to us and lost her words, actually and completely lost them, as she looked at Luke.

"Thank you," was all he said with a small smile. Her eyes fluttered and she stammered her next sentence, struggling to regain her composure.

"Y—you just look different… in a very good way. I mean…" She paused and her eyes came to mine. I gave her a warm smile to relax her. I wasn't a jealous person, and I knew the effect seeing Luke had on her because he had the same effect over me.

"Is it ready?"

"Y—yes, it is, Mr. Murray. Everything is exactly as you requested it. Bob will escort you there. And you'll need these." She handed him a folder of papers. "It's just a little something I put together to make sure everything is perfectly set up for you. Enjoy!"

Without a smile, Luke nodded his head and turned around to look at another man who was walking towards us, pale and balding with a bright smile.

"Mr. Murray! It's so nice to see you!" He reached out to shake Luke's hand and then turned to me. "And who do we have here?"

He reached his hand out to me as well but Luke didn't loosen his grip, instead he laced his fingers between mine, deepening our embrace. Bob's eyes connected with Luke's and he understood, tucking his hand back into his pocket. Caught off guard, I didn't know what to do, but Luke stepped in.

"This is Janelle." And then he added with a tiny smile, almost childish in nature, "And I would let her shake your hand but I'm not ready to let go of it yet."

My heart skipped a beat and I blushed. Bob's eyes ping-ponged between the both of us as he smiled brightly. I didn't know the type of relationship he and Luke had, but it was obvious he was surprised and delighted to see him act this way over me.

"Well, in that case, it's very nice to meet you, Janelle. I'm Bob, a long-time business partner of Mr. Murray's. Both of you can follow me."

Bob led us through the building and to the elevators. All throughout our walk, people greeted Luke, addressing him with the utmost respect, to which he always replied with a subtle nod of his head. It was as if the boss was in the building. We were the only black spots in a sea of white ones dressed in custom made suits and pricey shoes, but everyone from the lowest to the highest knew Mr. Murray had walked through the door and made sure to make contact with him.

I was intrigued. I was beginning to see the type of hold Luke had on people, whether male or female. I was so used to the man he was with me, that I'd forgot that his named meant something; not just in the hood but throughout the city. He made shit happen and people respected that. Whether they agreed with how he did it or not, the fact was they still wanted to remain in his good graces.

We were led into an elevator and went up to the highest floor. The entire time my stomach was bubbling with excitement. I could barely contain it. Bob was in front of us and we stood side-by-side, hand-in-hand behind him. Luke pulled me close to him so that I was standing in front and he wrapped his arms around my stomach. I felt him breathe in deeply and then lean down to kiss me on my ear before whispering softly,

"You smell so good."

I melted like hot butter.

When we stepped off of the elevator, all I heard was the loud sound of propellers. The wind whipped around us viciously but Luke held me tight, wrapping his arms around me to block out the cold. And then I saw ita helicopter. With my eyes wide, I turned to Luke and jabbed him in his stomach as Bob trotted away towards it with his head ducked down.

"Ow, shit, Nell! Yo' boney ass elbows hurt!"

"Where are you taking me?" I asked, giggling as he rubbed the place I'd hit him. I could no longer restrain my excitement or hold my peace. I needed answers now.

"I'm taking you away. This helicopter is going to take us to a jet. The jet is going to take us somewhere else. And we will be at that somewhere for however long it takes for you to get your plans straight."

I was confused.

"What plans?"

Looking away, Luke licked his lips and let out a low chuckle. I watched as he pushed his tongue through the inside of his cheek a bit before he began to speak. I was so on edge and he was killing me.

"Nell, when it comes to you, I'm not believing in doing no small time shit. You had grand dreams when I met you and I want them to be even grander now that you're with me. So I'm takin' you away and yes, it's a vacation and yes, I will enjoy your body." His lust-filled eyes fell below my neckline and I felt my skin prickle as he looked me up and down. "But I want you to make me a list of anything and everything you want for your career and I'm gonna make it happen for you."

I squinted up at him, a smirk tickling the edge of my lips.

"*Anything*?"

He looked straight at me with a deadpan expression, no smile, no laugh hidden behind his eyes, nothing.

"Anything. I don't care if you say you wanna be the fuckin' President of the United States… whatever you write down, I'm going to make it happen by any means necessary. I won't let you have any regrets because you chose me."

He spoke with absolute confidence and certainty, but there was a hint of dangerousness there. 'By any means necessary' he said, and I knew that was exactly what he meant. Whatever he had to do and whoever he had to get rid of for me to get what I wanted, he had no issues doing it. Luke was a dangerous man, and I knew there was a side of him that would scare me, a side I probably never wanted to see, but right then and there, I decided to put a blind eye to it—to not think of it. There was a lot of forgiveness in the heart of a woman when it came to her man, and we were no different.

"I have no regrets," I told him and kissed him gently on his cheek. The embrace relaxed him and he sighed.

"And that's how I want it to stay."

He grabbed me and pulled me towards the helicopter, both of us ducking down as we neared it.

"Can you at least tell me where we are going?" I yelled over the blaring sound of the propeller. Luke glanced at me, smiling so sexily that I momentarily forgot my question.

"I'mma take you to the moon, baby," he joked, and I rolled my eyes and laughed. But to be honest, I already felt like he had me there.

Janelle

*A*s much money as my family had, we didn't vacation often. Being the daughter of a, high-profile attorney meant that we maybe got one vacation a year and, even that was often shortened by whatever case my father was working on. So the thought of Luke dropping everything just to take me away to get my mind off my family problems was not only exciting to me, but it also made my love for him grow. Although he wasn't an attorney or a professional by any standards, he was just as busy and I knew it had to be costing him to drop everything in order to leave with me. Still, he did it without complaints.

"It's beautiful here," I said in awe as the small jet began to descend on an island that seemed nearly vacant outside of a few small houses and a large one that sat on top of a hill.

It was completely tranquil…so far removed from the hustle and bustle of the city, the overcrowded sidewalks, and the smoke and smog that littered the air. There was green vegetation everywhere, rainforests upon rainforests of trees, waterfalls, and wildlife. This was truly a paradise and the more I saw, the more I wondered if I'd ever want to go back home.

"You like it, huh?" Luke asked with a half-smile, almost as if he wasn't sure whether or not he'd picked the right place for our impromptu vacation.

I took my time pulling my eyes away from the sight in front of me and then turned to look at him, confused about the fact that he genuinely seemed unsure about my response. Was he crazy? This was insane! What man, that you know, could just whisk you off in the middle of the day to some island that resembled something that only Beyoncé and Jay Z could afford? I half expected little Blue to be running around or splashing in the water. It completely took my breath away.

"I don't just like it, I love it. It's amazing…"

The jet headed towards the biggest home on the entire island. Actually, calling it a home didn't do it justice. It was an estate! It was an all-white tropical style home with some obvious Spanish influences when it came to the structure. It couldn't be sitting on anything less than ten acres which included a beautiful garden, an infinity pool, tennis court… it was laid. It was the type of home that I could only wish to be able to afford once I fully stepped into my role as an attorney. If I worked hard enough, I knew I could get something just like it or better. Well… maybe not better but damn close!

"The president of the island must live there," I told Luke, pointing at the house that was now officially my dream house. "Or a celebrity! You think Beyoncé is in there?! Oh my GOD, if she's in there, I'm going to have a fit. Hand me my phone so I can take pictures and Google because I heard from the Beyhive that she was on some island vacay this week and if she's in there, I'm ready to go to jail TODAY! I can't believe—"

I wanted to say more, but then I noticed that the jet began to slow as it approached the massive white home, and all air stopped being produced in my lungs. I just knew I was about to faint. Looking over to Luke, I noted the sly smirk on his face and I was so overcome with joy that I almost hopped right into his lap. He knew how much I loved the queen! I was about to have a whole cow if he had really managed to fly me out to meet her.

"Calm down," he said, laughing hard as he looked at the growing excitement on my face. "This spot belongs to a queen but it ain't Queen Bey."

Crinkling my brow, I turned back to look out the window, still excited but confused about who it was that he'd brought me to meet. Luke continued to watch me, chuckling a little, but I ignored him. He was getting a kick out of making me wait. Evil ass.

The jet landed on a pad out from the property and I wasted no time grabbing my purse and standing up to get off. Luke cut his eyes to me, still humored by my eagerness, and then grabbed my hand to help me off. Once we stepped off the jet, I took in a deep breath and realized for the first time how much I missed the fresh air. The weather was perfect; there wasn't a cloud in the sky, and it was the perfect temperature outside: not too humid and a gentle breeze to give some reprieve from the hot sun. I didn't know places like this existed.

"Mr. Murray, it's nice to see you," a man said from my side. I turned towards the voice and saw an older black man driving a golf cart towards us.

"It's nice to see you too, Mr. Jerome. How's your wife?"

The man smiled deeply, showing the love he felt for his wife all over his face, and then nodded his head.

"She's better now. I thank you for the generous contribution you made to—"

"Don't mention it," Luke said, stopping him.

I gave him a curious glance, but he didn't turn to meet my eyes. I was smart enough to put everything together without him giving me any confirmation. Luke and his brothers took plenty of things illegally, but it seemed like they always gave back to the ones who needed it. They took care of the people around them. Who could fault them for that?

In the passenger seat was a woman dressed in a nice black dress that was cut right above her knees. She stepped off once the cart stopped and held up a bucket that was on her lap containing water. She held it out to me, offering me one but I politely refused. I was ready to get to the house and see what was going on.

"Would you like one, Luke?" she asked, and the way she referred to him as 'Luke' rather than 'Mr. Murray', like everyone else I'd met recently, gave me pause. I cut my eyes at the woman and noted the interaction between her and Luke, paying special attention to the glimmer in her eyes when she looked at him.

"Naw, I'm good. Thanks, Yancy," he replied back nonchalantly, but I continued to scrutinize the woman.

I wasn't jealous but I also wasn't dumb and she was cute. Yancy, as he referred to her, was about my height and had a thin build like me but… it just looked different on her. You know those thin chicks who still manage to look thick? That was Yancy. She had ass and breasts and, even though she didn't have a whole lot of either, when you placed it next to her tiny waist, she looked like she was built like a video vixen. She was pretty in the face and I noticed that right off but, being that I wasn't naturally jealous, it never occurred to me to think anything about it. But now, her almond-shaped eyes, beautiful brown skin and pouty lips had me second-guessing how close I wanted the Bernice Burgos lookalike to my man.

"This is my daughter Tiyancy," Mr. Jerome offered, urging my attention towards him. It was then that I realized he must have seen me staring. "Friends and family call her Yancy. She and Luke have known each other since they were babies playing in the sandbox." Mr. Jerome laughed and although I tried to give him and Yancy a genuine smile back, I could only manage a pressed grin. Luke squeezed my hand gently and I knew that he could read my discomfort in my face, which only made me feel even more awkward. Shit.

"Why don't we get going?" Mr. Jerome urged, tilting his head to the back of the golf cart, and I nodded my head with my eyes cast down. I was eager to do anything to get everyone's eyes off me.

Following Luke's lead, I jumped into the backseat of the golf cart and looked out the side at the scenery as it took off. Luke squeezed my hand again, this time shaking it a little so that I would turn to him. As soon as my face turned to his, he caught me in a kiss that was so sweet and gentle, I forgot all about what had occurred a few minutes before. Cupping my face in his hand, he deepened the kiss, showing me that he wasn't worried about who was around or who may have been watching. He was only worried about putting me at ease and he did just that. Once he released me, it seemed like it took forever for me to get my drunken eyelids to open. I was drunk on his love and every little bit I got of him only deepened my condition.

"Are you going to tell me who lives here?" I whispered in his ear as we neared the backside of the mansion, and he looked down at me, a question lingering behind his eyes.

"You don't know yet?" he asked, and I frowned at him to which he smiled and shook his head. "What kind of lawyer you tryin' to be... a prosecutor, right? The next time I'm about to get locked up for some shit, I'm going to personally ask for you to handle the case. I'll get away every damn time."

Before I could stop myself from pouting at the way he dissed the hell out of me and still managed to make it sound so good, the cart slowed to a stop.

"Welcome home, Mr. Murray!" Mr. Jerome said, holding his hands out. "Everything has been fully prepared as you requested it. If you need anything, you know you only need to call."

"What?!" I shot out, much louder than I'd wanted to. "Th—this is your place?"

Tilting her head to the side, Yancy turned to look at me and giggled a little. Even her giggle sounded a little too sexy for my liking.

"Oh, you didn't know? How cute!" she said, and I looked at her, ready to catch an attitude, but I stopped once I realized that she wasn't being rude or trying to throw shade, she actually seemed about as excited to see the look on my face as Carmella would have been had she been here.

"No, I didn't know... I mean, the thought occurred to me but I told myself that there was no way that—" I looked back up at the place and shook my head, not knowing what else to say.

Mr. Jerome and Yani went to grab our bags from a golf cart that I hadn't noticed was trailing us, and Luke took the opportunity to scoop me up in his arms, kissing me once again.

"You said a queen lives here," I reminded him and he nodded his head.

"One does. You… this is our spot now and you're the queen of this castle."

I wanted to cry. Like cry *real* tears. This type of thing didn't happen to anyone and it definitely didn't happen to me. I was Janelle, little ole smart ass Janelle. I wasn't the beautiful sister, truthfully, I didn't feel like I could hold a candle to any of my sisters. Carmella, Mixie, and Vonia were all drop dead gorgeous and, while I wasn't ugly, I was always the one who was harped on for being smart and I always hid behind that… telling myself that it was okay that I wasn't the first pick from the hottest guys when it came to the Pickney sisters because I was smart as hell and would be able to buy whatever I wanted one day to take the place of a man.

But Luke chose me and elevated me to a position that no one could take me down from. In his eyes, I was the most beautiful woman on Earth. He didn't have to tell me that, he made me feel it, and he let everyone around us know it.

"I have to do some stuff while I'm here. Go explore the house, get a massage, and then rest up. We'll go to dinner tonight," he told me, giving me another kiss as he prepared to walk away. "Have your list ready for me when I see you."

The list!

As soon as I stepped foot on the island, I forgot all about the list he'd asked me to make. He wanted me to write down my dreams so that he could make them come true. I looked up at the house once more and took a deep breath. Just looking up at it told me that everything that I may have been thinking might have been a little too small. It was time to dream big.

***

"Bitch, I hate you!"

Pausing, I looked at the phone in my hand before pushing it back up to my ear.

"Um… damn, Carm, what's that about?"

Vonia jumped in before Carmella could get a word out. "You know her ass is jealous. Shit, I am too! You just got done telling us about all this wonderful shit you doin' and you ain't even invite us out there with you!"

"Maybe that's because she didn't know she was going there, heffas!" Mixie jumped in, taking my side against my two crazy, jealous sisters.

"Exactly," I agreed, joining into the conversation. "I didn't know we were coming here. He had everything packed and ready for us to leave after we left the tattoo shop."

"Bitch, you got a tattoo without tellin' us, too?!" Carmella cut in, attitude still on one hundred.

"No! I got my bellybutton pierced. I was supposed to get one but punked out before I could. But *anyways*, I'm glad to see y'all are happy for me," I added with my mouth poked out. Leave it to my sisters to make me feel like shit for not inviting them on my vacation instead of being happy for me. I wasn't upset by it because I wasn't really surprised. Carmella and TreVonia were born spoiled so it would have been a shock to get anything different from either of them.

"Well, I can't speak for those other two but I'm happy for you. Especially after what happened with daddy," Mixie added in a low tone, and I knew it had to be because she was at home.

Her bringing up the situation with my father brought instant tears to my eyes. I wish I could say that I wasn't regretting my decision but part of me was. Since the last time I'd seen him, I'd tried to call him every day but he wouldn't answer the phone. I'd even called him a few times since I'd been on the island and he still sent me straight to voicemail. I wanted to try calling him on the phone in the house but I didn't want to trick him into speaking to me, I wanted him to answer the phone knowing it was me.

"I am happy for Jani," Carm added and TreVonia murmured her agreement as well. "I just wish that I was there, too. Shit, daddy disowned me, too. I could use some shit to take my mind off the fact that I'm all alone."

I rolled my eyes at her. "Carm, you barely called daddy unless you needed something and rarely came home for holidays. I'm sure you aren't missing anything."

"True but still… it's my daddy."

The line went silent as we all reacted in our own ways to the hurt in Carmella's voice. A single tear ran down my cheek and I wiped it away quickly, sniffling the rest away.

"He's not taking it well either," Mixie finally spoke, in a hushed tone.

"No, he really isn't," TreVonia added. "We didn't want to tell you guys because we figured it would make it worse for you, but daddy's isn't doing well without you two."

My heart squeezed tight in my chest and I closed my eyes, allowing a few more tears to escape.

"Just give him some time," Mixie added, as usual, trying to provide us comfort. "He'll come around. Just give him a little space to realize he's miserable."

After ending the call with my sisters, I got dressed and ready to go out with Luke. A stylist came to do my hair after my massage and mani/pedi. This was star treatment and I had no problem finding a way to get used to it. The estate was huge, so big that I hadn't been able to explore all of it. I couldn't wait to get back to walking around it and scrutinizing every little detail. Luke had definitely spared no expense when it came to décor and the level of detail in the architecture told me a lot about his taste. It also told me a lot about his net worth. I was used to nice things but nothing even close to this.

Taking a deep breath, I rounded the corner to the stairs, anxious about what Luke had in store for our night. When I saw Luke standing downstairs there was also a chauffeured car waiting behind him. I watched his eyes run down my physique as I sported the dress he'd picked out for me. I felt like the queen he said I was.

"Damn," was all Luke said as I walked down the stairway but, in my mind, my appearance was no match for his.

Luke was the type of man who could sport any style and rock the hell out of it. In a single day, he could go from hood chic to corporate swag and wear every style in between and still look effortlessly sexy. At the moment, he wore a tailored suit that perfectly fit his slim, muscular build. His long hair was braided into a single braid that ran down his back, and his goatee was freshly cut. His signature gold chains hung around his neck, his gold, diamond-encrusted Rolex glistened on his wrist, his ears sparkled with diamonds and his tattooed hands were bare except for a diamond pinky ring that he wore on the left.

His taste was impeccable when it came to how he dressed himself but also how he dressed me. The gown that he picked out for me was by some designer that I couldn't name, but I knew it had to be expensive from the moment that I saw it. When I put it on, it was like silk on my skin, making my small curves look better than they'd ever looked before.

"You tryin' to give me a fuckin' heart attack, huh?" Luke asked, laughing a little, but I saw the seriousness in his eyes as he looked me up and down.

"Not a heart attack. Just tryin' to keep your eyes on me for a little longer. That's all."

"Well, you get an A-fuckin'- plus," he replied, still marveling at me and I beamed, ducking my head slightly to look away as continued to stare. "You're beautiful. Shit… if I wasn't hungry as hell, we wouldn't be going anywhere but back to the room."

"We can save that for later," I laughed, grabbing his hand. He nodded, his eyes still serious as they pierced into my face. Then he let them drop once more to take in my body and licked his lips before turning away to lead me into the black Escalade that was waiting to take us to our next destination.

Instead of going to a restaurant off the property, the Escalade led us down a road right there on the estate. We stopped near a cabana right on the water; it was lit up by torches and in the center was a table lit by candles. My eyes widened as I looked at it in awe, once again rendered speechless by the fact that Luke had managed to plan all of this out for us. When it came to romantic men, Luke Murray was not the first thought that came to mind, but he was showing me that there was more to him than anything I thought I knew.

The food seemed endless and so were the drinks. By the time dessert came, I was nearly drunk off wine, working on my third glass even though Luke was only on his second glass of Hennessey, a 'man's drink' as he put it.

"So about this list," he started, taking a sip before placing his glass down and leaning closer to me. "Did you finish it?"

I gulped down the last of my wine before nodding my head and retrieving the paper from my purse.

"I didn't think it would be so damn hard to figure out what I wanted out of life. But after coming here..."

I paused, once again thinking about how much this experience made me think of greater goals. Luke smiled, almost like he could read my thoughts without me saying them so I didn't finish, I simply handed the folder up piece of paper to him and watched as he read through my list. Once he got to the bottom, a smirk crossed my face when I saw him pause and raise his brows.

"Hmm," was all he said but I knew exactly which line on my list had garnered his full attention. No lie, I was a little nervous about what his reaction would be once he saw it, but it was part of what I wanted and so I wrote it down. And then, a slow smile rose up on his face, starting at the edges of his lips before completely taking over his face.

"How many years until you hit twenty-eight?" he asked me smirking, and I ducked my head to hide my smile.

"Not too many more… but this is just my wish list."

"I can dig that shit," he replied and I couldn't help but laugh. "Your wish is my command."

He stuffed the paper into his pocket and I turned to look out over the water, still wearing the same goofy ass grin on my face. Somehow, even though nothing had happened just yet, I knew that he meant every single word he'd said.

Carmella

Zeke had me fucked up.

Yeah, I was somewhat to blame for having a total of two attorneys in my family and not asking either one to look over my contract but who would've thought his ass would be that slimy? Especially since he was dealing with his own sister's best friend. I couldn't believe this shit! Now, reading over the contract, I felt dumb as hell. Not only had I signed away my rights to review the promotions that any photographs I took would show up on, I'd signed a contract that was in effect for a total of two years. For two whole years, I would be the face of all of his porn advertisements. Hell, the way the contract was written, if he wanted to put me as the face of herpes cream, he had the right. *How could I be so fuckin' stupid?*

"Explain this to me, please," I fumed, slamming the advertisement down on the top of Zeke's desk. His eyes ballooned at my tone before he looked down at the photos. The wrinkles on his forehead relaxed and his lips cracked into a smile that I would have loved to slap right off of his face.

"Oh these? You're just seeing them, huh? They look great, don't they?"

Do you know his ass had the audacity to smile at me like I should agree?

"Great?!" I shouted, my angry black woman coming on in full gear. "You got my pictures on a fuckin' porn ad! Do you have any idea who my father is? This is fucked up, Zeke! You could've told me this shit."

I told myself when I was walking in there not to show out, but I was about to do just that and more. Zeke was staring at me like he didn't understand why I was so angry and I was looking back at him like he was dumb as hell. Why wouldn't I have a problem with this? Even if he didn't have to show me the ads my photo would be on, as a decent human being he could have let me check them out before plastering my face all along the east coast of the USA!

"Could've told you what, Carm?" he asked with furrowed brows, delivering a slight shrug with his question. "You post shit worse than this photo on your Instagram page for thousands of people to see. So just because I'm advertising a porn video, that you're not even in, it's a problem?"

See, it was niggas like this that were the sole reason women spazzed out in the first place. I came in here with every intention to be a lady and have a decent conversation, but he was about to have me show my whole ass.

"What I choose to do with my pictures on my Instagram page is one thing. If I decide to release a picture of myself ass naked, then that was a decision I made to show my body. But for you to use that as an excuse to make money off of me by selling sex is not acceptable!"

Zeke rolled his eyes and sat back in his chair, crossing his arms in front of his chest. "Carm, you were half-naked, wearing a thong bikini, bending over a desk with your ass and tits practically hangin' all the way out of the lil' ass shit we had you wearin'. What the hell did you think you were selling? Even without the word 'porn' on this piece of paper, that's exactly what it is." He shoved the papers towards me and I backed away with my nose twisted up, not even wanting to touch them anymore.

"Well, I'm done and I'm not doing it anymore. You can take the car and the condo that you gave me. I quit." Looking down, I reached into my purse to grab the keys to both and sent them sailing across Zeke's desk, right at him.

"You can't do that," he said, chuckling. There was an evil twinkle in his eye and I was instantly reminded about the way that Sasha had warned me about her brother. Why the hell did she give me that half-assed warning anyways? Why didn't she just come out and tell me? As much as I wanted to yell at her for that, I couldn't bring myself to call her and let her know how stupid I was for not being more responsible.

"Yes, I can!" I spat back and cocked my head to the side before pressing my hand into my hip. "I'm not bein' the face of any porn enterprise you have goin' on. I've embarrassed my family enough."

"Well, you'll be embarrassing them a whole lot more because you're under contract," Zeke reminded me and pushed the keys back towards me. "So take your shit and be ready to come in tomorrow and perform. We have some new stuff that we are on deadline to get out for the west coast. Your ad will be everywhere. Get ready to be famous."

My mouth dropped open. I really couldn't believe that someone as handsome and charming as Zeke could be so evil. But I guess he hadn't made all this money by not being an asshole.

"The west coast? But I go to school in Cali... I don't want my professors and colleagues there to see—"

"You said you wanted money. You said you wanted to be famous. I'm giving you all that. I'm holding up my end of the bargain and I expect you to do the same. We are all professional adults in this business."

And with that, Zeke lowered his head and began shuffling the papers on his desk in a dismissive way. This conversation wasn't over but I needed to regroup. If at any time I needed my older sister, it was now. Janelle had to be able to find a way for me to get out of the contract I'd signed with Zeke. There couldn't be a way that I was really stuck. Thankfully, she was due home from her tropical vacation with Outlaw and I would be able to ask her later on tonight.

***

"Carm..." Janelle sighed and I squeezed my eyes closed, expecting the worst. "You really should've let me see this before you signed it."

"Duh," I shot back, not wanting to sound bitchy but unable to sound any other way. "I didn't think that Zeke would try to fuck me over like this. He's Sasha's brother and he knows about daddy running for mayor... I just didn't think he would do this to me."

Janelle sighed again and I fought the urge to just hang up the phone. I was well aware of how naïve I sounded. Sasha was my friend but Zeke wasn't. To be honest, I didn't really know much about him so there was no reason for me to just have trusted him. Especially after his own sister had told me to watch out for him.

"People will screw anybody over when it comes to money. Look at Chris... as much as he claimed he felt about me, when it came to possibly losing his job, he only thought about saving his own ass."

My mind switched gears, all of a sudden, and I thought about that crazy night we'd had in front of Janelle's apartment. The day that both of us became fatherless daughters.

"Have you heard from him since?" I inquired, mainly because I was curious about Cree's family and how seriously they took that 'thug shit' they seemed to all abide by. That night, they'd allowed Chris to leave in his own car, but I wasn't stupid and I noticed that Yolo had decided to take off shortly after in Outlaw's car, driving in the same direction as Chris. Something told me that he wasn't just making sure that Chris was making it safely home.

"No," Janelle said after pausing for a short while. Something about her tone told me that she'd been thinking about Chris too. "But I wouldn't expect him to want to talk to me, to be honest. I return back to work tomorrow so I'll probably see him then."

"And if you don't?" I couldn't resist asking.

"And if I don't then... I don't know. He's not my concern anymore, Carm."

One thing for sure, Janelle was definitely in love and she had it bad. The Janelle I knew wouldn't have dismissed the idea that Chris could very well be somewhere dead, thanks to her new gangsta boyfriend. She would have wanted to know for sure that Outlaw had nothing to do with Chris being harmed. Janelle had always been the more morally upstanding of us all. The Janelle I knew wouldn't have let this go so easily by saying that Chris wasn't her concern. Then again, the Janelle I knew wouldn't have chosen another man over daddy either. Outlaw was changing her and I couldn't really say that it was for the worst. At least she seemed to finally have her own mind.

I held the phone in my hand, gripping it hard as I looked back over the electronic version of the contract I'd signed.

"So you're sure that there is no way to get out of this contract?" I asked her again, hoping for the best although expecting the worst.

"I mean… it's pretty straight forward. It's a two-year contract and you gave up your right to review images before they go to print or any authority you would have on where the images are placed. Pretty much, you signed something saying you would take photos for Zeke's company and he can do whatever he wants to do with them. Unless he allows you to pull out of the agreement, there is no way you will win this in court."

Now it was my turn to sigh and I did so heavily. "I'll talk to you later, Jani. I'm going to go ahead and get to bed. I have a long day of work tomorrow."

Before she could say anything, I hung up the phone and a single tear ran down my cheek. I tried to sniff the others away but, before I knew it, more began to fall.

"Shit!" I cursed, rubbing at my eyes.

I looked around at the beautifully decorated condo I was in. My prize for selling my soul to Zeke. The past few days I'd been sleeping at Cree's place, but I couldn't stand to stay there anymore because I was afraid that one day he would walk in the door ready to go crazy on my ass after seeing one of Zeke's ads somewhere. It was bad enough that he was constantly going off on me about the types of pictures I put on up on Instagram, this would send his crazy ass over the edge.

Standing up, I walked over to my dresser and pulled out a small piece of glass, a credit card and my magic powder. My party drug had turned into a full-fledged habit, but I wasn't prepared to admit it yet. More and more, I was using to get over my feelings about all of the bullshit going on in my life. After Cree and I really made it official, I'd managed to push the drugs away because I'd been staying with him, but everything happening around me now was too much. My father had disowned me, and now I saw that I was stuck in a contract that I didn't want to be in. And even if I could get out of it, I was in no better situation. Outside of what Zeke paid me, I was broke so I pretty much depended on him. My life had gone from sugar to shit.

And so I leaned over, plugged one nostril, and snorted my troubles away.

Sidney

*Y*ou would think I'd be happy but I wasn't. In fact, I was damn near miserable, but I didn't know what to do about it. And I was so ashamed of the shit that was going on that I couldn't talk to anyone about it. I didn't feel comfortable explaining to anyone how Sidney, the one with the slick ass mouth and all the good advice, was now in a position that was reserved for dumb bitches, sidechicks, and thots.

"Fuck!" I cursed after walking into Yolo's apartment and nearly stumbling over something that resembled a brick and was in the middle of the floor.

I had just come in from working a full night's shift and his living room was pitch black. Reaching out, I flicked on the light switch to stop from running into something else and killing myself. The room illuminated immediately and I saw the object of my pain wasn't a brick, it was actually a suitcase, a staunch reminder of the fucked up situation I was in.

"Turn it offffff," a voice moaned, and I gritted my teeth, annoyed by the voice. "Turn it off, please. I'm tryin' to sleep."

"What's goin' on out here?"

That was Yolo, walking in from down the hallway. Even in sleep, his pretty boy ass was fine as hell, dressed in some gray sweatpants and a wifebeater that snuggly fit around all his muscles. He had a matching

29

gray durag on his head to protect his beautiful waves. But even the sight of his perfect body couldn't change my attitude. Although I'd had a great day, just walking in this fuckin' place pissed me off.

"What's going on is I just came in from work and almost killed myself over this big ass suitcase that is right in the middle of the floor!"

I cut my eyes and looked at ugly ass LaTrese who was on the couch, now ogling Yolo's muscular frame and looking a lot less like the sleepy demon she had been pretending to be when I first walked in. Since she allegedly had no family and Yolo didn't want to go to the cops with what happened to her, he took it upon himself to take care of her and allow her to stay at his place while she recovered. In order to keep me satisfied that there was nothing going on, he'd also moved me in as well, telling me he didn't feel comfortable having her in his house without me there. I didn't see why he didn't just pay for the bitch to have a nurse stop by her apartment during the day. Actually, I'd suggested that and it seemed like Yolo was about to agree to it until LaTrese declared in a loud, obnoxious whine that she was scared to go back to her place because her ex may show up. That was all Yolo needed to hear. That idea was out and LaTrese was moved in.

"I'm sorry," LaTrese said, sounding sincere enough to fool Yolo but not me. "If I could have moved it from in front of the door, I would have but... I can't." She bent her head down and started pouting, pretending to wipe a fake tear from her eyes.

"Damn, Sid... I'm sorry you hurt yourself, bae, but you know she can't move heavy shit in her condition," he said, pleading with me to be nice. I snapped. Like *all* the way snapped.

"Bitch! If you couldn't move the shit, then how the hell it get in front of the door anyways? It wasn't there when I fuckin' left for work and I know it ain't been there all damn day. Now explain that shit, with your lyin'—"

"Sid!" Yolo shouted, stopping me from continuing. "Yo, it ain't that big a deal. You ain't hurt and I'll make sure it's not in front of the door anymore. Just turn off the fuckin' light and let's go to bed. Shit!"

Taking my sweet time, I first kicked the suitcase out of the way before walking over and turning off the light, walking right by Yolo without even turning to look at him. I couldn't believe that he would take that bitch's side! Was he my nigga or hers? Shit, I had no idea.

"The fuck you think you goin'?" Yolo said, and the next second I found a hand around my wrist, stopping me from walking by. I could barely see his yellow ass in the dark, but I could feel his presence near me and the heat coming off his body as he pulled me close. He kissed my neck, using full tongue and smacking loudly as he did it which put a satisfied grin on my face, not just because it felt so good, but because I knew that LaTrese had to hear it and know what was going down. And I was certain she knew when I heard her suck her yellow ass teeth. *Jealous bitch.*

"Get your ass in the room," Yolo told me, tapping me on the rear. "I got somethin' for all this shit you tryin' to start."

I wanted to tell him that I wasn't the one starting shit, but I kept my mouth closed for the time being. Yolo always made sure to openly show his affection for me in front of LaTrese, and I knew it was his way of letting me know that there was nothing going on between them. The problem was that I knew bitches like her didn't care about that shit. They'd watch you fuck your nigga and then wait for your ass to go to work so they could get in line to be fucked too. As long as she got a piece of Yolo, she saw it as a victory against me. She didn't give a damn about what he was doing with me.

"Sid, you gotta calm your ass down," Yolo started as soon as the door was closed behind us.

Ignoring him, I began pulling off my clothes to get in the shower. I wasn't in the mood to be reprimanded by him or reminded about how I needed to calm down and be nice to poor little LaTrese because she was going through a tough time. She was no different from anybody else and she'd made her own damn decisions. Her hard times were because of herself.

"We all in this together and we gotta have peace. If you're at odds with LaTrese while she's here, we will all be miserable. Just keep your cool and she'll be out soon. You do understand why I'm doin' this shit, right?"

No.

"Yeah," I told him, turning my back to him so I could properly roll my eyes.

"I'm only doin' this because she doesn't have anybody else." He came and grabbed me from behind, holding me tight as he talked into my neck. I shuddered as I felt his breath on my skin. He smelled so damn good… only Yolo's ass would spray on some cologne just to go to bed.

"I feel like I owe her because we—we had a child together and, even though he didn't survive, I told LaTrese that I'd always be there for her because I'm all she had. What kinda nigga would I be if I dated a woman for damn near ten years and just said 'fuck her' once we broke up, no matter what shit she got goin' on? I'm a stand up dude but I'm not gonna cheat on you or put you in a crazy situation. This is temporary. Just trust me," he said right before kissing me on the cheek.

I closed my eyes and nodded my head, hating myself for the millionth time for the control that Yolo had over me. He was the love of my life and he had me doing shit that I'd have sworn up and down I'd never do. This was the perfect example of it. I would have told any other bitch that she was stupid for letting her boyfriend's ex-girlfriend, who had made it clear that she wanted him back, move in. But here I was. I guess that's why they say you should never say never.

"You gon' stay down for me?" Yolo asked, kissing me again on the neck, right below my ear. My hot spot.

"Yeah," I replied, eyes fully drunk and pussy soaking wet. "You know I will."

And I always will.

✳✳✳

"Are you going to the store? I have some stuff I need you to get."

Squeezing my eyes closed, I kept my back turned to LaTrese mainly to keep myself from diving on top of her ass and pummeling her face in with my fist. For some reason, her living on Yolo's couch for the past week made her think that I was her personal maid. Every time she laid eyes on me she had to open up her big fat mouth with a request. And most times, it was shit that she could do her damn self.

Like making her a glass of water or a sandwich. Out of all the damn things that had happened to her ass, broken fingers weren't one of them.

"Well, if you have stuff you need, you need to call one of your lil' ugly friends to come over here and bring them to you. I am not the maid."

"My lil' ugly friends?" LaTrese parroted with attitude, the attitude that she consistently had when Yolo wasn't around but managed to hide whenever he was in hearing range.

The bitch wasn't smart, and I knew exactly what she was trying to do. Too bad that it wouldn't work. Yolo may have had his heart on his sleeves, but his brain was securely in his head. He wasn't stupid enough to fall for her tactics and the sooner she realized it, the sooner she could get the hell on.

"Yes, your lil' ugly ass friends. Get them to come bring you your shit because I really don't care if your ass eats," I grumbled and snatched an apple from the fridge.

I chewed it angrily. Sinking my teeth in it was enough to stop me from wanting to haul off and pop LaTrese right against the side of her neck.

"Bitch, listen, it's obvious that Yolo wants me here so you're going to have to get with the program," LaTrese spat, propping herself up on the couch so that she could look directly at me. "And the program we goin' by is the one that means you do what I say when I say do it. You fetch when I tell you fetch, okay bitch?"

I almost choked on a piece of the apple as it went down my throat.

Did she really just call me out of my name? Did she really say what I thought she'd said? And in my man's house that she was staying in? Had this bitch lost all of her natural mind?

"Da fuck did you just say to—"

Midway into my sentence, I stopped talking because my mind told me *fuck what she said, go with what you heard and beat that hoe's entire ass'*. I snapped.

In five seconds, I was on her ass and I punched her so hard that her head flew back into the back of the sofa, nearly knocking against the wall. She yelped loudly, sounding very close to the painful whine that a mangy mutt makes and then snapped her neck forward to glare at me while holding onto her cheek.

"You might be living here right now but I'm Yolo's girlfriend which means that I run everything up and through this shit. You better learn your muthafuckin' place before I do it for you."

Standing up, I pressed my hands against my thighs and wiped them off. I didn't even like the fact that had to touch her but chin-checking her for talking reckless did make it somewhat better.

"I'm going to tell Yolo what you did," she threatened me just as I was about to walk out of the door. "I'm going to tell him and he'll beat your ass for this."

I shrugged and then turned to look at her right before walking out the door. Truly, I didn't give a damn if she did tell Yolo, but there was one thing that I knew which, obviously, she still had to learn. Yolo wasn't as stupid as she believed him to be.

"Tell him whatever you want to, bitch."

Outlaw

"*M*uthafuckas, stand da fuck up! Outlaw's in this bitch!"

Walking into the room, I made my rounds, dapping up my brothers. A vacation was good and shit, spending it with Janelle was the icing on the cake, but I couldn't lie and say a nigga wasn't glad to be home and back to business.

"Damn, nigga, you done got a tan?" Kane asked and I laughed at his crazy ass.

"Since when you known niggas to tan?"

"And you glowin' and shit!" That was Yolo's joking ass. I swung on him and he ducked out the way, laughing his ass off before handing me a cup. Everyone sat down and prepared for our card game. This one was much different from the others. Instead of chillin' together to prep for a hit we had scheduled the next day, we were chillin' to discuss our next moves. And, thanks to my trip, I was able to score the perfect equipment to get our next job together. Sure, the vacation was about Janelle and giving her some time to cool off and get her mind off the fact that her sorry ass daddy disowned her, but part of it was for me to get some things in line. And those things were the reason we were meeting tonight. We just had to get the pleasantries out of the way.

"Yolo's right though. You are glowin', nigga," Cree chimed in, his eyes low as hell as he pulled from a fat blunt. "That lil' trip did ya some good, huh?"

"How the hell would you know if I was glowin' or not, nigga? Ya eyes are barely open. Da fuck you got in that blunt?" I asked him and he waved the blunt towards me for me to try it out.

One pull had me mellow as hell. Now I knew why Kane was in such a good mood. Either that, or he and Teema were getting along much better than I'd thought.

"How's my niece doin', Kane?"

His usually tight, serious face broke into a smile and he ran his hand over the top of his fresh low-cut before nodding his head and replying to me.

"She's good… great," he corrected himself, clearing his throat. "I paid for Teema to go on some girl's trip with her friends so that she could enjoy herself and give me and Kenya some time alone."

My brows rose up to nearly the center of my forehead. "Word? So you alone with Kenya? She still alive?"

"Hell yeah, she still alive!" Kane screwed his eyes tight when he asked his next question. "What you think I don't know how to watch my daughter?"

"Naw, nigga, I think you just *got* a daughter. And before her, I never even seen yo' ass look at a kid. Much less, look after one," I laughed while turning off the ringer on my phone.

The rules were that we were to turn them completely off when we had business meetings but today was Janelle's first day back at work and I wanted to make sure I was available if she needed me. My brothers had gotten rid of that dumb ass Chris muthafucka for me the night that everything went down. Yolo followed him home and Tank caught up with him later. I didn't mention it to Janelle, but she was smart. Once he stopped showing up to work, she would put two and two together and I wasn't sure what kind of backlash would come from that.

"Bruh ain't never even watched none of my kids neither. I could've let you have some practice with your niece and nephews," Tank added with a smirk. Kane didn't even respond to him and instead waved him away with his hand. He knew none of us wanted to watch his bad ass kids. He barely watched them without one of their mama's around.

"Anyways, let's get to business because I got shit to do. Grandma watching Kenya right now and I don't want her watchin' too much more of that Maury and Jerry Springer shit. What you found, Outlaw?"

Smiling, I took one last pull on the blunt in my hand before handing it off to Cree so I could enlighten everyone on the new job that I had planned out for us. If everything went right, this hit would keep our money right for the next year or so, we wouldn't have to do shit else, and I could properly focus on making all of Janelle's dreams come true. She had some shit on that list I asked her to make that threw me for a loop and, honestly, she said some shit that I wasn't thinking she even had her mind on. But when I told her that I would make sure it would all happen for her, I meant that shit.

"The only problem I have with this," Kane started running a single finger along his goatee as he thought out the rest of his sentence, "is that we aren't enough. We'd need to bring in more men just to get this shit done."

"That ain't no issue though, bruh," Cree piped in, always ready to take my side. "We got cousins that we can throw into the mix to help us out. This shit seems like it's right up Gunplay's alley."

"You wanna trust that crazy muthafucka to help us with some shit like this?" Kane's brows lifted as he asked. "The shit we do is thought out, calculated, and we gotta depend on each other to stick to the rules in order for it to work the right way. You really think he's the one to pull into this shit?"

"Hell naw!" Yolo took the opportunity to respond. "We already got one crazy nigga that don't take orders well on our team." He looked at me with a pointed expression and I stuck my middle finger up at him. "Why don't we just use Jamal and Benny?"

"Jamal?! The nigga who fucked up on the last job we had him on? And Benny probably won't do shit with us after getting shot in the armored truck robbery."

Kane cut his eyes at me and I was about five seconds away from getting ready to punch him in his shit, but I stayed in my seat. Ever since making things official with Janelle, it seemed like I was able to handle my temper a little better. She brought a nigga like me peace and also showed me the benefit of family. She was hiding it well but I saw how devastated she was about her pops turning his back on her. She idolized that nigga and for her to lose him just because she loved a nigga like me, it fucked me up inside. It only put the pressure on for me to be the only nigga she needed. I had to think smarter about how I did things. I couldn't nut up over dumb shit anymore.

"We'll need both of them to get in on this job. I'll talk to Benny and, as for Jamal, I think he realized his fuck up and learned from it. He'll be good, we just need to do more training and run-throughs. We been doin' this shit for a long time, but Jamal hasn't. He'll need more practice than we will," I replied, leaving no room for anyone to come against what I was saying. Kane included. I'd thought out every last detail of this hit, and I knew there was no way we could fail. We were doing it and that was it.

Keeping my eyes focused on Kane, I sat back in my chair and crossed my arms in front of my chest. Kane stuck a toothpick in the side of his mouth and chewed on it thoughtfully while he kept his attention on me. Yolo, Cree and Tank sat silently around us, the air in the room awkwardly thick as we all waited to see where this would go. Would this turn into another stand-off where I would finally have to give this nigga a dose of his own medicine and punch him in his shit, or would he see things my way?

"Look at lil' bruh, talkin' like a boss," Kane said finally, a smirk crossing his face. "That's all I ever wanted you to do was to step up, bruh." He said that last part in a low tone as if meant only for me to hear. Then he turned and looked around the table, eyes on each of our brothers as he spoke.

"Okay, it looks like we'll be doin' this shit. Outlaw got everything thought out to a tee and there ain't shit that I'd add to it. Let's get all the equipment we need in order so we can do this by the timeline he put in place."

I smiled and nodded my head. "Trust me. I got all this shit under control."

"How you feelin'?" I asked Janelle before dropping my jeans and pulling my shirt over my head.

She raised one brow and looked at me as she continued to hold her book in her hand. She looked cute as hell with her glasses on and a messy ass bun on top of her head as she lay in my bed reading. Ever since we returned from our vacation, she'd been staying with me and I didn't really want it any other way. It was hard for the type of nigga I was to admit that I was better with anyone by my side, especially a woman. But that's how it was. I was better with Janelle. The only thing that fucked with my mind is that I was always wondering if she was better with me.

"I'm good," she replied and placed the open book down on her lap. "And I'm not about to have sex with you... I got a lot of catching up to do after missing a couple days of work."

"Y'all still investigatin' me?"

Pursing her lips, she looked like she didn't want to respond right away. I knew I was putting her in a fucked up position. She wasn't allowed to talk about her cases with anyone, especially the person who was being investigated. But what happens when the person you're investigating happens to be the same nigga lying in the bed with you at night? The easiest answer to this situation was for her to quit her job, but she hadn't mentioned wanting to do it, and I couldn't make her. I needed her to come to that conclusion on her own.

"We... we haven't been given anything new to work on since I was last at work," she replied carefully, as if she was afraid of saying too much. That shit put me on edge. Why the hell did I feel like we were already at a point in our relationship where we were keeping secrets?

"I've been put in charge of diggin' up all kinds of information on you but—" She paused and then let out a heavy sigh before lifting herself up higher in the bed. "Honestly, Pelmington wants you all to go down for this. He has it bad for you and your brothers and won't even let us focus on anything else other than you guys. So…"

Janelle lifted her head and gave me an uneasy look that told me she was about to say something she didn't want to say. Chances are, it was something that shouldn't have been said. And I was right.

"Did…did you do it? Did you and your brothers—was that you on the film?"

She lifted her eyes and looked at me straight, trying her hardest to pierce straight into me and look inside of my soul. But I wasn't new to this. Maybe I was new to the love shit but, this part right here, this questioning me about the things that I've done or what I did… it wasn't something I wasn't prepared for. I wouldn't lie to Janelle, I'd promised her that. But that didn't mean I would always tell her the truth.

"Don't ever again ask me no shit like that again."

In true Janelle fashion, she cocked her head to the side and squared up on my ass quick.

"You don't ask me about my work and I won't ask you about yours," she posed, pulling her arms together and crossing them in front of her to show she meant business. Then she pushed her glasses up higher on her nose before folding her arms back again. She was such a fuckin' nerd and stubborn as hell, but I loved it so I really couldn't say shit about it.

"How the hell do you think that's gonna fuckin' work? You're investigatin' me 'bout some shit that could have me and my brothers locked up for life, and you expect me not to ask you about it?"

"I expect you to trust me," she replied, shutting me down instantly.

Trust. That was some more shit that didn't come easy for me but I knew she was right. I needed to trust her but the problem was, I wasn't sure I was ready for that. I'd shown her where I laid my head, she knew more shit about me than anyone else I'd ever fucked with. But she still hadn't met my grandmother and I hadn't really introduced her to my brothers yet either. I told myself that it was because I wanted to keep Janelle to myself and protect what we had. But was that shit really true? Or was it because I didn't completely feel at ease around her?

"Trust you," I repeated more to myself than to her. "You expect me to trust a woman that's investigatin' me. A woman who works for the one muthafucka in the world who wants to see me get the death penalty." Then something occurred to me and I switched gears.

"I told you I bought you your own building so you could start your own practice. You don't even have to work with that nigga anymore. Why haven't you started makin' plans on that shit? You haven't even asked to go see the building."

I bunched my brows together as an uneasy look crossed Janelle's face once again. She licked her lips slowly and looked down, dodging my gaze. My chest got tight and I felt the familiar feeling of rage creeping into me, burning the back of my neck. I swallowed hard and tried to push it down as I waited for her to respond.

"I—I haven't brought it up because..." she paused and licked her lips again. Her lips weren't that muthafuckin' dry. Her ass was stalling.

"Because what? Spit that shit out, nigga."

"Because I don't want to quit my job—"

"WHAT?"

If ever I wanted to punch a hole in a fuckin' wall, it was right now. How could she not want to quit? She said she wanted her own practice. In fact, it was the top thing on her fuckin' list! Now she had it and didn't want it? Women never knew what the fuck they wanted. You could give them the whole damn world and they'd want the galaxy. It was never enough. Except her ass was backwards as fuck. I was trying to give her the world and she wanted a lil' podunk ass town in Nobody Village. She could have her own shit, but she wanted to work for that yellow neck ass nigga, Pelmington?

"I'm learning a lot and I need the job experience if I'm going to have my own firm," she explained, but I really didn't want to hear it. "I can't just leave and start my own thing after a few months in a real job. I have no experience at all! I need someone to learn from and Pelmington is one of the best."

"And he's investigating your fuckin' boyfriend. You don't think that shit is an issue?"

I stood, hovering over her, my eyes blazing into the top of her forehead as she looked down at her hands, searching for the answer somewhere in her palms. One thing for sure, I wasn't going to keep giving her shit just for her to refuse it.

"You had this on your list as one of the things you wanted!"

"But I didn't want it *now*," she argued back. "I'm grateful for what you did, but it's not the time. I don't have my father around to show me how to be a good attorney so I have to learn from working with one. If I had my daddy then… then I could do it but he won't even answer my calls and—"

Her voice cracked and a second later a tear fell down her cheek. *Shit.*

"I just need you to trust me. I would never betray you, but I can't quit right now. And I can't talk to you about what I'm working on. You just have to understand that I'm with you because I love you and I wouldn't let anything happen to you."

It was some of the realest shit I'd ever heard come from her lips. And, instantly, I was rock hard.

"Damn."

Janelle giggled as she looked at the tent in my boxers that was getting higher and higher the more she stared at it. She turned me on with ease and, even when I was supposed to be mad at her ass, I couldn't be for long. When she lost her dad, I made it my position to protect her and be there for her always. That type of love and commitment didn't go away because of a simple argument.

"So let me see what dat slick ass mouf do," I teased and ran my tongue over the top of my bottom row of teeth.

"You got rid of the golds but you still got a yuck mouth, huh?" she smirked but pulled her glasses off, tossing them on the nightstand next to her. "If you were gonna still be nasty, you might as well have kept them in."

"You want me to put them back in?" I only half-teased because if she said the right thing, I'd go get my shits put back in asap. She pulled her rubberband out of her hair and let her medium-length tresses fall to her shoulders as she shook her head.

"Nah, I like the grown man, professional shit you're on. Turns me on."

As if to show how much she was turned on, she pulled off her top and showed me her perky tits. Her nipples were so hard and round in the center that I wanted to lean over and just pluck one into my mouth. I pushed off my boxers and my dick boomeranged out of them, a drop of pre-cum was already glistening on the tip. Janelle leaned over, not missing a beat and grabbed the base of my dick before aiming it at her mouth. She stuck her tongue out and licked the cum from my dick in a sexy way that almost made my knees buckle.

I couldn't understand niggas who cheated on the one they planned to give it all to. My baby was a lady in the streets and a major freak in the muthafuckin' sheets. There wasn't a damn thing I wanted to do that she wasn't game for doing. I could come up with the wildest shit and, even though she might look scared as hell, she was down to try it.

"Let me tie you up," I found myself saying, running my hand through her hair right after she sucked my pole in between her jaws. She frowned and then pulled away.

"Huh?"

I didn't repeat my statement. Instead, I went to the Gucci duffle I'd brought in with me and reached in, pulling my hand out with a rope in my grasp.

"You just carry shit like that around with you?"

I chuckled a little but didn't reply back. Instead, I walked over to her and grabbed her by her hands, tying and tightening the rope around her wrists before looping them through the frame of the bed. Janelle kept her eyes on me, breathing evenly as she watched me intently, waiting and wanting to know exactly what I had planned. Once the rope was tight enough, I backed away and admired my work. She was naked, except for her panties, and tied with her hands crossed at the wrists, her perky titties in the air, mine for the taking.

Almost.

Reaching into the bag, I pulled out another rope and then tied her ankles to the opposite end of the bed, spreading them apart so her legs were wide open. I'd contemplated tying her legs up by her hands but decided against it. She was definitely flexible enough, but I'd save that for another time.

"Finished?" she asked, as I took another step back to admire my work again. This time I clicked my tongue against my teeth in satisfaction.

"Yeah, I'm done," I told her and then turned off the lights.

A nigga was hungry. And it was time to eat.

Teema

"*B*itch! I'm havin' the fuckin' time of my liiiiiiiife!"

I screamed to the top of my lungs, not giving a damn who could hear me. After having the worst luck that could ever come to any woman on God's green Earth, I was finally in a place and space where I felt like things were going perfectly.

Kenya was with her father. Can you *believe* that?! That definitely was a statement that I'd never thought I would say. But anyways, she was with her father and Kane sent me away to Cabo on a girl's vacation with Cyndy and Miyani. Everything was paid for by him. That meant that we were free to eat, drink, and do whatever the hell we wanted and not worry about the bill. I had gone from being homeless to living like a damn Kardashian! It was the true Cinderella story. I went from rags to riches, and it was all thanks to the baby daddy I'd spent the last few years hating.

"I can't believe how things are workin' out with you and Kane," Cyndi said as she sipped from her margarita while lying down looking at the beach. Miyani hummed in agreement next to her, and I nodded my head.

"Cyn, I can't believe this shit either. When I went to him for help… hell, I didn't know what to expect but I didn't expect much. But I had no other choice. Turns out, he had a change of heart and now he wants to make up for lost time. He wants to be the father that Kenya deserves, and should have always had, and he wants to give me some time off from always handling things on my own."

Sipping from my pina colada, I had to swallow back the tears that had come to my eyes just that quickly. No one could have told me that this would be my life. After whooping my mama's ass for stealing money from me and my child and getting us evicted, I just knew that shit would be over for me, that I'd probably have to resort to selling my body to get by. But now Kane had come to the rescue once again. He was never there when I wanted him to be but it seemed like just when things got too bad for me to survive it, he showed up. Just like he had when we first met.

"Well, all I know is I'm glad that I'm one of your besties so I can be along for the ride," Cyndi said, smacking her lips and once again Miyani agreed, still not saying much which made me look over at her.

"Yani? Bitch, why you so quiet?"

"Girl, my bad. I'm texting this guy I met last night," she answered, exhaling softly and trying to tuck away the smile from her lips.

"Last night?! You met someone while we been out here and didn't bother telling us?"

Sighing, Miyani rolled her eyes and I rolled mine right back. It was just like Miyani's pretty ass to find somebody so quickly. We hadn't even been in Cabo that damn long and already she had a nigga sniffing at her ass. With her long, jet black, straight hair and greenish-brown eyes, Miyani was one of those chicks that was just too exotic looking to be ignored. She was gorgeous and it took a long time for me to really

49

be her friend because of how I always felt about myself.

Miyani was Cyndi's friend first and mine by default because I'd grown up distrustful of women like her. But once I met her, I realized that Miyani was cool as shit. She was down to Earth and, just like Cyndi and I, she had been raised in the projects. And let me tell you, when you're raised in the projects, your good looks didn't always work in your favor. Most times it made you a target, and that's exactly what happened with Miyani. But because of that, she was a down ass chick and her ass could fight like a MMA champ. She was the perfect example of why you shouldn't judge someone just by looking at them. She was a beautiful bitch but Barbie she was not.

"Well, the reason I didn't mention it is because his ass isn't even interested in me. I can tell." She snorted and rolled her eyes again. "I think he's just the least shy out of his group of friends and that's why he approached me. But he keeps mentioning how we all should hang out tonight. I asked him about just him and me kicking it because y'all may be busy, but he's adamant about bringing the two of you along. So my guess is that one of his boys is interested in one of you and was just too shy to make the connection."

"Humph! I hope it ain't me because I ain't got no time for no shy niggas," Cyndy let it be known and I knew she wasn't speaking anything but the truth. Cyndy was known for eating men alive if they didn't come at her correctly. She needed someone confident enough to deal with her mouthy ass.

"I don't care if he's shy. It actually seems kinda cute."

Both Miyani and Cyndy looked at me wearing the same exact

expression of their eyes pulled tight and their brows bunched into a frown with their lips open into a perfect 'o'.

"What?" I shot out after waiting for them to say whatever was on their minds and not getting any type of response.

"Um…" Miyani looked from me to Cyndy and then back to me again. "Teema, the only reason we are here is because of Kane. We figured you were trying to work things out with him… you're not available."

I snorted through my nose and raised my glass to my lips, frowning at the both of them.

"Why the hell am I not? Kane is *not* my man. He's Kenya's father and we are living together only until I can get my shit together. We are not sleeping in the same bed and he's not my man! We haven't even talked about being anything more to each other than what we are… Kenya's parents."

There was a thump in my chest after I finished my lil' speech and a lump also formed in my throat, though I wasn't really sure as to why.

"So the two of you haven't…" Cyndy made a wide-eyed expression with her brows straight in the air and I sucked my teeth.

"Hell no! Kane hasn't even come at me that way, Cyn. His focus has been on Kenya. Where it should be."

The lump seemed to get bigger and I cleared my throat before taking another sip of my drink while Miyani and Cyndy continued to watch me. Then I caught them exchanging glances as if communicating silently amongst themselves. This time Miyani was the one to speak up.

"Okay, but you're living with him so you think he would be okay with you dating while you're in his house?"

"No one said anything about dating!" I reminded Miyani. "I don't even know if I'm ready for that. But if I can get my life in order, I'd be open to it. I haven't been on the market in a while because I've been killing myself to take care of my daughter by myself. Now that I have help, that gives me time to focus on me, lose some of this weight, invest in looking better and feeling better... once all that happens, the niggas will come."

"Humph," Cyndy grunted and then sat all the way back in her seat, lifting her feet up so she could be in full lounge position. "All I know is that I've never known a nigga to be okay with his baby mama dating another nigga while living in his house. Matter of fact, most niggas act an ass off their baby mamas dating period! And the type of nigga Kane is... he ain't havin' that."

Rolling my eyes, I reclined as well and pulled my new Versace shades over my eyes to block out the bright, but beautiful, sun.

"I don't give a damn what Kane is or isn't havin'. He's not my nigga to be worried about the shit that I choose to do so he can stay out my business and keep his opinions to himself."

My comment was met by silence from Cyndy and Miyani but it spoke volumes, almost like I could hear their disagreement in the air. But then Cyndy, never one to hold her tongue, decided to speak and she dropped a dose of realness on me.

"All I know is... if I had a baby daddy handling things like *this*, fronting the cost and shit for me to live like queen of the world just because I pushed out his lil' munchkin, I would care what he thought about the next nigga before I made any moves that might land me back in the poor house."

I swallowed hard and folded my lips into my mouth, not wanting to let on how much her statement effected me. She was right. As much as I touted myself as being the independent woman who made my own decisions because I took care of myself and earned my own shit, that wasn't me anymore. Everything I had was because of Kane and, without a job opportunity in sight, it would be that way for a while. Though I didn't want him to have a say in my personal life, I did need to make sure whatever decision I made didn't land me back on my ass.

"*If* I find anyone worth dating, I'll see what he thinks about it," I said finally, feeling like I would be meeting Kane halfway and also covering my ass. "But that's a big if. Besides, he and I are friends now… or we are trying to be. So I don't mind getting his opinion."

I looked over at Cyndy and Miyani just in time to see them exchange glances and I wanted to throw my glass at them, but instead I lifted my hand in the air to signal our personal waiter to make me another one, tucked my shades further back on my face and looked over the ocean, enjoying the scene. I didn't care what they thought or what their opinions on my situation with Kane was. We were friends and that was it. Nothing more and nothing less. I didn't have a say when it came to his life and he didn't have a say when it came to mine.

***

Everything about the vacation was top of the line. The food, the room, the drinks… hell, even the people looked like they were crème de la crème! So when I walked in the small sports bar style restaurant located on the resort, I wasn't scared to admit that I felt a little unsure of myself. Looking down, I smoothed my hand over the beautiful Prada dress that I'd purchased at one of the boutiques earlier, courtesy of the allowance Kane had given me to shop with, and pinched my lips into my mouth. I looked the part but I didn't feel comfortable. Just a few days ago, I was sporting styles I'd found on the clearance rack at K-Mart. Now I was mixing and mingling with the super rich and privileged. It was fun but… was this really me?

"Bitch, stop," I heard Miyani say and I lifted my head, surprised when I saw her eyes were on me.

"Stop what?" I shrugged a little and tucked a stray piece of hair behind my ear.

Aside from being beautiful, Miyani was also a beast when it came to hooking up a hairstyle. She did her hair, Cyndy's, and mine before we left for the bar and, even though I didn't like wearing so much weave, I had to admit that my look was on point. I had long Remy waves rolling down my back to the point that it almost touched the start of my ass. I knew I looked good but I still couldn't shake the fact that I felt so damn uneasy.

"Stop looking like you're about to throw up," Miyani explained, rolling her eyes to the ceiling. "I know this isn't your usual scene, and I know you're about two seconds away from running out of here but you look good, smell good, and you need to get used to being in places like this. You deserve it and you're finally getting a piece of what you deserve."

"Exactly," Cyndy added. "Let your hair down and relax. Even if you make a fool of yourself, we're far from home. Too far for anyone here to know you and bring it up. I mean…I will but you don't have to worry about anyone else doing it."

"Shut up, Cyn! There they are…Heyyyy, Lamar!"

I turned my attention to the spot where Miyani was now walking towards and sucked in a breath as I put one foot in front of the other, following her while also avoiding meeting eyes with any of the men at the table.

"Shit, they are foooiiiine," Cyndy said from under her breath, making me look up.

And damn, was she right! I locked eyes with a dark-skinned cutie who resembled the actor Lance Gross but was a bit more muscular. Like most of the men in the club, he was wearing a sports coat but his was white linen and looked beautiful against his dark skin. And his teeth… they were about as bright as his jacket. I almost lost my breath when he smiled deeply, immediately captivating me by his charm. His hair was low cut with a deep wave that added to his allure. I loved me a man with waves! It just did something to me that the regular old haircut didn't do. Now I could appreciate a fresh line-up too, but his swag was on another level. He had a thin goatee that accentuated the juiciest lips I'd ever seen on a man. Well…a man outside of Kane, but he wasn't in the picture right now.

"That's him. The one I've been texting, Lamar," Miyani whispered, jabbing me in the side. "And next to him is Javier. He's the one who is interested in one of y'all, I think. I can't remember the other one's name." Cyndy grunted loudly.

"Shit, Lamar ain't tell you which one of us that Javier is interested in? Damn, I hope it's me because his ass is sexy!"

Swallowing hard, I mentally agreed with Cyndy although I didn't say anything. I hoped his ass was interested in Cyndy also because I couldn't even begin to think of how I was going to open up my mouth and say anything worth hearing to a man that damn fine.

"No, Lamar didn't say which one, he just kept saying shit like 'my boys, will be there so make sure you bring your friends with you'. But the other one is cute too…"

Her voice faded away just as we were about to approach the table, and I took the opportunity to look at the man sitting on the other side of Lamar. He definitely was a looker too. Brown-skinned with baby eyes that looked sexy on him. He was definitely the more low-key of the three because instead of looking at the three of us, he simply glanced in our direction before turning away and bobbing his head to the beat. I frowned slightly at him, wondering what his deal was. Yeah, I was feeling some type of way about being out of my element but I knew damn well I at least looked the part.

Lamar stood up and smiled wide, his full attention focused on Miyani. She may have thought that he invited her out just so his friends could hook up with either me or Cyndy, but she was obviously bugging. Judging from the huge grin on his face and the way his eyes seemed to dance and sparkle when he looked at her, he was definitely vying for Miyani's attention.

"Hey, Miyani—"

"You can call me Yani," she corrected him, barely looking him in the face. I almost sucked my teeth at the way she was acting. For someone so smart, Miyani never seemed to see when a guy was feeling her even when he was right in her face showing it to her, like Lamar was doing at the moment.

"Okay, well...Yani, hey," Lamar said with only a hint of a chuckle, probably from embarrassment from how Miyani was now sitting at the table with her eyes on her phone instead of him. "Anyways... ladies, these are my boys, Javier and Othello."

Javier smiled at me and nodded his head slightly which made my heart flutter like butterflies had erupted right in my chest. And then, just as I was about to take the seat ahead of him, he turned to look at Cyndy, and his smile deepened as he stood up and thrust his hand towards her.

"You can actually call me Javi," he said. "And your name is?"

Trying to hide my pout, I reasoned with myself that I wouldn't have had shit to say to Javier anyways and took the chair in front of the quiet, distant, and very uninterested friend, Othello. Once I sat in my chair, he only barely gave me a look, allowing his eyes to quickly cascade over my appearance before swiveling around slightly, turning his face away from me.

"Well, these are my friends, Cyndy and Teema," Miyani finally introduced us after pulling her attention away from her phone.

"Miyani, let me buy you a drink," Lamar requested and grabbed Miyani's hand to lead her to the bar. Cyndy and Javier sat chatting for a while and I tried to act like I was part of their conversation before they left to head to the bar. Leaving me alone with the weirdo friend who didn't talk.

Fuck my life.

Janelle

*M*y eyes darted to the clock for like the tenth time and then I started to do something that I swore to Luke that I'd stop doing. I began to bite my nails.

Shit.

I tucked my fingers underneath my thighs and pressed them firmly against the cream leather seat I was uncomfortably shifting around in, trying my hardest to keep my promise alive. But my nerves were scrambled and it was all I could do to appear that I was keeping my cool. Granted, I was doing a piss-poor job at that, but I was definitely trying.

Pelmington had called an emergency meeting, requiring all of us to meet with him in the conference room at precisely this time. Actually, he was about five minutes late. Uncharacteristically late. And that's what had me so not at ease. The only time he called us into the meeting room was when there was a break in the case and that's the *last* thing I wanted. Our primary focus for the past month was on how to nail the Murray brothers for the armed truck robbery. If there was a break in that case, that meant that Pelmington had stumbled on some evidence that could pin them for the crime. There was no way I could let that happen.

"Nervous about something?" a voice said from behind me.

I took my time turning around and was met by Tatiana aka Blondy. But I guess I didn't need to call her Blondy anymore. The only reason I came up with that name was because I had wanted Chris, and she seemed to be my main competition when it came to nailing him down. I wasn't worried about all that right now.

"No, I'm not nervous. Just eager to get back to work." I gave her a weak smile along with my lie and began to turn around.

"Mmhmm," was all she said but it seemed like there was more to it.

Like, I felt like I should have been turning around to mush that bitch in the face, but I kept my cool. It wasn't what she said but how she said it. Just stank like she was low-key calling me a liar. I decided right then that with or without Chris being an option, I still just didn't like the bitch.

"Okay, everyone, I'm here."

Just that quickly, Tatiana was the least of my worries and all of my attention was on Pelmington. I had no idea what I would do if something came through giving him the right to lock Luke or one of his brothers up. I was at the bottom of the totem pole, a brand new assistant district attorney. There was little I could do to combat anything Pelmington was about to put in motion.

I watched him intently as he walked in front of us all, his hand holding a cup of some undoubtedly expensive sugary coffee drink, and his other hand clasped on the edge of the desk behind him. Lifting up onto his toes, he sat on top of the desk and let out a heavy, protracted sigh, and my heart leapt a little in my chest. He didn't seem happy. So whatever he had to say about the case was bad news, which meant good news for me. The sooner we could get the heat off of Luke and move on to the next case, the better.

"So I have a bit of bad news," he started and I sat up in my chair, eager to listen and trying hard to hide my relief. "Your peer and co-worker, Chris Havarty, is missing. His mother issued a statement this morning asking anyone who has any information on his whereabouts to come forward."

My stomach flipped and then flopped about three times before I felt the radiating glare coming from behind. Trying to remain casual, I turned and once again locked eyes with Tatiana who was giving me a peculiar look that made me question how much she may have thought she knew about the nature of my relationship with Chris.

"According to his mother, this isn't part of Chris's character to be gone this long without speaking to her, missing work and not contacting family. She's extremely worried and, the fact that he's not even called into work to explain his multiple absences has me worried as well. I've offered up our investigative services to help her look into his disappearance. Chris was one of the best we had on the team and it's the least I could do. But…if any of you have any additional information to offer, I ask that you please come forward."

I felt a kick on the back of my chair and I turned around once again, this time frowning.

"Shouldn't you know something?" she whispered in a tone that sounded more like a hiss. "Weren't you dating him?"

Instead of answering her, I turned around and looked at

Pelmington, pretending to listen although my mind was now elsewhere. Obviously, Chris and Tatiana must have been on talking terms for her to know that we were dating. What else had he told her?

"Now I know he was close with a few of you. Janelle, you were close with him, right?"

Swallowing hard, I nodded my head, trying hard to keep my composure as all eyes turned to look at me. I could almost see the smug look that I knew was on Tatiana's face. Before I could respond verbally to Pelmington, she cleared her throat loudly, making sure that even if I couldn't see her, I could hear her.

"Yes, Chris and I were friends but… I haven't heard from him in a while," I replied, choosing my words carefully. I definitely did not want to admit to the fact that I was among the last few who had seen him alive. My eyes misted with tears but, luckily, Pelmington seemed to take it as me getting emotional over Chris's disappearance and came over to place his hand on my shoulder and offer his support.

"I know it's hard for you. Just… if you know anything, let us know."

After that, we were dismissed to commence work and I stood up slowly, not wanting to seem so eager about how I wanted to leave, not only the room, but out of the doors and never come back. As much as I wanted to learn more about what it meant to be a lawyer, I was strongly contemplating doing my own thing. Just like Luke suggested.

"So when is the last time you saw Chris?" Tatiana quipped just as I was making my exit. She walked around until she was standing right in front of my face, her blond hair pulled in a ponytail so damn tight it made her eyebrows look a bit more arched than usual.

"I don't see why that's any of your business."

She cocked her head to the side, the white girl's equivalent to the neck snapping that black girls did when it was time to fight.

"Oh? Well, I happen to remember Chris telling me that he was going to see you right around the time he stopped showing up at work. I think your birthday. Yeah... that was it! Something about letting you pick out some jewelry? What happened that night?"

I had to stop myself from reaching up and grabbing the owl necklace that I still wore around my neck. Although Chris hadn't bought it, I'd gotten it that night. It was the night that changed everything. My whole life. Still, I struggled to keep my face neutral, knowing that Tatiana was a trained attorney and would be trying to read any and everything she could through my expressions.

"I'm not sure why you're so focused on the relationship I had with Chris," I replied back with a slight shrug. "He's missing. Therefore, we have better things to focus on than your catty girl drama. His life could be in danger or worse. Focus on trying to find him instead of trying to get the details about the relationship that we may or may not have had."

Feeling confident that I'd spun her ass when I saw the way her mouth dropped open in surprise, I twirled around on my heels and headed in the opposite direction, leaving her nosey ass behind me. But even though I had succeeded in getting her out of my hair this time, I knew that she would be back later. Tatiana was like a gnat. She would disappear for a few minutes, but best believe she was somewhere hovering around ready to be annoying again.

***

"I hope being his girlfriend doesn't mean I'll have to keep coming to shit like this," I muttered, tucking my glasses on my nose as I stared down at my phone.

"Bitch, what are you doin'?" Carmella yelled, swatting at my phone. I moved it out of the way and gave her a nasty look. "I hope your ass ain't workin'!"

Snorting, I rolled my eyes, crossed my legs, and pinned my eyes right back on my phone. "I'm not working really. I'm reading up on some case law so that—"

"Her ass is workin'!" Sidney chimed in and I poked my mouth out at her.

Although I would rather have been somewhere cuddled up in my bed reading on my iPad instead of my small ass phone, here I was at the club with Carmella, Sidney, and Sidney's loud ass, ghetto friend Faviola. The Murray brothers were throwing a party to celebrate the fact that it was a Friday—in other words, it was just another reason to be in the club—and everybody and their mama was trying to get in to the hole in the wall club in Brooklyn. I'd decided not to go as soon as Luke had mentioned it, but Carmella called me up and reminded me about the dozens of women who would be lined up to ride his dick and told me that I better be there.

So here I was... sitting in the lounge section wearing a semi-sexy dress and not at all sexy shoes because my feet hurt like hell from tiptoeing away from Tatiana all day. I looked around at the other women at the table: Carmella in her normal clubwear, looking like a damn runway model; Sidney, looking more feminine than usual, in a pair of short shorts and strap up gladiator flats along with a sequin top; and Faviola in her ghetto-fabulous attire of high-waisted coochi-cutter shorts, complete with her rounded ass cheeks hanging out, a loose fitting shirt with a plunging neckline, and her placid blond hair in soft ringlets down her back. At my age and with my profession, I would have never imagined this would be my crowd, but here we were.

"Look at that bitch all up in Tank's face! I should smack the fuck shit out of her ass!"

I was ready to dive for cover when I heard Faviola pop off but Sidney was ready for her, grabbing her arm before she could run over and demonstrate for us all what it meant to smack the 'fuck shit' out of somebody. Carmella burst out laughing and I eyed her, wondering why she was in such a good mood, then I shrugged and chucked it up to good sex.

"Favi, calm the hell down! Ain't you pregnant? You ain't supposed to be fighting!"

"Pregnant?" I blurted out and eyed her stomach, trying to hide my disgust at how she was acting and how she was dressed while she was supposedly carrying someone's child. I'd heard a while ago she was pregnant but since she was still sporting a flat ass stomach, I'd assumed the worst had happened.

"Yes, I'm pregnant," she announced with a smile on her face. "With Tank's child, too."

"Yes, this much I figured," I replied, pushing my glasses up on my face and returning my attention to my phone.

"You know, you a little snobby and shit, but you'd be pretty if it weren't for them coke-bottle ass glasses."

"FAVI!" Carmella and Sidney both shouted at the same time, each of them giving her matching looks of surprise and disapproval.

"Shit… she's being rude as hell though," Faviola replied with a shrug and I chose to ignore her, pressing the button to lock my phone. I was ready to find Luke and tell him that I was about to go home. I couldn't do the club scene tonight. I wasn't in the mood to drink, and I had a lot of other things on my mind.

"I'm going to go powder my nose," Carmella said, suddenly standing up from the table. "I'll be back."

I didn't think nothing of what she was saying until I looked up and saw Sidney and Faviola exchange knowing glances as if there was some secret that I wasn't privy to. I was about to ask them about it but was interrupted from my question when my phone began to ring.

"Hello?" I answered quickly, seeing that it was Luke calling. My eyes searched the club for him, but he was nowhere to be found.

"Come over to where I am. In the corner," he said and instantly I began searching the club again, trying to find him.

And then there he was. Hidden in the shadows, across from where the DJ was and leaning up against the wall. My heart tingled in my chest with the love I felt for him. I nearly floated from my seat over to him, not even paying attention to the crowd I had to walk through in order to get to where he stood.

"Just stand here with me," he asked and pulled me close to him.

He was dressed pretty low-key tonight with a fitted cap low on his head, nearly covering his eyes, but I could still see they were rimmed in red from all the alcohol he'd been enjoying. Maybe even some weed. His neck was adorned with his multiple gold chains, but he had on a simple t-shirt and jeans with a colored bandana hanging out the back pocket that I wanted to ask him about but decided against. His shoes were anything but low-key. In normal Luke fashion, he had to be wearing the most expensive ones in the city, and I knew they were custom-made because that's the only way he wore them.

I leaned on his chest, taking in my fill of his cologne, happily finding myself getting drunk on him. He cupped my ass with one hand and pushed me closer so that I could feel the bulge in his jeans, and I felt myself gush into my panties.

"You not really feelin' this spot tonight, huh?" he asked and the only thing I could do was shake my head. I didn't trust myself to be able to speak just yet.

"You'll understand that the same way you help people… I help people. People in the hood need to know how to have a good time. It's a break from dealing with bullshit all day. When my brothers and I come here, it's not just about clubbing and shit. We pay for drinks, provide a little weed, get the place lit. They know if the Murray brothers coming through, it's time to celebrate life. I just want you to be apart of that, okay?"

I planned on nodding my head 'yes' but before I could get the motion out, I felt Luke fumbling with the hem of my skirt. Less than a few seconds later, his hand was between my thighs and he was slipping a finger inside of my panties.

"Luke, what are you… I can't—"

Fuck!

He started rubbing against my clit and it began to feel too good for me to stop him. He leaned closer to me, disguising his lustful act and pushed his face into the nape of my neck, kissing me softly as I moaned in his arms.

"Feel good, don't it?"

His cocky ass. He already knew what the deal was, but he needed me to admit it. I wouldn't give him the satisfaction though. I kept my mouth closed.

"Oh?" he asked and my eyes began to flutter open when I felt his expert fingers probe a little deeper, work a little faster. He ran his thumb over my nub, and my bottom lip began to quiver.

"You not gon' tell me that it feel good? It don't feel good to you?"

This time I wanted to respond, but I physically couldn't. I opened my mouth, waiting for the words in my mind to come out of my mouth, but they hid behind my impending orgasm. I could barely take any more.

"That's the spot, or you want me to stop?"

"Don't stop," I purred against him. "Don't ever stop."

He snickered, fully enjoying having me at his mercy. I hated him in this moment but loved him still. And then, while probing inside of my hole with two fingers, he ran his thumb over my nub once more before pressing into it, making me squirm into his chest.

"Fuck…"

"Let it go, Nell," he beckoned me. "C'mon, Janelle… let that shit go."

Seconds later, I was convulsing into him, my leg shivering and my body quivering. His ass had made me cum right there inside of the club but I couldn't make myself begin to care while I was in the middle of it. I pressed my face into his chest and cried out as he continued to run his finger over my nub, cupping my ass with his other hand and kissing the top of my head as I came down from my high. I tried to catch my breath while he cleaned his fingers by dipping them into his mouth, one-by-one.

"That was just the appetizer. Something to hold you over until we get back to my spot, a'ight?" I nodded my head weakly and took a deep breath as he backed away from me and winked before going back to join his brothers, the scent of me still, undoubtedly, on his fingertips.

When I finally got myself together enough to turn around, I walked back to the table noticing that both Sidney and Faviola had smirks on their faces although they refused to meet my eyes. My cheeks got hot but I sat down without saying a word. Maybe they didn't know anything…they couldn't have *seen* anything, right? We'd been pretty discreet.

"So…you still ready to go, Janelle?" Sidney asked finally, smiling a little as Faviola giggled beside her. "Or did Outlaw find a way to keep you here a little longer?" She finished, raising two fingers in the air suggestively, and I gasped.

Dropping my head in my hands, I couldn't help but laugh along with them as they made fun of the not-so-private moment I'd had with Luke in the corner of the club. These two weren't anyone I would have picked to chill with but this was my new crew, and I was learning I didn't have to be so uptight all the damn time. Right?

Sidney

"*H*ow far along are you again?"

Faviola grunted and rolled her eyes dramatically then flipped her long, platinum weave behind her back before turning her attention on me. Still, I couldn't pull my eyes away from her flat stomach. According to my calculations, she should have been at the end of 4 months…if not 5 months along and she still had the same thin, athletic physique that God had blessed her to have before being pregnant.

"I'm about 20 weeks. If that asshole would come with me to the doctor, we could actually see what we were having but… you know that nigga ain't trying to be a father."

Biting my bottom lip, I thought back to the night before when Tank was over and I caught him alone and mentioned him being a father again. The way his eyes lit up…there was no way he was still giving her issues about being pregnant.

"Have you asked him about going with you to the doctor since the first time when you had just found out?"

Faviola looked at me briefly, pressed her lips together and then placed one of her hands on her hip. I could tell without her saying a word what her answer would be.

"You haven't mentioned it at all, huh?"

"Why are you so interested in my business? What Tank and I

have going on doesn't concern—"

Standing up, I put my hand in the air to stop her right before she got started on her sassy black woman rant that she was only about to spew in order to throw me and squash the conversation.

"I'm not concerned or bothered by whatever the hell weird ass shit you have goin' on with Tank. I'm worried about you. A lot of stuff can go on when it comes to having a baby, and it's important to go to your appointments to make sure you're healthy. At 20 weeks, you're about halfway along and—"

"I appreciate you bein' worried and shit, Sid. But I got this. I'm takin' my prenatals, and I even think I may have felt a little movement the other day. I'm good," she finished and then turned back to look into the mirror and primp her already perfect hair.

Sighing, I sat down on her bed and decided to drop the subject for now. I couldn't rid myself of the thought that something had happened with her baby, but to push her further would mean that my own secrets would come out. Before there was a LaTrese in my life making me miserable and destroying what could've been between Yolo and I when I was only a teen, I had gotten pregnant. Scared that I'd made the biggest mistake of my life, I took some pills that I'd gotten from the clinic that told me it would easily abort the pregnancy. I didn't know any better so I took them and went on with my life.

In the middle of a basketball game, I passed out on the court after suffering from the most severe stomach cramps I'd ever had. When I went to the doctor, I found out that I'd finally miscarried. My mama whooped my ass to the point that I could barely even focus on the pain, and she made me promise not to tell my father or anyone else about what I'd done. I obeyed her every word and I didn't tell anyone, not even Yolo.

The fact that Faviola was pregnant but was not progressing brought all those memories back. She was so certain that everything was fine, but I knew firsthand that it took more than a positive pregnancy test to bring a healthy baby into the world. So many things could go wrong between that point and delivery. She needed to check and make sure everything was alright, but I couldn't make her.

"Tank has me plannin' some barbecue for this weekend so I can meet all his kids." She rolled her eyes and looked at me through the mirror.

"And his baby mamas?" I pushed, knowing that I was going to hit a nerve but wanting to know anyways. If the baby mamas were going to be there, I would have to make sure I was around to run interference and keep Faviola from whooping one of their asses.

"Hell to the *fuck* no, they ain't invited over here! He's supposed to round up all the kids and bring them over. I'll have some hotdogs, hamburgers, and chips ready and that's it."

I cocked my head to the side and smirked a little. "So you and Tank tryin' to work this thing out, huh? He's lettin' you meet the family and shit… it must be official."

Faviola kept her eyes on her own image in the mirror but her lips curled into a genuine smile. It was nice to see my girl happy. She damn sure had been through a lot of men in order to get to that point. And trust when I say *a lot of men* but you know what they say: hoes need love too.

"That's my bae," was all she said but the look on her face and the light in her eyes spoke volumes. She was in love with Tank's ole babymakin' ass and, whether they'd made it official or not, there was romance happening. Maybe even love.

"What's goin' on with you and Yolo anyways? He still got that crazy bitch over there?"

I was about to answer her when I stopped, dropping my mouth open. The way she said 'crazy' reminded me of something that I had pushed to the side for the past few weeks because I was so busy dealing with my new roommate: LaTrese's ugly ass.

"GIRL! You just reminded me about something!"

Before she could say anything, I ran to my room and grabbed my small backpack that I carried around. By the time I was back in her room, I had the pill bottle in my hands and plopped my ass right on the bed so that I could open them.

"The hell goin' on with you? You gotta pop a pill before you tell me what that bitch is up to over there? Damn, what she putting you through?"

Faviola finally dragged herself from the mirror and sat down on the bed next to me. She reached out and grabbed a few of the pills I'd dumped on the top of her comforter and fingered them with a frown.

"These are some pills I found in LaTrese's house when we went over there to get her. The label scratched off so I'm looking on that pill identifier site you told me about so I can see what they are for."

"You talkin' about that site I used when I was tryin' to poison homegirl I found out was messin' with my nigga back in the day?"

Pausing, I looked up at Faviola and rolled my eyes. "Yes, bitch. That's the one."

"Well, you don't even need that site for these. Bitch, these are Lithium pills. I know because they tried to put my sister, Diane, on them shits when she was in middle school. They thought she was crazy but that hoe was just ghetto as hell."

Scrunching up my nose, I looked up at Faviola and was about two seconds away from reminding her that her sister Diane was currently in prison serving time for stabbing her ex boyfriend's pregnant fiancé. Thankfully, the baby and the fiancé survived but there was no question about it: Diane was crazy. And to be real, Faviola wasn't too far removed from Diane her damn self.

"Why they wanted to give her Lithium? What's it for?" I asked, even though I was already looking on Google for the answer. Who knew what ratchet shit would come out of Faviola's mouth, especially when it came to Diane.

"They said she was bipolar, depressed, schizophrenic… girl, name it and they said she had it. Diane was diagnosed with all kinds of shit."

Sucking my teeth, I dropped my phone on the bed after reading the entire reason for a person to be diagnosed with Lithium pills.

"I bet that bitch beat her own ass."

I'd been thinking it for a long time but hadn't mentioned it to anyone, especially not Yolo. At the moment, he was so consumed with the fact that someone had touched LaTrese, and his need to get revenge for her, that I couldn't say anything contrary to what she claimed happened. But shit didn't add up for me when I walked inside of her house and it still didn't. She'd told me she was going to find her way back in Yolo's life and she had. It wasn't the way I would have thought she would have, but when it came to a crazy bitch like LaTrese, there were no rules to the game. Leave it to her bipolar, depressed, and schizophrenic ass to come with some off-the-wall shit.

"So you think she beat herself and then stuck a pole up her *own* ass to make it seem like she was raped in order to get Yolo's attention?" Faviola asked slowly while looking down on the bed as if thinking to herself. "You know what, I believe that shit. I would've done it too if I needed to."

Yes. She was definitely Diane's sister and her ass was definitely crazy.

"I'm going to ignore you sayin' that stupid shit and refocus back on LaTrese. This bitch is certified crazy and now I have proof."

Faviola smacked her lips and then nodded her head. "Yes, you're right. But what are you goin' to do about it? You gon' tell Yolo?"

I shook my head. There was absolutely no reason to tell Yolo at this point because he would only feel sorry for LaTrese about her mental issues and wouldn't believe anything about her doing the shit to herself. And on top of all that, I would look like the crazy ass snooping girlfriend who was rooting through her stuff to find something to fight about.

"That's right," Faviola said, running her forefinger along the top of her lip. "We need more evidence about this bitch to prove how crazy she is before we go to him."

Um... what?!

"Favi... I'm goin' to just drop it. At least I know what I'm dealing with. And she's almost fully healed from her self-inflicted injuries so she'll be out soon. Crazy bitch..." I couldn't get over the fact that she'd probably beat her own ass just to get a nigga's attention. Females did the dumbest shit.

"What did you say her ex's name was? I need his full name." I watched as she grabbed the laptop off the side of her bed and opened it. Her fingers were already moving a mile a minute, her long ass stiletto nails clacking across the keys before I could answer her question.

"I didn't because I don't know his name. He's some nigga she was messin' with when—"

"No need!" Faviola cracked her knuckles first and her neck second and then started moving her fingers back along the keys. "Bitches like her put every damn thing up on their Facebook page. I'll find out who he is."

Leaning over her shoulder, I watched Faviola get to work doing some shit that I wasn't even comprehending. Although most women my age lived on Facebook, I was more boy than girl and I didn't know shit about the site. I didn't even have a Facebook page and had never thought about opening one either. I rarely took pictures and I was positive that I couldn't count up five people who gave a damn about what I had to say. There was no point in me even trying to open a Facebook page. Might as well be talking to myself.

"AH HA! Here he is. Calvin Tolbine... damn, his ass is fine!"

One thing for sure, Faviola was right. Calvin was sexy but he kinda resembled Yolo in a way, except that he was a little shorter. Still, he was a definite pretty boy like Yolo, was light-skinned with light brown eyes like Yolo... hell, his style was even similar.

"When she said she was attacked again? Two weeks ago, right?" I nodded my head. "Well, this nigga got pics sayin' he was in Croatia two weeks ago. Now how his ass beat her up from Croatia with them short ass arms? I'm confused."

Bingo!

"She is such a fuckin' liar. I can't stand her ass, I swear," I muttered as I took the laptop from Faviola and began scrolling through the pictures that Calvin had taken from his vacation. There was a blond in many of the pictures. She was drop dead gorgeous and, from the looks of it, she was his new chick. He wasn't the least bit worried about anyone from his past.

"She claimed he used to beat her. I'm thinking she was lying about that too," I added.

Pulling up one of the photos, I enlarged it so I could take a good look at his face. Although you couldn't tell from looking at someone whether or not they were a woman-beater, Calvin didn't strike me as one. In fact, he didn't look like someone I would match up with LaTrese at all. From his pics, he was outgoing and had a surfer-dude type vibe. Definitely nothing close to matching Yolo's thug swag.

"Girl, that bitch lyin' about everything. Take it from me, and I feel like I can tell you what that hoe thinks because she thinks just like me—" I rolled my eyes. "—when a bitch like her wants a man, *anything* goes. She'll say whatever the hell she needs to say in order to make sure that he's focused on her and not you. So if she gotta lie… *hell* yeah! That's the easiest thing to do. A lie is some easy shit to do. And from what you told me about this bitch sticking a rod up her ass, she's on a whole 'nother level. That's Diane-type crazy. You may wanna watch out."

With Faviola's warning still weighing on my mind, I continued to scroll through Calvin's pictures until I got to one of him and LaTrese. The photo struck me as odd because of the fact that, even though LaTrese's stomach was flat, both of them had their hands on her belly.

Was this crazy girl pregnant from him too?

It seemed likely. I scrolled down to read the comments but they wouldn't show up. Something wasn't right.

"Why can't I see the comments under the photo? It says there are 16 of them."

Faviola, who was now in her closet trying to find something to wear didn't even glance in my direction before she answered.

"We aren't friends so some things you aren't gonna see. I can add him if you want."

"NO!" I shook my head. "LaTrese might see it some way and know that we're on to her."

Faviola only mumbled something under her breath about how she didn't give a fuck what LaTrese thought, and I turned my attention back to the photo, wondering how I was going to find out the real deal behind it. One thing for sure, I wasn't the only bitch sitting around with secrets. LaTrese had more than a few of her own, and I was definitely not going to stop until I got to the bottom of it and got her ass out of Yolo's house.

Carmella

"*T*hem bitches know you or somethin'?" I asked, attitude on fleek as Cree and I sat at down at a semi-private table in one of the many upscale restaurants in Manhattan.

Rumors were swirling that the restaurant we were in was frequented by celebrities, including Jay Z, Drake, Kanye and a few other rappers who I'd kill someone in order to be in their videos. But even if no one was in attendance tonight, I was all set to have a great time with Cree, who I hadn't seen in a couple days. However, a group of thirsty females were sitting at a table across from us and wouldn't stop staring at him like his ass was a celebrity.

"Calm down, Mel. Shit ain't that serious," Cree replied, tugging at the brim of his fitted cap.

"It may not be that serious but the shit sure is disrespectful," I said, loud enough for them to hear as I glared right into the eyes of the boldest one. She rolled her eyes at me and whispered something to her friend before picking at whatever nasty food she was neglecting that was on her plate. Heffa was too busy staring at my man that I was sure her food was cold. I couldn't believe these hoes now-a-days. They were bold as hell.

"How you gon' have an attitude about them hoes staring at me when niggas be tryin' to eye fuck you on the daily? And it ain't like you give a shit... always givin' them more and more to look at on your fuckin' Instagram page." He screwed up his face like something repulsed him and I rolled my eyes, realizing that I'd fallen right into a trap.

Cree had been more pushy than ever about me not taking sexy photos on my Instagram page. He didn't see it as a career like I did but I was getting a few dollars for advertising from small business owners and I knew if I could grow my followers, I would soon have top names like Fashion Nova asking me to wear their clothes for a nice price. In my mind, what I was doing was no different from a Victoria's Secret angel walking down the runway in lingerie so how come they got praised for doing it and people looked down on me for what I did?

"I really don't feel like having this conversation. At the end of the day, we are dating but I pay for my own shit and make my own money. What I do is the same thing I've always done since the day we met. You can't be mad at me when you knew the deal coming in." I crossed my arms in front of me and Cree gave me a blank, unreadable look.

The waitress came over in the midst of the tension between us and asked if we were ready to order. I hadn't had a chance to look at the menu because I'd been so upset about Cree being the center of attention for the table behind us but before I could open up my mouth to say that I needed a moment, Cree began to order. But get this... he ordered for himself and he ordered for me. How the hell did he know what I wanted to eat?

"Okay, I'll get that right out for you. And..." she looked at me. "I'll make sure to top off your drink."

Smiling, I nodded my head and then cut my eyes back to Cree.

"How did you know what I wanted to eat? You didn't even give me a chance to look at the menu!"

"Mel, you need to chill," he said in calm tone. "I've been dating you for a minute now. You think I don't know what you wanna eat? I thought that was the type of shit that chicks go crazy over… a nigga knowing them like they know themselves. Now you wanna start some shit because I actually know what I'm dealin' with?"

I knew I was acting like a bitch and I also knew why. I was feigning for a hit. I mean, it wasn't like I was a cokehead or anything like that. I didn't *need* it to the point that I would rob and steal in order to get it but it relaxed me when I was on edge and helped me to have a good time. I tried not to use all that much around Cree so the lil' bit I had before I met him at his place had already lost its effect.

"I'm going to go to the bathroom. I'll be back," I told him and walked away with my purse in my hand.

Less than a few minutes later, I was back at the table in a much better mood. Not even the girl's sitting across from us could fuck up my vibe.

"Bae, flex your muscles a little bit… give them hoes somethin' to look at," I joked and Cree looked at me like I'd grown a third eye out of my forehead.

"What?"

"Just toy with them a little. It'll be funny!"

"Hell naw," he laughed. "You on some bogus shit right now and I ain't walkin' into that trap."

Rolling my eyes to the ceiling, I cut into the chicken breast on my plate. Cree knew exactly what he was doing when he ordered it and I had no problem telling him that. The waitress had only just set it down in front of me and I was wolfing it down like it was my last meal. Cree smirked as he watched me but didn't bother to say 'I told you so' although he'd been right.

After leaving the restaurant, we took a walk down the street instead of heading back to the car. It was a beautiful night and so many people were out enjoying the city. Everything around me looked more vivid, colorful and lively than it had been before. Cree grabbed my hand and I smiled hard, knowing how out of character it was for him to show affection publicly. He was the low-key brother who always hid behind the big personality of the others. He didn't like being the center of attention and he didn't wear his heart on his sleeve. He was his own person, content with being himself and didn't care who judged him.

On the corner we were nearing, there was a small band and a man singing a blues song that seemed not all that familiar to me but, in my current state, you couldn't tell my ass that I didn't know the words. Grabbing tighter onto Cree's hand, I pulled him down to the corner and then turned to face him so that we could dance. I held him tight and swayed my body back and forth while closing my eyes and singing made up words to go along with the song.

"The hell you doin', Mel? You straight wildin', yo." He chuckled but fell into step with me, holding me tight. We were in our own world and I was so comfortable in his arms.

"You crazy as hell, you know that, right?"

I giggled at him. "I'm crazy over you."

"That's some corny shit."

We didn't say anything to each other for the next few minutes, just continued enjoying each other's company until someone decided to try and ruin the night.

"Awww, look at this shit right here. Ain't that sweet?"

Something about the tone of voice made me eyes open up and I twisted my neck around to see who the voice came from. When I saw it was the lil bird ass hoes from the restaurant, I snapped.

"The fuck you doin'? Following us?!"

Cree tugged on my arm as I pulled away from him. "Mel, ignore them bitches. We got shit to do and I ain't seen you in a minute, ma."

"Naw, I ignored these hoes earlier but it's obvious they want my attention," I told him, shaking my arm loose from his grasp. "Well, you got it bitch. Now what it is?!"

The bold one, the obvious leader of the crew, began to laugh and flipped her hair behind her back.

"Bitch, ain't nobody really worried 'bout you like that. We just find it funny as hell that a Murray brother would be fallin' for a fuckin' porn star."

No, this bitch didn't!

My neck snapped back like I'd been hit as my brain flipped her words over and over again in my mind. Her little evil sidekicks beside her began to cackle in laughter, obviously tickled by what she said. I saw her open her mouth to say something else but I didn't even give her a chance to speak. Kicking off my heels, I took off, lunging straight for that bitch's throat. And I wasn't even a fighter but the blow in my system was telling me that it had my back and we were about to beat this bitch's natural ass.

I clipped her in the jaw with a mean left hook that she wasn't expecting and she fell backwards. Grabbing onto her hair, I rabbit punched that hoe three good times to the face before her knees got wobbly and she fell backwards. I kept my firm grip on her hair as she fell to the ground and dove on top of her punching her from left to right. It was at that moment that her friends decided to jump in, trying to pull me off of her.

The crowd gathering around us did nothing but excite me and the adrenaline rushing through my veins definitely helped. I knew I could beat all these bitches if I needed to. I felt just that powerful.

"WORLDSTARRRR!" someone yelled and I knew that we were being filmed. That juiced me up even more. Hell, I was giving a show worth recording. *I was beating this bitch's ass!*

Until somebody punched me dead in my ear.

Whap!

All I could hear was white noise for a second. That bitch literally knocked my eardrum out of commission. Not missing a beat, I reached out for her and missed but my long nails got caught up in the fabric of her dress, ripping through it enough to knock her off balance. She stumbled over her heels and nearly fell to the ground. This was my chance! Launching in the air, I was about to jump on her when I felt someone grab me around my waist and lift me up.

It was Cree.

"Let me go! I almost got that bitch!" I screamed and then hocked up a wad of spit, shooting it out in her direction.

The beautiful bandage dress I'd decided to wear that night was now pushed up around my waist, exposing my lace panties. But they were nice and clean so what did I have to be embarrassed about?

"Let them hoes fight!" someone yelled out and I felt Cree get tense. He lowered me to the ground and the look in his eyes sobered me in an instance.

"That's right! Let them hoes fight. Especially that thick one. She was about a second away from showing her pussy!"

The man who was talking began to screech out a laugh and I watched as fire flashed before Cree's eyes. Pivoting around, Cree tugged his hat low and ran over to the guy who wasn't even aware of the danger about to come upon him.

"Cree, no!" I screamed.

It was too late.

Reaching to his side, Cree pulled out his gun and knocked the butt of it into the man's jaw, crushing it instantly. I'd seen this scene before but seeing it again was not any less horrifying. I almost threw up and had to cover my face with my hands and turn around. There was no way I could continue to watch as Cree brutalized the man who was now a bloody mess on the ground.

"Fix ya fuckin' dress and let's go," Cree ordered once he walked back up to me, wiping his gun with a piece of material he'd torn from the man's shirt. I didn' say a word, simply fell into step beside him.

"You made a fuckin' fool of yourself and pulled me into your shit. Now I got videos on the street of me crushing that nigga."

We had reached the car, finally. I slipped in fast, pouting because I didn't understand how Cree was acting like this was all my fault.

"I was only defending myself. Those girls—"

"Who gives a fuck about them? I thought you were proud of the shit you did!" Cree yelled out, smashing his fist against the steering wheel. "So she called you a porn star. I guess when you show your ass on the Internet all day, you can't be mad about that shit."

This was no time to correct Cree and let him know that she actually was more likely referring to the ads that Zeke had put up with me advertising his porn business and not actually my Instagram. But letting him know that tidbit of information surely wouldn't make anything any better.

"I'm sorry," I whispered, feeling like taking the high road so we could stop arguing. My high was gone and I felt like shit. Now he was making me feel guilty on top of all that.

"Sorry don't cut it, Mel. You out there fighting in the street like one of them ratchet bitches I said I'd never fuck around with. Murrays don't date and dine bird ass chicks and you know that shit. It's a fuckin' embarrassment. That's the kinda shit you on?"

He turned to me and I looked him in his eyes, wanting to cry but no tears came. Then something flashed through his pupils and he grabbed me by my chin, deepening his stare into me.

"You high?"

"Huh?" I retorted, pulling my face away. "No, I'm not high. Just tired as fuck and... I feel bad for everything that happened. You're right about me actin' just like those ratchet bitches out there. And I didn't even have a reason to do all that because I know you know what you got."

"Yeah," Cree replied back but his brows were bunched together like he wasn't really listening. He had other things on his mind and I prayed he wouldn't press me about whether or not I was high.

"Let me get you home. I had some other shit planned but... I just need a minute. I'll have someone drop your car off to you later tonight."

Him saying that broke my heart. I'd ruined our night and whatever else he had planned all because I couldn't control myself. That was the bad side of using blow. It made me have the best time of my life but it also had me on a hundred at all times. I was always ready to fight because it made me feel invincible. Well, Cree had put an end to all that.

"I don't wanna go home right now," I whined, leaning over to grab Cree's hand. He let me but his fingers didn't close around mine.

"Where you want me to take you?" He kept his eyes on the road, not even attempting to turn to look at me. His tone was blank and emotionless, like he was speaking to a stranger.

"To your house."

He shook his head. "Not an option."

Crossing my arms in front of me, I looked out the window the entire way to my condo. All I could think about was that I couldn't wait until I could get home and better my mood by snorting a few lines. It wasn't what I wanted... I would have rather been with Cree but since that was no longer an option for me, I was left with no other choice.

Teema

*B*ora Bora was beautiful but, to be honest, I was ready to get home.

While Cyndy and Miyani were enjoying spending time with their new boos, I was alone. Normally, I would have appreciated the quiet time because being a single mother to an toddler meant that it didn't come often. However, this was supposed to be a girl's trip and both of my girls had abandoned me for some dick.

"Would you like another drink?"

I looked at the waitress like she'd lost her mind. Of course I wanted another drink! I was lying by the beach, alone and practically twiddling my thumbs because I had nothing to do. Without a verbal response, she got the hint and hurried off to grab me a refill.

"I was going to ask you if you wanted another drink but I guess you got that covered. So would you like some company?"

The voice was familiar but not familiar enough for me to place who it belonged to. Shielding my eyes from the sun, I looked up and found myself staring right into Othello's eyes. I almost sucked my teeth and rolled my eyes, but I managed to keep it together. For a second, I thought I would be getting some real company, not some weirdo quiet boy who had sat across from me and ignored me the entire night while my friends had the time of their lives with his boys.

"Yeah I guess so," I replied with a slight snort and then grabbed my shades to place them back on my face.

Regardless to what my mouth said, it should have been obvious that I wasn't at all interested in his ass. I wasn't certain that having him sitting by me was any better than sitting alone. It wasn't like he was someone I could talk to.

"I, uh… I wanted to talk to you about the other night. Been tryin' to catch up with you. Cyn told me I could catch you here."

Instead of responding, I snorted again and kept my eyes ahead on the waves in front of me. I did make a mental note to cuss Cyndy's ass out later on though. I'd personally told her and Miyani how boring Othello was and how pissed I was at the fact that I'd gotten the only lame friend so why would she point his ass in my direction?

"I know the other night wasn't all that good because I ain't really say shit…" he chuckled. Like a nervous chuckle and I couldn't help glancing in his direction. And I have to say that I'm glad I did! Homeboy had the most beautiful smile with perfect, straight and white teeth that I hadn't noticed the other night. Mainly because he hadn't talked or smiled the whole time.

"…I didn't say much mainly because I wasn't sure how to approach you really," he continued and I turned back to look at the water, wondering where the conversation was going and also wondering why I was getting a tingling feeling in my stomach the more that he spoke.

"I'm actually the one who had Lamar text your girl about meeting up. I mean, he was feeling her anyways but I asked him to make sure that she brought her friends along because I wanted to chill with you. But then… after you got there, I realized I ain't really have shit to say."

He laughed again and this time a smile started to tease the edge of my lips. I gave in to it and gave him a slight smile, turning partially so that I could meet his eyes.

"Well, you could have said anything. We were just sitting there and you barely looked at me," I replied, licking my lips slightly—not to be sexy but because they were dry as hell and I'd left my chapstick in the room. However, I couldn't ignore the way that Othello's eyes dropped to my lips. It made me feel a little antsy when I saw his eyes shine with lust.

"Looking at you is kinda hard, to be honest. You're beautiful and… to be honest, you had a nigga tongue-tied. So how about we start over?"

Pausing, I gave him a long look even though I already knew the answer. In just a few minutes he had me intrigued, and I wasn't ready to admit it, but I was enjoying his company so far.

"Okay, let's do that," I replied, nodding my head. "I'm Teema and I'm 26-years-old, I am also a single mother of an almost two-year-old beautiful little girl named Kenya."

Cyndy told me all the time that I shouldn't lead introductions with the fact that I was a single mother because she said that I'd make men run before they even got a chance to know me. But my stance was…if the nigga ran because I had a child, then he wasn't the nigga for me. I wasn't hiding my baby for no one, didn't matter how perfect his teeth were.

"That's amazing. I actually have a daughter too… same age. She lives with her mother, but we are pretty much best friends so we work out the custody well."

Uh oh… he got a friendly baby mama. They probably still fuckin'.

I almost wanted to roll my eyes. But then again, would I rather he have baby mama drama? I contemplated which would be the better option and before I could come to a conclusion, Othello cut into my thoughts.

"And by best friends, I mean we are just that. We tried a relationship but decided we were better off as friends. But by that time, my daughter was already born. Matter of fact, she was born before we even got into the relationship. She's a product of a one night stand," he explained and my eyes went wide.

"Wow…" It was crazy to me that strangers could have a baby and raise her together when Kane and I were deeply in love but Kenya coming along split us apart.

Othello and I spoke for hours and I quickly realized that his daughter was the key to getting him to open up. By the time the sun started to set, I felt like I knew her although I'd never seen her in person. We swapped pictures of our daughters and then went on to other things so that we could learn about each other. I learned that although he lived in Miami, he was in New York often for work. It was after midnight before we decided to part, but we made plans to meet up the next day. I went to bed with a big ass smile on my face.

***

"When do y'all leave?"

"Early tomorrow."

"Well, I guess I got the rest of this day to give you the time of your life."

I smiled so hard that I was probably showing all my damn teeth. Othello pushed a glass of champagne in front of me and I grabbed it, sipping a little to help get the goofy grin off my face. The past few years since ending it with Kane, no man had approached me in this way. Obviously it was because I'd been traveling in the wrong circles. In the hood clubs that I frequented with my girls, I got no attention but a few nights in uppity ass Bora Bora and I had a man telling me all the right things.

"And what do you have planned?" I asked Othello.

He looked at me and smiled, showing off those perfect teeth again and shook his head.

"It's a surprise."

The surprise turned out to be a helicopter ride over the island that was nothing short of breathtaking and amazing. Othello had a license to work a helicopter as well so for part of the ride, he took over and I nearly died before I realized that he knew what he was doing. When he finished, he sat next to me and pulled out a black rectangular box from his pocket.

"What's that? Oh no... I can't take it," I told him, shaking my head. We hadn't even known each other that long. It was way too early for gifts.

"Don't do that. C'mon… I spent all morning looking for something special for you and this just fit. When I saw it, I knew you should have it. It's not a big deal really. I'm not broke as hell so it's not as big as what you're thinking." He pushed the box at me once more and I sighed before taking it.

When I opened it, I saw the prettiest bracelet ever. The charm at the end was of a mother holding a baby. Tears came to my eyes. From all the talking we'd done the day before, it was obvious he'd picked up on how important Kenya was to me. Seeing the charm made me chest ache. I missed her and it wasn't as obvious to me before as it was right then.

"This is beautiful, O. Thank you."

There was silence between us as we stared in each other's eyes and I knew we were both thinking and wanting the same thing. I closed my eyes once I saw him lean towards me, knowing exactly what was coming. His lips were so soft but still had the roughness of a man. He took control of the kiss, leaning in and slipping his tongue in between my lips. I was just about to really get into it when he pulled away.

"There will be time for that," he said and I knew he was alluding to sex which made a funny feeling flip around in the pit of my stomach.

Yes, I'd been all into that kiss but I wasn't sure I was ready for whatever we had going on to be more than that. It was all I could deal with right now. Plus, the last person I'd even had sex with had been Kane. Actually, he was the *only* person I'd ever had sex with. I'd never even thought of going there with anyone else.

Oh God... Kane!

As soon as he entered my mind, I began to feel guilty about what I was doing with Othello. It was like I'd started a whole relationship while he was back home, taking care of our child. Wait... but why was I guilty? Kane was not my man. Like really... he was *not* my man!

"Can I take you to dinner? I have a surprise in store for that, too."

Giving him a weak smile, I nodded my head but my mind was still on Kane and thinking about him made me feel uneasy about whatever it was that I was trying to do here. I hadn't talked to him about how he felt about me dating or moving on with another man and, Cyndy and Miyani were right. He was fronting the costs for this trip and everything else in my life. He deserved to know.

Othello looked out the window and I took the opportunity to grab my phone to text Kane and see what was up with him. Kinda feel him out before this continued any further.

Hey... you datin' anyone?

I watched the bubbles form on my screen, indicating that he was texting me back.

Naw.

But if you found someone that interested you... would you date her?

There was a slight pause before the bubbles returned.

I guess so. Why?

Biting my lip, I wondered how I should address this.

Well, I was thinking about dating someone and wondered how you felt about that.

There it was. It was out there and the only thing left to do was to wait for him to reply back.

I don't own you. Do what you feel, ma.

Crinkling my brow, I read his return text about three times before pushing the phone back in my purse. What did that mean? Was he being sarcastic? How was his tone? My phone vibrated and I grabbed it up, hoping that he'd given me a little more to go off of.

And I'mma do the same. You do you and I'll do me.

Sucking my teeth, I rolled my eyes before pushing the phone back down to the bottom of my purse. 'You do you and I'll do me'? I don't know why but that statement had me pissed off. What was he trying to do? And with who? Shouldn't he be concentrating on building a relationship with his daughter?

"You okay?" Othello asked, giving me a look of concern. I nodded my head and tried to relax my face.

"Yes, I am," I replied. "I'm more than okay."

He smiled and I smiled back at him, taking it a step further by grabbing his hand. I was bugging. Here I was sitting next to the perfect guy who was making it obvious that he wanted me but I was second-guessing that and feeling all guilty because of Kane, the same man who had abandoned me when I needed him most. Sure, he was making up for it now with the trips and everything but I wanted more. I wanted a relationship and, at some point, a family. If Kane wasn't willing to give me that, it was fine. But I wouldn't wait around wasting the best years of my life when there were plenty of men out here who would.

Janelle

*H*ave you ever had to sneak around your man? If you have, I bet it was because either you were cheating, doing something you weren't supposed to be doing, looking at something you weren't supposed to be looking at, or maybe even buying something you shouldn't have been. Well, not me. I was sneaking around and trying to hide from Luke because I was trying to work, and I knew he would not be too enthused about the fact that the primary object of our investigation at my job was him. Not even him *and* his brothers…just him.

Pelmington had other attorneys working on investigating the other four Murray brothers, but he was constantly up my ass about information and updates on 'the Outlaw'. Why Luke seemed to be everyone's favorite brother, I didn't know. From talking to Pelmington, it seemed his reason for focusing on Luke was because he was known as the wildest and most unpredictable. In other words, he was the one most likely to make mistakes. He was flashy and arrogant so he would do things to deliberately piss off the Feds, police, or whoever was investigating them at the time.

"What the hell you doin'? Hidin' from a nigga?"

I was so preoccupied with what I was reading that I didn't even hear him walk up on me. The paper I was holding in front of my face wasn't about Luke or his brothers specifically. But it was about their parents. Apparently, their mother had come from a pretty wealthy family and lost it all when she decided to be with their father, who was raised by a single mother—one who worked her ass off to provide for him—but nonetheless was never at the top of any high society invitation list. But that wasn't the most intriguing part of it all. Luke's father was just as bad as his sons when he was younger and had a slew of mugshots to show for it. Luke never told me much about his family so I was gobbling up all of the information I could, ferociously reading as much as I could. Which…is why I didn't hear Luke walk up on me until he slid right on the couch next to me.

"No, I'm not hiding," I replied slowly, closing the folder that I was reading from.

Luke's eyes went to it and his brows rose up in the air. I felt him tense up beside me and I knew he wanted to say something about all of the secrets that I still had. I couldn't expect him to understand why I couldn't share the details of my job with him, but I just needed him to understand that I would never betray him. He had to understand that the moment anything came up that would incriminate him or his brothers, I would do my best to get rid of it. He must've understood that because in the next second the distant look escaped from his eyes and his expression returned to normal.

"Pack all that shit up. I wanna take you out," he ordered, pressing against my leg with his forefinger. I flinched and rubbed at the spot on my leg that was now throbbing.

"Out? Where? I still have a lot of reading to do."

"All that reading shit is done. I wanna take you to the movies."

The words didn't even seem natural coming out of his mouth. Luke wasn't a 'movies' kinda guy but here he was claiming that he wanted to take me to one.

"A movie? Which movie you want to take me to see?"

He made a funny look, letting me know he was everything but at ease and then cocked his head to the side.

"Some chick flick that'll probably get my thug card taken away if any of my homeboys see my ass in there, but I know you'll want to see it anyways. Figure this might earn me some points and shit." He smiled, a cocky half-grin, and I shook my head. But then the smile on his face dropped a little, and his eyes tore away from mine. I crinkled my brows in concern.

"I'll have to leave in a couple weeks for work."

Now it was my turn to get rigid. He'd never discussed what he did for a living, and he'd definitely never admitted that he'd done any of the things he'd actually been accused of, but we both knew I wasn't stupid.

"For work?" I repeated, wondering if there was more he was going to say.

"Yes. In 'bout a couple weeks or less I'll be leaving. So until then… let's do some shit so we can get out this damn condo sometimes."

Standing up, he grabbed onto my hands and pulled me until I was standing in front of him. I looked up so that I could admire the love in his eyes.

"I know that you like to hide a nigga, but I'm done with that shit. I'm ready to get out the hood and do something that doesn't involve me flying your ass across the country just so we can be together out in the open," he told me, and I knew that even though he said it with a little bit of humor, he meant every word.

Ever since being with Luke, most of our time spent had been done while holed up in, at first my apartment, and now his condo. Outside of the things we did on our trip and the occasional club parties in Brooklyn, we never went out together in public. Mainly, that was on me. I was afraid I'd see someone from work. I could lose my license to practice law for not coming forward about a personal relationship that I had with the man who the State was investigating.

"Take a shower and get ready. While you were down here in the basement hidin' from a nigga, I put a lil' somethin' special that I bought you on the bed."

I raised my eyebrow at him. "You picking out my clothes now?"

He began to laugh and my heart swelled in my chest. It wasn't often that people could put a smile on his face, much less make him laugh. It was a sight to see, and it made me feel so good seeing it that I almost got jealous thinking about anyone else who had the pleasure of witnessing it.

"Naw, I ain't pickin' no clothes, ma. I'll leave that shit to you."

I took one look at him and then ran up the stairs, eager to see what it was that he'd gotten me. On the bed was a large box along with two smaller ones. My big ole eyes wouldn't let me do anything but grab the biggest box, and I tore the top off quicker than I would let him tear my panties off that night in thanks for buying me gifts.

"Whoaaaa!"

I pulled out a pair of high ass red bottom heels. I didn't know anything about labels but everybody knew a pair of Louboutins when they saw them, including a nerd like me who had never valued clothes that came from anywhere but Target. I clutched the heels close to my chest and closed my eyes, hugging them tight. Never in life would I have had the nerve to drop hundreds of dollars on a pair of heels, no matter how good they looked and how much I wanted them to be mine. But here I was with a pair of my own.

Slipping them on my feet, I shrieked with joy and fell back on the bed with my legs in the air, kicking my expensive ass Louboutin-clad feet. Then I remembered the other boxes and grabbed them, opening them quickly. Inside of each box was another teal blue box.

"Tiffany's!"

I nearly screamed before ripping open the box and revealing a pair of diamond earrings and a matching diamond necklace. Pushing my head in my pillow, I shrieked again. Yeah, it might have been a little thing to some chicks but, to me, this was *everything*. Never in life had I received anything this expensive from any man I'd dated. And, even though my daddy always bought us nice things, he taught us not to be materialistic. A part of me always wanted to be like Carmella, decked in designer gear from head-to-toe and spending my whole paycheck to look that way without having a worry in the world, but I'd die before I reached the register.

"Aye, stop all that screaming and shit and go wash ya ass," Luke said from the door. I froze in place and sat up on the bed, facing him. He was wearing a big ass grin that told me he probably had been standing there for much longer than a few seconds.

"How long have you been standing there?" I tried to cover my embarrassment by rolling my eyes and pulling on some fake sass.

"There are a lot of nice things that I'll be giving you," Luke replied, ignoring my question. "Ain't no need to act like that. This shit is just what I want you to wear to the movies. We got a long way to go, and I have a lot of things in mind."

Smiling hard, I stood up, slipped the shoes from my feet and carefully laid them back in the box before giving him a big fat juicy kiss and hopping my happy-go-lucky ass in the shower.

***

I looked good and smelled good, but I felt crazy as hell on the inside.

Twisting my feet around in my Louboutin shoes, I fidgeted with my fingers as Luke and I waited in line for popcorn and a drink. I wanted to decline the in-movie snacks, but I'd already told Luke how much of a necessity it was that I had all kinds of food with me in the theater whenever I went, so if I declined to have food this time, Luke would know it was because I was uncomfortable being seen in public with him. I couldn't make him feel like that. Even if it were true.

"What all your greedy ass want to eat?" Luke joked, poking me in my side. I caught his stare and could tell that he knew I wasn't feeling completely at ease but was trying to roll with it anyways.

"Just popcorn and soda." I gave him a small smile and he nodded, stepping forward.

"Damn, that nigga is fine as hell," I heard some woman remark as Luke ordered for us at the counter. I stopped myself from turning around to stare at her, but my ears were definitely tuned in on every word that left her and her friends' mouths as they continued to speak.

"He is. Damn…he look familiar too. I don't know where I know him from though."

"Bitch, the *news!* That's Outlaw Murray. Him and all his brothers fine as hell. I'd fuck him in my nigga's bed if he asked me to!" a third voice exclaimed and by this time, I couldn't help but cut my head to the side to look at who it was speaking. The thirst was getting a little too real.

"That *is* him!" the first girl said at the same moment that I turned around to look at her and her friends. They were the typical clubbish type, thick and curvy and dressed like their pussies were open for business. I rolled my eyes and turned back around, walking up closer to Luke and pushing against him to make it obvious who I was with.

"Couldn't handle all the talk 'bout ya boy, huh?"

I looked up with my eyes wide and was met by Luke's cocky ass smirk. Huffing out a breath, I rolled my eyes, but he only laughed and draped his arm around my waist before kissing me gently on the lips.

"Will that be all?" the man at the counter said and Luke nodded his head. I took the opportunity to look at the counter and saw that he'd ordered damn near everything behind it.

"Who is all this food—"

"Janelle?"

My blood went cold in my veins and I froze in place, instantly recognizing the voice behind me. I took a few steps back and then slowly turned around, connecting with Tatiana's eyes. There was another girl to her side, I didn't recognize her but she looked almost identical to Tatiana so I figured she must be her sister.

"Tatiana... hi!" I said a little happier than I should have, being that she was the woman who had threatened me and was trying to dig all in my personal life. And now she was being given all the pieces she needed. I watched as her attention went from me to Luke who was paying for our snacks at the counter. I followed her eyes and saw Luke glance first at me, giving me a peculiar look, and then at Tatiana. Instead of saying anything, he turned back to the counter, grabbed his change and stuffed it in his pocket.

"So...this is who you're dating now. How long has this been going on?"

I panicked and my mouth started moving before my brain could tell me that I was making a mistake. Never, ever, ever reject the one you love for a bitch who isn't worth giving a shit about. Never.

"Tatiana, it—it's not what you think. I'm just..."

My voice died off when I felt a rush of air pass behind me. Luke had gathered all of our snacks and was walking away like the stranger I was pretending him to be. He didn't even give me a second glance as he walked down the hall alone towards the movie that he'd picked for us to watch together. I caught the eye of the three women who had been ogling Luke, and they were each giving me stares and smirks that said a million words although they weren't saying one. It was obvious there was now trouble in paradise and, in their minds, he was there for the taking. And I'd made it that way.

"Um…" I stammered, my thoughts merged. I didn't know what to say to Tatiana because my mind was now focused on Luke. He was pissed and he should have been. Here I was in a position where I was putting something else before him.

"I think it is what I think. You're dating Luke Murray. How unethical of you." An evil smile crossed Tatiana's face, one that mirrored the one on her sister's although she shouldn't have known me from a can of paint. Or maybe she did.

"I—"

"Your secret is safe with me," she cut in and shrugged slightly.

Before I could say another word, she walked away with her sister shadowing her. I didn't know whether to feel relieved or not about Tatiana having the fate of my job in her hands. That was definitely the last place I wanted it to be.

By the time I found where Luke was sitting inside of the theater, the movie had already started and he was shoving popcorn in his mouth at a rate that seemed too fast for him to actually be able to taste it. Since being together the last few weeks, I'd seen so much growth in his character, especially when it came to his ability to use restraint. I just hoped that some of that would come through today and I wouldn't be greeted with a face full of popcorn as soon as I sat beside him.

"That was fucked up, Nell," Luke finally said, not even bothering to lower his voice. A few people around us turned to look in our direction, but one look from Luke told them they needed to mind their own business.

"I know...I'm sorry, I just—"

"No excuses. That was fucked up."

Swallowing the lump in my throat, I sat back in my seat remembering the man that I was dealing with. Luke didn't give excuses for his behavior, and he didn't accept excuses for anyone else's behavior. If you did something, you had to own up to your shit. And that's what he expected from me.

"Just remember when all these muthafuckas ain't around—when you really need something or someone to help your ass out—I'm the one who you expect to be there. And I'd drop whatever shit I'm dealing with in order to be there."

"I'm sorry." I ducked my head down and sunk my shoulders. "This is just new to me."

"I know," Luke replied.

Pushing two fingers under my chin, he lifted my head and kissed me gently on the lips, changing my mood and shifting my emotions in the way that only he could. I couldn't even think of being with anyone else besides him. But I had to figure out this work thing and my personal life because he was right. There was no way that I could continue to hide him anymore. If I chose to be with him, I had to choose him in every situation, no matter what craziness that brought about.

The next morning, I was called into Pelmington's office before I even got a chance to put my things in order at my desk. Sucking in a deep breath, I collected my folder that had all the details about Luke, figuring that Pelmington wanted to ask me, once again, about the status on the case. Time was passing and word was that the Murray brothers had another job planned so I knew that was most of the reason that Pelmington stayed on edge. He wanted to get ahead of them before they made another move.

"Good morning! I—"

My mouth clamped shut when Pelmington swiveled around in his chair to face me wearing anything but the smile I was used to seeing. Instantly, my mind went to Tatiana and then to Chris. Did Tatiana tell about Outlaw even though she said she wouldn't? No, she was evil but she wouldn't go that low. But the other option wasn't better. What if he wanted to ask me about the nature of the relationship I had with Chris?

"Janelle, I respect your father and learned a lot from his career so I'm going to just cut straight to the chase with you. It has been brought to my attention that you have a personal relationship going on with the focus of our current case, Luke Murray."

My mouth nearly dropped open and I struggled to keep my composure.

That bitch!

"As you very well know, that is an ethical violation, especially since you didn't report it on your own and was trying to hide it. Is it true that you are dating Luke Murray?"

Pelmington wasn't a prized prosecutor for no reason. He had a stare that could make even the most hardened of criminals squirm, and I was nowhere near being a hardened criminal. I was about to either shit in my pants or break out in tears. It was taking everything I had in me to keep it together in front of him.

"I…"

Just when I was about to speak, I thought about what Luke said to me the night before. There was no way I was going to deny him or the relationship that I had with him.

"It's… it's true."

The look of disappointment, disgust, and anger on Pelmington's face was unmistakable, and it was just about as hurtful as when I'd seen my father look at me the same way. The only two things that I'd cared about in life were my family and my job. Being with Luke felt like the right thing for me, but he was shifting my life around in ways that I'd never planned for. Still, my addiction to him was true. I would rather have him than be without him.

"Am I fired?" I asked Pelmington after a long moment of silence. His lip curled up in repulsion but he shook his head.

"The only reason I won't fire you is because of the reputation that your father has. I know that he's planning to run for mayor and I don't want to be the initiator of a scandal that will destroy him. I'll leave that to you," he added the last bit with venom and I felt every drop. "But you're off the case and anything else concerning the Murray brothers. I don't even want you speaking to anyone who is working on their case. I will not have you mess this up for me just because of some childish, immature error in judgment. Now clean out your desk and go to the third floor. Leave the papers you have on the Murrays on top of your desk."

This time my mouth did drop open, and I almost fell over. The third floor was where the interns and paralegals were housed. They didn't even have law degrees and I had graduated at the top of my class! There was no way I should have to be down there, especially since there were so many other places I could sit on the same floor as the other assistant DAs and be out of the way. Pelmington was punishing me.

Picking up my mouth from the floor, I stood up and walked out of his office, devastated about the way my life was going. When I got to my desk, I started organizing all of my things, stuffing what I could into my briefcase, and putting all of my files regarding Luke and his brothers on the top of the desk. About ten minutes into packing up my things, a large brown box landed right on top of them. I looked up at the person who'd placed it there and locked eyes with Tatiana.

"Figured you might need this," she said in her typical snobbish way, crossing her arms across her chest as she smirked at me.

In an effort to keep what little job I had left, I pressed my lips together and didn't respond. I knew that anything I said to her would get right back to Pelmington. She was going to try anything she could to get rid of me.

I could just have Luke get rid of her, I thought but then reprimanded myself in the next second. I couldn't get him involved in the disappearance of yet another assistant district attorney.

"It's just like you to run your mouth about things you don't understand. I'm really not surprised," I couldn't resist saying. "You've had it out for me since the man who you wanted didn't want you."

That struck a nerve and I could tell by how red her face got. If she was planning on being a top attorney, she had to work on those reactions.

"Well, too bad you chose a thug like Outlaw over him. Look how far you've fallen. You can take the ghetto girl out the hood but can't take the hood out the ghetto girl, huh?" she shot back and I swear I came *this close* to slapping the shit out of her. But it wasn't necessary. Yet.

"Why don't you just remember the things that 'a thug like Outlaw' is accused of and stay the fuck out my face? I'm sure you don't need any reminders of the things that he may be capable of."

The redness on her face deepened and her eyes widened at my words, letting me know she caught everything I was saying. Without another word, she swirled on her heels and nearly ran over to her desk, returning back to her own business, which is where I needed her to be.

With a sigh, I looked back down at my desk and began packing everything into the box that she'd left there, trying to ignore the fact that all of my colleagues were staring at me. It was obvious that Tatiana had passed around the news of what was going on. This would all pass soon... not really soon but soon. Until then, I'd just push through it. I was a fighter, but I also knew that if I ever got tired of fighting this bullshit, I had a problem-solver in my corner. Luke was there for me just like he said he always would be.

Sidney

"*I* got that nigga," Yolo said, walking in the room. "I got that nigga that did that shit to LaTrese. I know exactly where he is."

Looking at Yolo from under the hood of my eyes, I wondered if he expected me to either shout gleefully or jump for joy. It didn't really matter because his ass wasn't getting either one. I didn't care that he had finally made contact with the man who LaTrese *said* abused her. I just wanted her ass out.

"Thank you for being so patient with me. I know this shit ain't easy... but you gotta understand, she ain't got nobody. I can't just leave her hangin' like that."

I fought the urge to roll my eyes at Yolo. I felt like I was being more than accommodating. In fact, I felt like I was being stupid but the only thing keeping me quiet was because I wanted to keep her close in order to see what this bitch was up to. Not only that, I knew if Yolo put her up somewhere else, I wouldn't be able to watch what was going on between them. I trusted Yolo but I didn't trust her slick ass. She was the type of bitch who would drug and rape a nigga just to prove a point.

"Yeah... so when is all this gonna be handled so she can go?" I asked, trying not to seem as eager and uncaring about LaTrese's situation as I was.

Yolo gave me a sideways look that said he knew what my true feelings were.

"I gotta go out there and check the last of her bandages. They should be good and that nigga should be brought to me by this weekend… so then everything is a go. It'll be over and we'll be back to normal."

I watched him as he took his shirt off and started changing out of the clothes he had on in order to throw on a t-shirt and some gray sweatpants. Yolo was sexy as hell in every way to me and there was nothing more that I wanted than to be alone with him with our lives back to normal but I knew as long as LaTrese was around and well, that shit wasn't happening. She would find a way to balloon her ass back into my relationship as soon as she got the chance.

"Are you sure that this guy did that to her?"

Yolo pulled his shirt down and checked it for wrinkles before he looked up at me. His pretty ass had to be the only man in the world who cared if the clothes he slummed around the house in had wrinkles.

"What you mean?"

"I mean… you don't think it's kinda crazy that this random ass nigga comes out of nowhere and beats her ass for no reason? He don't even look like the type to put his hands on nobody!"

I blurted the words out before I got a chance to think about what it was that I was saying. For a second, I prayed that Yolo wouldn't think about what I'd said but he wasn't the ordinary thug. He had a degree to show for his intelligence.

"What do you mean 'he don't look like the type'? How you know what he looks like?"

Might as well come clean.

Placing down my phone, which I'd been holding in my hand, I rolled over on the bed and sat on the edge, sighing deeply before I decided to speak.

"I looked him up on Facebook."

"You did what?! Why would you do some shit like that?" Yolo frowned up his brows at me like it was really a crazy thing to do.

Um… *any* woman with a brain would do some research on Facebook when it came to her man and another woman. I wasn't the first and wouldn't be the last. Between Facebook and Google, women were catching niggas and their sidechicks, groupies and hoes up in all kinds of shit and I wasn't any different.

"I was curious and something about her story don't seem right to me. You know she's taking Lithium? It's a medication for people suffering from bipolar disorder," I further explained. "Here, I can show you the pills so you can see for yourself."

"What?!" Yolo barked and I froze in place before swiveling around to look at him. Why the hell did he seem so angry?

"You really need to mind your own business, Sid! This shit doesn't concern you. And you already saw what his ass did to LaTrese… you really wanna get mixed up in that shit?" He sighed heavily and shook his head. "You stressin' me the fuck out, Sid. And it ain't even supposed to be like that between us. You supposed to be my peace after I'm done dealin' with this shit but you keep tryin' to become part of the damn problem. Just stay out of this shit!"

I knew that I should've just let it go. Not because Yolo was right but because the last damn thing I wanted was that bitch, LaTrese, to hear me arguing with my man but I couldn't help it. I wasn't the typical female and I didn't get crazy over the little things but men had a way of pressing buttons and making even a cool ass chick like me act out. And that's exactly what Yolo did.

"How the hell you gonna blame me for tryin' to help you with this bullshit situation you got me in? *We* are together: you and me. But you done moved this bitch in here because you feel some connection that should've died long ago with y'alls dead ass relationship! Now I played the side chick while you was with her and promising me that I was the one you loved but I'm done with all that shit now. I'm not about to sit quietly and watch this bitch work you like a fuckin' idiot about some shit that she probably did to herself!"

Yolo's fury showed all over his face but he didn't say a word. Not one damn word. Instead, he walked over and grabbed his medical bag before leaving out of the room. I couldn't stand his ass. This was his way of handling every conflict that he ever had in his life: he'd just walk away. Then he'd surface later, after he thought that I'd calmed down, and start with the 'baby, pleases' and 'come back to mes'. I wasn't feeling it this time.

I heard what sounded like someone crying and decided that it was time for me to get my ass out of the room and see what Yolo and LaTrese were up to. Before opening the door, I took a few quick breaths to calm myself down and prayed that I wouldn't lose my man after killing his ex-bitch because of whatever ploy she was pulling now.

115

When I opened the door, I saw Yolo sitting at LaTrese's side, patting with a cotton swab at some small ass cut near her eye that he'd repaired with stitches as she sobbed and rubbed tears from her eyes.

"I just don't understand why she hates me so much! I haven't given her a reason not to believe me!"

This bitch. I should've known that she'd been ear hustling through my convo with Yolo and would use it to her advantage as soon as she could.

"Calm down, man, before you bust these stitches back open. Sid supports you just like I do and she wants to make sure that we get this nigga for everything he did. Right, Sid?" Yolo asked looking at me with his eyes tight, daring me not to agree with him.

Hell naw! After the fight we'd just had, he had the audacity to test me in front of this heffa? Not happening!

"Actually, I don't think he did this to you at all, LaTrese. I think your bat shit crazy ass is seeking attention and you did this to yourself."

Yolo's eyes widened. He didn't expect me to lash out in the same way any other woman would because I'm 'no drama Sid' the one who sat quietly as his side piece for years and never spoke out about anything or caused him any problems. I was the one who always agreed with whatever he did without criticizing him for how he allowed people to take advantage of his kindness. But not this time. My life had changed, my patience was running thin and I'd found my voice.

"Sid, what da fuck?"

"Yolo, what da fuck?" I parroted, rolling my eyes. "Listen, if you wanna let this bitch use you like a fool, that's on you. But I'm not about to sit around and watch it happen."

I placed my hands on my hip and cocked my head to the side as I glared at him. It was something I'd seen Faviola do plenty of times when she was about to get ratchet but not something I'd ever thought I'd be doing myself. But here I was. Next thing I knew, I'd be calling her to stand by while I ran up on some bitch.

Standing up, Yolo walked over to me as LaTrese looked on, doing a piss poor job of hiding the smirk on her face.

"Sid, just trust me," he said, giving me a look that I guess I was supposed to read. But I couldn't see past the bullshit going on around me.

"Hell naw, I'm not settling for that anymore. It's either me or her and that's it. Either kick her ass out or I'm leaving."

Never give a man an ultimatum. I knew that shit… it was one of the first rules of arguing. Especially with a Murray. You never gave them an ultimatum because they'd always call your bluff. Without saying a word, Yolo shook his head; his eyes full of disappointment and then stepped back, as if to say that I could go. My chest ached and I wanted to take back what I'd said but one look at the smug look on LaTrese's face made me change my mind.

"I'll be out in less than an hour," I said and turned around to pack my things and leave.

***

I woke up the next day and had to pee like a racehorse thanks to the fact that I'd spent all night drinking and talking to Faviola about the LaTrese situation. The bad thing was, my fucking toilet wasn't working correctly thanks to the apartment manager being a stupid ass and I couldn't hold it long enough to nigga-rig it like he'd showed me.

"Gotta use your bathroom!" I yelled, bursting into Faviola's room. If Tank had come over in the middle of the night and was naked in her bed, she'd just have to forgive my ass because a bitch needed to pee!

Sitting on the toilet, I exhaled heavily as I let everything out while staring at the ceiling. I knew that today I'd have to deal with Yolo because there was no way he was going to let me go a full day without returning his calls before he popped up on my ass. I wasn't looking forward to it. After giving him all the evidence about LaTrese, he still seemed like his ass wanted to take her side so what was there for me to do? I knew for a fact I didn't want to be in a relationship like that. I'd played sidechick to that bitch for long enough already and I'd be damned if I was going to do it again when I was supposed to be Yolo's main chick!

Looking down, I reached for the toilet paper so I could clean myself but stopped short when my eyes caught on something in the trashcan.

"What da fuck…"

Frowning, I cleaned myself up and then hurried to straighten my clothes and wash my hands.

"Sid, why you usin' my bathroom?" Faviola asked through the door, just as I was finishing up and trying to get my words together for her ass. "I have to—"

"You have to what?" I shouted, swinging the door open. "Change your tampon?"

Faviola's mouth flew open and I saw in her eyes that she was trying to work up an excuse to explain the wrapper that I'd seen in her garbage. Realizing there was none, she sighed heavily, her shoulders drooping pitifully. If I hadn't been so upset about the fact that I now knew she'd been lying to me for months, I would have felt sorry for her.

"I—I think I lost it."

Her revelation came out as a whisper that I could barely hear but, although I wanted her to repeat the words to make sure that I'd heard her right, deep down, I already knew I had.

"Lost it? The baby?"

Faviola nodded her head as tears started streaming down her cheeks. She walked back into her room and sat on her bed. The sight of her nearly broke my heart. I've known Faviola for a long time, and the thing about her was that she never let anyone see her down. She was the epitome of crazy, but she was also the epitome of a strong woman. No matter what bullshit anyone put her through, she always bounced back immediately but, this time, I was seeing the vulnerable side of her that she often hid.

"I really was pregnant... I didn't lie about that. I wasn't just trying to trap Tank, I swear." She paused and wiped at her nose. I walked into the bathroom and grabbed some tissue before handing it to her.

"Some weeks ago, I started to have the worse stomach pains. I didn't know what was wrong but I was too scared to go to the doctor. I guess I didn't want to hear anything bad so I just dealt with it. Then I started to bleed...deep down, I knew some shit was wrong because I haven't been feeling pregnant for a while. No cravings, no weight gain… shit, I look fly as ever right now." She wasn't lying. She did.

"Favi, you gotta go to the doctor still. If you had a miscarriage—" She shuddered at me saying the word. "If you had one, you still need to be checked to make sure that everything passed through and won't make you sick later on. I know this is hard and I'm so sorry for you, but this just gives you an opportunity to work on the relationship you have with Tank and get your shit together before you decide to have a child again. But still, I'm so sorry."

I wasn't a crier at all but watching Faviola so emotional as she collapsed into my arms made me want to break down and join her. I knew how it was when I lost my baby. Even though it was because of a decision that I'd made, part of me had wanted to keep it and I still mourned the loss of the child Yolo and I had created.

"Let's get ready so we can go to the clinic and get you checked out."

"I can't!" Faviola cried, pushing her face into my shoulder. "I just don't want it to be true."

"Favi, ignorin' this shit isn't going to change the circumstances, but it could make it worse. Let's go. I'll drive."

Faviola's doctor's appointment was hard to get through, but the good news was that we learned she would be alright, and there were no complications after the miscarriage. She fell asleep as soon as we got onto the road, and by the time I was around the corner from our spot, she was snoring lightly. Which was a good thing because I pulled up at the same time that Tank and Yolo jumped out of a bright blue Maserati that was parked right in front of the door.

Sighing, I glanced from Tank's face to Faviola, who was sleeping peacefully after crying her heart out for the last few hours. I tried to play out in my mind what I was going to do to help her out in what was about to be one of the hardest situations she'd ever faced.

"Where y'all comin' from? She sleep? No wonder she ain't been answerin' the damn phone," Tank said, peering through my windows over to the passenger side. I placed my finger to my lips to urge him to be quiet and quickly got out of the car, still avoiding Yolo's eyes. It didn't stop him from walking over and standing right next to his brother, inviting himself into our conversation.

"She—she had a really hard day," I started, hesitating because I wasn't sure about how much I should tell him. "Don't be too hard on her. She has somethin' to tell you about the baby, but it ain't gon' be easy—"

"What about the baby?" Tank butt in and I could hear the panic in his voice. His eyes searched mine and I saw them grow wide with dread as he understood the words I hadn't even said.

"Fuck!"

He dropped his head in his hand and then ran it across his beard, staring at Faviola who was still sleeping in the car, not even aware of what was going on outside. Yolo put his hand on his brother's back to relax him and I took the opportunity to look into his face. The sadness I saw there told me that he was thinking of the child he'd lost. The one he'd had with LaTrese. I pulled my eyes away from his face, pressing my lips together to avoid the pain of knowing he was thinking about that child instead of the one that I'd made with him. But that was my own fault.

I watched as Tank walked over to the other side of the car and opened the door. Faviola stirred a little right before he plucked her from the seat and cradled her in his arms. Her eyes flickered open in surprise and then settled on Tank just as he bent down to kiss her on the forehead. I continued to stare as he walked her up the stairs, using her key to open the front door before they disappeared inside leaving me to deal with Yolo. I knew then that Tank loved her. He would make sure that Faviola was alright.

"I'm sorry about your friend. I know how it must feel," he said. I looked down instead of into his eyes.

"She'll be fine. Favi is strong."

"So are you." I snorted at his flattery, wanting to play hard rather than accept it for what I knew it was: his way of apologizing.

"LaTrese still at your place?"

He dropped his head and stuffed his hands in his pockets. He didn't even have to say anything, I knew the answer just from his actions. My eyes teared up but I sniffed the tears away. My emotions were fucked up from the morning I'd had with Faviola, but I'd be damned if Yolo saw me cry over this bullshit.

"Yeah, I just wanna get this shit out of the way with her ex and then she can go. But trust, that's all it is."

I wanted to slap the shit out of him for being so stupid.

"She's playing you, Yolo! Do you really think that her ex really did anything to her?" I asked him, frowning so hard that my forehead throbbed. After everything I'd said to him and shown him, he still felt like LaTrese was telling the truth about this whole ordeal. I couldn't believe this shit.

"Listen, I believe what you sayin' Sid. I just have to be sure 'bout a few things. It's not just about what she told me. I don't expect you to understand, but I expect you to trust me."

Looking up into his eyes, I felt dumb as hell because I knew what I was going to do even though I wanted to punch my own damn self in the face for doing it. Have you ever felt weak for a man? I mean, like so weak that he could be telling you some bullshit but you'll convince yourself that it wasn't so because it was easier to be with him than to be without him. That's how I felt when it came to Yolo. I knew I wouldn't play this game with him and LaTrese for much longer, but I also knew that he was the one for me, and I wanted to stick around just in case he started to see that sometime soon.

"Come here," he said but didn't waste any time pulling me close. Leaning down, he kissed me deeply and I returned it, pushing away all of my thoughts of feeling out of place, dumb, and weak to the side.

"I love you, Sid."

"I love you too," I replied. The words were so familiar to my tongue, it was like they glided right out.

"Aye, you got me tomorrow?" he asked and I nodded. "We gon' do the couple's tournament?"

Smiling hard, I nodded once again. Tomorrow was the Murray's Fall basketball tournament and, for the first time since they'd started sponsoring the event in Brooklyn, they were including a quick tournament of couples vs. couples basketball. I didn't know who else was playing, but it was a given that Yolo and I would ball out.

"I'll be there," I reaffirmed and he grinned at me, showing off damn near all of his beautiful white teeth.

Reaching out, he looped his fingers into the belt loop of my jeans and pulled me closer to him, flipping around so that his back was on the car and I was leaning on his front.

"Are you comin' back home to me then?"

I paused, not sure about how I wanted to respond. On one hand, I didn't want to see LaTrese's ugly ass face but, on the other hand, I didn't want to leave her alone with Yolo any longer. It was stupid enough that I had an argument earlier while she was in the house and then left the two of them alone. Bitches like her loved to see shit like that because then they thought they had a chance.

"Yeah, I'll come back. Since you drove with Tank, just let me pack up a few things and then I'll drive us both over there."

"Hell naw," he remarked, startling me. I looked up, unsure of what to expect when I glanced into his face but I was happy to see a smirk.

"You don't need to pack shit," he continued, pulling a black card out of his wallet. "It's been a minute since a nigga broke bread on you for real. Let me treat you…remind you that you're still and always will be my queen."

Ducking my head, I tried to bite down on the smile coming up on my face. I was caught up in so many emotions but the largest of them all was love. It would never go away.

"I hate your ass," I told Yolo, pushing him lightly as I sat back down in the car. He jerked me by my arm and pulled me out before scooping me up into his arms to carry me to the passenger side.

"I know it," he countered before kissing me gently on the lips.

Carmella

*O*ne line of blow was beginning to not be enough. Some days, not even two.

It was becoming harder and harder to get high these days, but I had to do it in order to perform the way I needed to at work. Have you ever tried to take off your clothes in front of a room full of people, and look sexy while doing it, but know that your image would be flashed across the country in porn-related ads that your professor and classmates would see? If you have, then you know how fucked up it felt to be me right then. It was one thing to pose in sexy lingerie on my Instagram page. It was another thing knowing that my image would be used to promote the release of 'Ms. Juicy Booty 45' when it hit the shelves.

"Arch your back a little," Jake, the photographer, coached me in between clicks.

I did as he asked, pushing my breasts high in the air, while delivering my best seductive look. My head was in the clouds and I didn't feel a thing. In fact, I was actually having a good time and feeling myself. That was how it was when I was high. It gave me the courage that I needed to get the job done. In fact, I felt downright sexy posing in front of the camera and hearing from Zeke how gorgeous I was while I did it. A couple of times, he even smacked me on the ass and made me giggle, which turned into some of the best photos of the entire shoot.

"Alright, I think we got what we need," Jake announced and I was happy to hear it.

By this time, my high was wearing off and I needed to re-up on my nose candy to keep my high going. I was heading home so I really didn't need it but the feeling was so good…a little bit wouldn't hurt, right?

Now I know I swore that I wasn't an addict. Cocaine was a party drug and I was a party girl. Nothing has changed; the story was still the same. The only difference was that my job had become a big party, and I needed to use it more often to wrap my head around what I needed to do. As soon as I was done with my contract, I was done with the drugs and back to my normal life. After speaking with Zeke, he agreed to shorten the contract to six months, but he crammed so many shots into each day that my head was spinning. His ass thought he was slick. All he did was push two years worth of work into those six months.

"How you feelin'?"

I turned around just before going into my changing room and came face-to-face with Zeke. Although I wasn't really feeling him all that much, my high was giving me a major attitude adjustment and was allowing me to at least stomach his ass for the time being. I shot him a smile and sighed deeply before responding.

"Tired, but I'm good. Thanks."

Just as I was about to turn back to walk into my changing room, Zeke reached out and grabbed me by the arm. I frowned slightly when he tugged me around, but before I could say another word, the next thing I knew his lips were pressed up against mine. I was too stunned to move and it seemed like he took the fact that I wasn't pushing him away as approval to continue. He inserted his tongue into my mouth and flopped it around like a dying fish, and that's when I finally came to my senses and pushed away from him.

"Zeke! What the fuck?!" I shouted, darting my eyes back and forth down the empty hallway to make sure no one was around watching. Reaching up, I rubbed his wet kiss from my lips and frowned into his eyes, wondering what the hell kind of explanation he had for this.

"Damn, Carm, don't act like you don't know I been feelin' you," he replied, his light brown eyes in a slight frown as he looked down at me like I was in the wrong for calling him on his shit. Leave it to a nigga like Zeke to pull some shady shit and then beat me getting mad. Being shady seemed to be his M.O.

"I don't give a fuck what *you've* been feeling! I'm in a relationship and I didn't ask you for that. You don't just go pushing your lips up on people like that!" Then something occurred to me. "You know, technically, this qualifies as sexual harassment. I could report this…or you could let me out of my contract."

It was a dangerous game I was playing because outside of a little bit of the money I saved up, I was broke. Still, I believed in me and I knew I'd find a way. Zeke had given me a way out of the contract I had with him and I would be a fool not to take it. With a smug look on my face, I placed my hands on my bare hips and looked up at Zeke, still standing in the thin bikini I wore for the shoot. I had the upper hand here and it felt good. The problem was…the haughty look on Zeke's face didn't match the way he should've been reacting, knowing that he'd just fucked up majorly.

"Naw, that ain't gonna work," he started and I was about to interject right before he continued. "I know for a fact that you've been coming to work high as fuck every single day. What's your poison?" He wiped his thumb against my nose and I slapped it away. "Powder, huh? Well, check your contract. We have a clause at the end about drugs. If it's found that anyone was taking them while working for us, your contract is forfeited but we keep the images and you have to pay back your advance as well as compensate us for the time you spent using the car and living in the condo. Can you cough up about... twenty thousand dollars right now?"

My smile melted away from my face just that quickly. This nigga was the fuckin' devil incarnate. He had me again and there was nothing I could do. Even if I had it, there was no way I could pay him back that type of money. I needed it to survive off of.

"Fuck you."

"You're welcome to. Any time you want," Zeke let slip right before I stepped into my changing room and slammed the door behind me, right in his face.

This was some bullshit and I knew that if I told Cree about it, he would take care of Zeke and I would never have to deal with him again. There was just one problem with that: Zeke was my best friend's brother, and she'd never forgive me if I let Cree hurt him. Fuck... I'd never forgive myself. I didn't want Zeke *dead*, I just wanted him out of my life. And I knew if I called Cree on him, dead is what he'd be.

"Muthafucka done blew my high," I muttered, rumbling through my small make up bag to pull out my stash.

Reaching down, I grabbed it and looked at it, mortified when I saw how little was left. I didn't have much to begin with, but that never really bothered me because I didn't use consistently and I wasn't dependent. Now, I could literally feel myself on the verge of panic as I stared at the clear plastic bag. And I hated to admit it but needing it for work was the furthest thing from my mind. I needed this shit for *me*. It helped me cope with and ignore the devastation of not having my daddy there to depend on. I'd never tell anyone but I was probably calling his ass more than Janelle was, and he was ignoring every call. I never was the type to depend on him to pay for my bills or anything like that, but I still liked knowing he was there…but now he wasn't. The drugs helped me deal with that but now they were almost gone.

What the hell was I going to do when this ran out?

***

"You a'ight?" Cree asked me, reminding me that he was in the room.

It was a day later and I'd used the last of my blow before leaving work the day before so the withdrawals were settling in. In my head, I was doing a good job of hiding them, but the look of suspicion in Cree's eyes made me think twice on that. He seemed to almost be able to see through me. We'd made up since the date night from hell where I showed my entire natural ass—literally—but still he seemed to be acting differently around me.

"Yeah I'm good. Why?" I began to fidget with my hands and then slowly pressed them down together in my lap, realizing that my nerves were bad. When I looked back up, Cree was staring right into my face, his thick and dark brows curled into a slight frown.

"Because I've been talking to you and you're not listening. You're staring at the wall...biting your fingernails and shit. Now you're fidgeting. Is there something that you need to tell me? Some shit you hidin'?"

The question hung in the air for a lot longer than it should have because I couldn't respond. I rolled my eyes to the ceiling as if searching for the answer somewhere among the dried paint, but when I brought my pupils back down and locked them with Cree's beautiful light brown eyes, I still had nothing to say. Not anything that he would believe anyways.

"I'm not hiding anything. I'm just distracted...about work," I added and then instantly regretted it. The last topic I wanted to get on was work. I still wasn't sure if Outlaw had told him about the reality of what I did, and I'd been avoiding the conversation for a while now.

"Work, huh?" Cree grunted, giving off a dry chuckle at the end before sitting down across from me. "You mean the porn palace?"

I should've known Outlaw's big ass mouth couldn't be contained. Of course he'd told his brother everything.

"It's not the porn palace, Cree. I just have to finish up the photo shoots that I'm contracted to do, and then I'm free to go. And these could really be good for my career—"

He snorted and I cringed. I didn't like the idea of anybody talking shit about what I did for a living...even if I talked shit about it too.

Nobody said anything about where he'd been the past few days when he was so-called 'working'. I knew the type of stuff the Murray brothers were involved in, but you didn't see me judging.

"Your career, huh?" he said in a mocking tone as he leaned over and unzipped a Gucci duffle bag at his feet. "You mean your job advertising pussy?"

Even though I was ready to snap on his ass, I couldn't help but admire the way that his beautifully toned arms flexed as he reached down to open the duffle. He was sexy as hell right then, and it almost cured me of all my withdrawal symptoms. With his beats headphones that matched his entire outfit draped around his neck, and his low cut curls on the top of his forehead, it was easy to see that he was definitely related to Outlaw and Yolo, the more stylish of the Murray brothers. But Cree had a style that was all his. Even now, he was wearing black and red biker gloves to complement his rather relaxed outfit of basketball shorts and a simple tee. On his feet were Converses. Only Cree could make this shit look fly as hell.

"I don't advertise pussy, Cree!"

"Well, what do you call it?" He lifted his eyes to meet mine and I folded my lips into my mouth, pissed off at the fact that I had no idea how to respond to him.

"I don't like that you criticize what I do. I've never criticized…"

My voice died off when Cree pulled open the duffle bag and revealed what was inside of the bag. It was stocked full of drugs. *Lots* of drugs of every variety: pills of all kinds of colors, weed… and powder. What the hell was he doing with this? I knew for a fact that the Murray boys didn't run drugs at all. They dealt with taking shit. Was Cree doing some extra stuff on the side?

"W—what is that?" I asked him, trying my hardest not to start salivating when he reached in and pulled out a large Ziploc bag full of coke.

It was enough to last me for a couple months, easily. Immediately, my mind began working on how I would be able to get my hands on it. I didn't need a lot…just enough to last me until I could connect with my supplier back home in Cali and figure out how to get him to send more to me.

"This doesn't belong to me…you know we don't do no drug shit. I'm holdin' it for my cousin. He was in the city and had it on him but had to make a run upstate. I told him I'd keep it safe until he gets back." He looked up at me and I jumped to relax the wide-eyed expression on my face. "Look, I know that you probably don't feel comfortable havin' this shit around so I can take it to my other place and—"

"No!" I said a little louder than I really wanted to. "I mean… I don't mind it, really. I've never seen that much drugs in my life, but it's okay. I trust you."

Biting down on the corner of his lips, Cree tried to hide the smile on his face but I saw it and loved it.

"Well, the good thing is you said you couldn't spend the night tonight so you won't be around it long." He shrugged.

"I'll spend the night!" I replied and then inwardly cursed myself for being so eager. "I'm just happy to see you. I miss you."

Licking my lips, I stood up and slid into Cree's lap. He wasted no time scooping his hand under my short skirt and palming my ass. I teased him by brushing my lips against his but waited until he took charge and dived in, sucking on my bottom lip before pushing his tongue inside to deepen the kiss.

I did miss Cree and there was no one else that I wanted to be with more than him, but things were difficult between us because I didn't feel comfortable being around him when I was high. And these days, I was high more than I wasn't. I hadn't been spending the night with him as often because I'd started using before bed, and I knew I couldn't do that around him. It was one thing to snort a line when we were at the club or something, but I knew if I did it too much he'd pick up on the changes in me. Cree didn't seem like the type to judge, but I didn't want to find out.

"I missed you too, Mel."

He pushed his hand forward and right through my panties, sticking one of his fingers—and then two—right inside of me. I gasped, and he sucked on my lips again before pulling me into a deep kiss as he stirred my honeypot. I dripped my honey all over his fingers, loving the feeling of him touching me more than anything in the world.

"Let's go to the room," he grunted against my neck, his voice deep and raspy. Sexy. He was the epitome of sexy…everything about him made me think of sex. Cree could ignite my body with one touch and I instantly belonged to him. There was no other thought in my mind but him when he commanded my emotions in this way.

Except for now.

Now, I was painfully aware that while he was giving me the

pleasure that my body craved when he wasn't around, right below me was something that could make the feeling even better. I couldn't resist it. I cut my eyes to the powder that was sitting inside of the plastic bag that Cree had left on the coffee table. Somehow I had to find a way to get to it.

"Have you ever fucked while high?" I asked him, pulling away from our kiss. Cree curled his brow at me but then slowly began to nod his head.

"Yeah...I mean, I've fucked you a few times while high off some weed. Shit like that." He shrugged, and I bit my lip. I glanced back at the bag on the coffee table and then quickly back to him before he could catch me.

"I mean, have you ever thought about trying anything stronger? Like...a lil' coke?"

"Hell no." His answer came fast. "Besides weed and the shit Yolo mixes up, I ain't tryin' shit else. 'Specially not no damn coke."

My heart dropped, but I hid my disappointment well...or at least I thought until Cree sighed and shifted as if he was trying to push me off of him.

"I'm about to leave. Gotta meet with Outlaw 'bout some shit right quick and I'll be back."

He moved from under me, sliding me off his lap before plopping me right back on the sofa where I'd started. Part of me wanted to stop him, jump on top of him and convince him to finish what he'd started. To be honest, things had been off with us for the past couple weeks, but I hadn't been too worried about it because I'd been too busy dealing with things in my own way. But then there was the other side of me that was still eyeing that plastic bag, hoping that Cree would hurry up and leave so that I could dive into it and take some for myself. There was so much, there's no way the little bit I would take would be missed.

So instead of stopping him, I sat my ass right on the couch and watched Cree stand up, pecking into his phone absentmindedly, not even noticing how I was about to break into a sweat waiting for his ass to leave. I mean…damn! Time seemed to slow down or something because it seemed like he was dragging his damn feet. I watched him, my eyes ping-ponging between his back and the bag on the table.

"Yo, I'll be back but it'll be late. Don't wait up," was the last thing he said before the door closed on his ass and I all but celebrated.

I tried to wait at least ten minutes to make sure that Cree was at least out of the building and in his car, but I swear every minute felt like an hour. Shit…I needed a little something from the bag to help me wait the damn ten minutes!

"Fuck it," I muttered to myself and reached over to grab the bag.

Not wanting to waste any more time, I popped it open, grabbed a pinch of dust into my hand and snorted it up quickly. Dropping back on the couch, I tried to let that be enough, telling myself that I should wait a little longer before I dove back inside but only a few seconds later, I found myself back inside, scooping a bigger amount out and sprinkling it into my palms so I could take a deep inhale. The euphoria came fast and I was so giddy that I almost giggled as I sucked it all in, enjoying the way it stung going down.

I was so caught up in pleasure that I barely heard the door when it opened. By the time I looked up, Cree was standing right in front of me. Staring hard. So hard that I almost felt like his eyes were lasers, splitting my face into two.

"I fuckin' knew it. I *fuckin'* knew it."

Running my hand over my nose to get rid of any debris that may have still been there, I darted my eyes over to the table, noting that I'd placed the bag there and, from where he stood, it appeared closed. He couldn't know what I'd been doing...could he?

"You knew what? I was just—"

"Don't fuckin' lie!" Cree yelled, his eyes pulled into slits and his lips in a sneer. Walking over, he snatched the bag off the table, noting that it was open, and lifted it to his eyes.

"I set this whole thing up because I knew you was on this shit. I just didn't know it was this bad," he said and I felt my heart tug at the disappointment and hurt in his voice. "Now you gotta go."

I frowned deeply, wondering if I'd heard him correctly.

"Huh?"

"You heard me," he replied, his voice a little more steeled in tone. "Get da fuck out. I don't want you here anymore. I don't want to see you ever again."

Teema

I was super nervous about the day because after speaking to him every day, and nearly all day since I'd been back in the States, Othello was coming to visit. What had me on edge, however, wasn't only the fact that I'd be seeing him, it was the fact that I'd be seeing him with Kane right in the same vicinity. It wasn't my idea to invite Othello to the park, it was Cyndy's fault. She was coming to the park with Javier, who was also in town, so when Othello found out that I'd be there too, he decided to tag along. I didn't have the heart to tell him no but now I was wondering if that had been a smart move.

"What you dressin' up for? We goin' to the damn park not the fuckin' club," Kane grunted and I rolled my eyes hard, keeping my back to him.

"I know where we goin' but I have someone meeting me there and I wanna look nice," I replied back as if it were any of his business.

"Better not be no nigga," I thought I heard him say.

"What?"

"Nothing."

Turning around, I cut my eyes at Kane right before he turned and walked down the hall away from where I stood in the bathroom finishing my make up. At his feet, Kenya toddled behind him, trying her hardest to keep up with her father's long strides. I decided to let

Kane's little comment go and exhaled heavily before turning back to look at myself in the mirror.

One thing was for certain, Kane was not my man, and he couldn't tell me what to do. Yes, I was going to be meeting up with Othello at the park today, but we weren't dating so it wasn't that serious. And not just that… I had already made the decision to slow things down with Othello. I'd even put the bracelet he'd given me in an envelope to return to him when I saw him. I knew he had feelings for me, but I wasn't ready to explore them yet. Something was holding me back from really wanting to take that next step into the direction he was leading me into. Still, he was fun to talk to when I was lonely and we'd been doing that more and more since Cyndy and Miyani didn't live close by and were always busy with work or one of their many niggas.

"You ready to go yet? I wanna catch up with my brothers before everything starts," Kane snapped for the fiftieth time this morning. He was in a bad mood and had been in one for a while. It was pissing me off.

"Didn't you just hang out with them all last night? Shit…y'all can't breathe without each other?"

"You shouldn't talk about not bein' able to breathe…them lil' ass shorts you got on. Da fuck you dressin' so hot in the ass for?"

Gasping, I swiveled around and caught Kane leaned back on the wall diagonal from me with his arms folded and his eyes on my shorts. Feeling a little put off by his statement, I grabbed at the hem and tugged, wondering if they were really all that short. I'd lost a few pounds the pass few weeks and was celebrating by showing off my body a little more, but I didn't want to be pegged as a hoe.

"They aren't that bad! My ass ain't hangin' out!"

"Tell me somethin' tho," he started, ignoring my statement and switching gears. "You meetin' up at the park with that nigga you been sneakin' around and talkin'?"

I huffed out a breath and rolled my eyes yet again.

Here he goes with this bullshit.

"If you're talkin' about Othello, yes, I'm meeting him at the park. But I haven't been sneaking around and talking to him." It was a lie. I had been sneaking and I was mortified that I now knew that Kane had caught me. "It's not that serious Kane. He's just a friend. Really."

Kane snorted, bunching his brows together as he looked me up and down.

"Friend my ass. The nigga got a dick and I bet it can stick. If he ain't gay then I ain't hearin' shit you got to say."

I cocked my head to the side and smirked at Kane's little elementary rhyme. "You tryin' to take up rapping now?"

"Don't fuckin' play with me, Teema. I mean this shit. And I don't want that nigga around my daughter!" His fists balled up at his sides, and I had to blink a few times to realize that Kane was really taking this to a level it didn't have to be on. Othello was cool and I'd briefly entertained the idea of dating him but the spark just wasn't there.

"Kane, first of all, I am not your property for you to be telling me what to do and who to see. And as for Kenya, I'm glad you want to be a father to her now, but you can't tell me who can and cannot be around my child. I was her mother and the only decision-maker before you stepped in, and I did a damn good job without you!"

His eyes lowered into slits and it was like I felt heat on my cheeks from the way that his eyes bore into me. Kane had always had a quick temper. Especially when it came to my slick ass mouth because he didn't know how to deal with it. And now here we were, at the start of another argument that Kane would squash by emphatically stating what he wanted me to do without leaving room for a response to go against his wishes. He wouldn't argue back, he'd just lay down the law like he was judge and jury. Big head ass.

"I said I don't want that nigga around my daughter and that's muthafuckin' it! If you wanna be hot in the ass and shit, that's on you but I won't have her watchin' her mama be a hoe!"

That was it. I was about to fuckin' lose it. Did this nigga really say that I was being a hoe because of *one* man he knew I was talking to?

"Fine! Fuck that tournament. We'll just go somewhere else because I don't even wanna see ya lil' ugly ass face anymore!"

"You ain't goin' nowhere with him so cancel that shit. He ain't comin' to the tournament and you not goin' nowhere with him. I don't know that nigga and neither do you," Kane replied back with his arms crossed in front of his chest, looking like a big ass child having a temper tantrum.

I really couldn't understand what was going through his head right now. He'd gone from acting like he was my jealous ex-boyfriend to now acting like he was my father. If this was how it was to have an involved baby daddy, I wasn't sure that I wanted it.

"You can't tell me where to go and you damn sure can't tell me what to fuckin' do!" I fumed ready to meet him on his childish level and start stomping my feet and pouting like the child he was treating me like.

"Try me. Muthafuckin' try me, Teema, and I swear I'll lock your lil' ass in here."

Cocking my head back, I looked at Kane like he'd lost them all. He *had* to have lost them all if he was really threatening to lock me in the house so that I wouldn't go out with another man. I swear I couldn't stand his ass when he got like this. He seemed to think everything was his way or the highway but that wasn't how I rolled. I would not be ordered around like I was his personal slave.

"I'm doing what the hell I want to do Kane because you don't fuckin' own me so do what you think you gotta do," I told him, snaking my neck with every word.

He was going to learn today that Teema Joy Ellison was not to tested and not to be threatened. I made my own rules and did whatever the fuck I wanted to do.

***

If I've never told you anything, I'm going to tell you this because it just may save your life. Never, ever, *ever* test a Murray. You'll come out on the losing end every time.

"Cree, can you come pick me up? I'm at Kane's. You still got a key to his place, right?"

"Pick you up? Why that nigga can't get you?"

Sighing, I was almost too embarrassed to explain my situation. "He locked me in the guest room and I can't get out. Only thing I got is my phone because he wanted me to cancel the date I had with this dude I been talking to."

I called his bluff because I didn't think his ass would follow through but he did. While I was in the bathroom finishing my make up, Kane's ass reversed the lock on the guest room door so that it could be locked from the outside and then pushed my ass in there. Before leaving with Kenya, he told me that I needed to cancel the date I had with Othello because I wasn't going anywhere until he got back and then he left. I halfway thought about calling the police and telling them I was being held hostage but I wasn't that stupid.

"Y'all crazy as hell. Why don't y'all stop fuckin' around and just get back together?"

Blinking a few times, I squinted my eyes and scrunched up my nose.

"Um… it's cliché to think that I would want to get back with him just because he's Kenya's father. What we had is over. Plus, Kane ain't tryin' to be with me like that anyways."

"Oh, that's why he locked your ass up, huh?" Cree joked, chuckling a little on the other side and my heart fluttered a little as I thought about what he was implying. Did Kane still have feelings for me?

"Who knows what goes on in your brother's crazy mind. I'm sick of his ass," I huffed out, rolling my eyes.

Sitting down on the bed, I nibbled on the cookies that Kane had left in the room for me and then took a bite of the peanut butter and jelly sandwich. Reaching over, I grabbed a bottled water out of the small mini-fridge to wash the sandwich down. Yes, only that nigga would lock somebody up in the guest room but make sure they had snacks, magazines and other reading material to keep them company. He was a thoughtful asshole at least.

"Stop giving him such a hard time, Teema. You know better than I do that Kane has a hard time expressing himself. We all do but that nigga probably got it the worst. You gotta see into what he's not saying. He told you that he didn't want you goin' out with another nigga and he locked your ass up to keep you from goin'. He meant that shit. He don't want you dealin' with no other nigga but him."

"How romantic," I sassed. Cree laughed again.

"Hey, I'm just tellin' you that nigga is still feelin' you. Think about it."

"Well, he can be feelin' me from a distance," I told Cree, sucking my teeth. "Can I stay at your place for a few days? I need a break from his ass. Would your girl be okay with that?"

Cree went silent for a minute and I thought it was because he was trying to tell me that his girlfriend would have a problem.

"I mean, if she has an issue with it, I don't have to stay—"

"No, it's not that. Her and I aren't together anymore. You can stay as long as you like," he said finally and I was instantly curious about his business and what he had going on.

"Really? I didn't see that coming."

"Yeah, she got a lot of lil' habits I can't vibe with."

"You mean a coke habit?" I blurted out and the line went silent.

"How you know 'bout that?" he asked, his tone different.

I paused and licked my lips, wondering if I should tell him the truth about how I'd found out about his girlfriend's addiction. I probably should have come forward about it instead of holding it in all this time.

"I ran into her once, before I knew she was your girlfriend. She was using back then," I revealed. A few seconds passed between us without Cree saying a word.

"I'll be there in a few to get you and then we can head to the game," was the last thing he said before hanging up the line. I placed the phone down wondering if I'd put my foot in my mouth.

Sidney

*L*ooking at the trophy that Yolo and I had won from the basketball tournament, I wondered if I was making the right decision about what I was about to do. Everything was good between us... better than it had been in a minute. We'd balled out at the tournament just like we thought we would. Of course, the Murray brothers brought home every award, winning the team competition and Outlaw brought home the prize for the slam-dunk competition. Cree won the most free throws during that competition but the best part of the day was playing along with Yolo for the couple's competition.

Afterwards, we went back to his place and had loud, passionate sex. And when I say loud, that's exactly what the hell I meant because I wanted LaTrese to hear everything going on and know that we were the happy couple she wanted us not to be. Judging from the ugly ass look on her face the next morning, I was sure that she was well aware of everything that had gone on in that room the night before.

But now, here I was sitting with Faviola, Janelle and Carmella, about to do something that might mess up all the progress that I was making with Yolo. Still, I had to do it.

"Guys, I don't think this is a good idea. We can get in a lot of trouble for accessing someone's personal information." That was Janelle's ole law-abiding ass. The only reason she was even over here was because Carmella had said that she was a lawyer and had certain access to things that we might need.

"Girl, we don't care about gettin' in no damn trouble! We know we 'bout to break into some shit and that's what we 'bout to do!" Faviola snapped, flipping her hair in Janelle's direction. Janelle gave her a stank look but didn't say anything.

It was a few days out from when Faviola had gotten confirmation that she'd lost the baby but she'd bounced back fast. Every now and then I checked on her to make sure that she was okay and I could've sworn that one night I heard her crying in her room when I came over to get some clothes. But Tank had been coming over to be with her nearly every night. She was in good hands as long as he was around.

"Here it is! I got her mama's name," Carmella said and I ran over to where she was to lean over her back and stare at the computer screen. "I thought you said her mother was dead."

She frowned at me and I frowned right back before shrugging slightly. "That's what Yolo always said."

"Well, it says right here that she's not dead. She's in some psychiatric clinic though."

Faviola ran over and read the name. "I know that place! Diane was admitted there a few times."

"Your sister was in a psychiatric hospital?" Janelle chimed in, looking at Faviola like she now understood more about her. Faviola cut her eyes at Janelle before replying.

"Yes, bitch. And?"

"Oh nothing," Janelle replied back but I knew from the look on her face that she was thinking Faviola's ass deserved to be there, too. I would have laughed at the exchange had I not been so focused on the records that Carmella was going through.

"Jani, call and see if you can get access to the records for a woman by this name." Carmella pointed to the screen.

Janelle's eyes widened and she wanted to refuse until Faviola waved her fist in her face in a threatening manner.

"Fine... but you guys should know that this is illegal and we could—"

"Bitch, you datin' a fuckin' criminal. Why don't you tell his ass what's illegal?" Faviola snapped and this time I couldn't help laughing. Janelle pushed her lips tightly together and grabbed her phone.

About an hour later, I had more information on LaTrese's crazy ass family than I ever needed. Her mother was dead alright. The online records hadn't been updated though because it was unclear exactly how she'd died. The case had been formally declared a suicide, however, stating that she'd saved up all her medication, after pretending to take them, and then overdosed. She was in the psychiatric facility for poisoning her husband, LaTrese's father, and then setting their house on fire. She'd actually set the house on fire with LaTrese in it but they'd been able to save her before it burned down. Was it bad that I secretly hoped they hadn't been able to save her ass?

"He accepted the friend request!" Faviola piped up and I turned to look at her.

"Who?"

"LaTrese's ex nigga. I wanna see the comments on that pic," she replied, staring at the computer as she scrolled through some images.

"FAVI! I told you not to do that," I told her but still got up to look over her shoulder.

I'm so happy for you guys! Congratulations on the baby!

I heard you're having a boy. Congrats to you both!

So the bitch *had* been pregnant by another man after her and Yolo broke up. But what caught my attention was the last comment.

This picture is so beautiful. I'm so sorry for you guys' lost. Just know your angel baby is in heaven now, shining down on you.

"Damn, she lost that baby, too," I said, feeling a little sadness for LaTrese in spite of everything else going on. As much as I hated her, I wouldn't wish that shit on any woman. Especially not twice.

"I wonder what happened," I said and everyone around us went quiet. I knew they were thinking the same thing. No matter who you were and where you were in life, hearing about a woman losing a baby, especially so far along in her pregnancy, just affected you in a bad way. It was sad as hell.

"Well, I'm going to find out," Faviola said, grabbing her phone. I looked at her curiously, wondering what the hell she was up to now. She had all kinds of tricks up her sleeve.

"What are you doing?"

"I'm calling him! His number is listed on Google. A lot of people's numbers are listed on there. You have to request to get it removed. It's how I found out about one of Tank's ugly ass side pieces one time," she replied nonchalantly like it wasn't nothing.

"Favi, you can't—"

She stuck her finger in the air and put the phone on speaker as someone picked up the other line.

"Hello?"

"Hi, Mr. Tolbine?" Faviola started using her best white lady voice. "My name is… Janelle Pickney, I'm an assistant district attorney in New York and I just have some questions about someone you may know."

Janelle looked like if you blew your breath on her, she would fall over. Like, she literally looked like she would die.

"Um… yeah. I'm happy to help if I can, Ms. Pickney."

"Thank you, Mr. Tolbine—"

"You can call me Calvin."

"Thank you, Calvin," Faviola continued, smiling slyly. "Now the person of interest is a Ms. LaTrese Manandez. Do you know her?"

Calvin snorted before answering, his voice considerably different than the light-hearted tone he'd had before.

"Yeah, I know her. Wish I didn't," he added under his breath.

"Oh?" Faviola licked her lips the way messy chicks did right before they were about to get some of the juicy tea. "Well, can you tell us more about your relationship with her? LaTrese… I mean, Ms. Manandez is being investigated for… murder."

Janelle looked like she was about to have a stroke.

"I mean, burglary," Faviola corrected herself quickly in order to save Janelle's life. "Sorry, I got the files mixed up. Even an uptight, stick-in-the-booty attorneys such as myself can mess up sometimes." That was an obvious dig at Janelle's scary ass.

"Well, if you were investigating her for murder, you'd be right," he added. "She is a damn murderer."

"Oh? Can you expand—"

"Expound," I whispered.

"I mean, can you expound on that a little?"

"I sure can. LaTrese was my girlfriend for about a year. She'd just gotten out of a relationship and said she lost a child and blah, blah. I was a friend to her and then it turned into something else. She got pregnant and around six months, she went into labor and delivered our baby. He was stillborn. I never got to see my son alive."

Faviola visibly gulped and I knew she was thinking about the baby she'd lost.

"And you blame her for that? For losing the baby?" she asked. I looked at her, knowing it was something that she probably wondered about when it came to her situation.

"Yes, I do," he affirmed aggressively. "Because I found some shit in the bathroom… some medication used for abortions. When I confronted her about it and called the police, all these secrets came out about her being crazy and her family being a bunch of loonies. Instead of going to jail where she belonged, they took her to some crazy hospital to get help. But that bitch killed our son. I know she did. LaTrese is the type of chick who craves attention and sympathy. We were going to break up and then she got pregnant and played the role of the abandoned pregnant woman and I got back with her. And then we were about to break up again and she all of a sudden goes into labor days later and delivers the baby, saying that I couldn't leave her during a time like that. She's a fake, a liar and she's crazy. Whatever you said she did, she did that shit."

I couldn't believe what I was hearing. This was way more serious than I had thought it to be. All of a sudden, I realized that I didn't want to know any of this. I wish I never dove into LaTrese's past. The things coming out could hurt a lot of people, especially if what I was suspecting was true.

"Do you think that she'd done this before? You mentioned her having just lost a child when the two of you got together," Faviola asked but her eyes were focused on me. They were filled with tears that had yet to fall.

"Yes, I do. Without a shadow of a doubt, I feel like she did." Hearing him say that crushed me. My eyes filled with tears and when they fell, I wiped them away, realizing that I wasn't the only one in the room crying. Faviola, Janelle and Carmella were all wiping tears from their own eyes.

"Hey, you won't need me to testify will you? I haven't seen that bitch since they took her to the crazy house and I really don't want to see her again."

"No, you're good. I think we have all we need," Faviola told him and then ended the call.

"I have it all here… all the records from her stay at the psychiatric clinic," Carmella said, pushing her laptop screen towards me. "Sorry,

Jani. I used your credentials to access the records."

"It's okay," Janelle replied back still rubbing at her eyes.

"I don't want to see them. I know everything I need to know." I pushed the laptop screen away and stood up to walk to the window.

Some things were better left unknown and unsaid. This was one of them. If Yolo found out that LaTrese may have actually killed his child, it would tear him up inside.

"Are you going to tell him?" Carmella asked the question that I knew everyone was wondering about.

"Truthfully, I don't know. If I tell him, he'll kill her. I know he will."

"But if you don't, Calvin will be killed because of that lyin' ass bitch. You said that Yolo wanted to move on his ass this weekend, right?"

I nodded my head. My hands were tied. I had to tell Yolo. I just hoped that whatever happened once he knew the truth wouldn't lead to the destruction of us both.

Janelle

*L*ooking in the floor-length mirror in the bedroom, I smoothed my hand over the front side of the dress and then shifted from heel-to-heel, scrutinizing my appearance. I looked perfect, that much went without saying. Luke had completely upgraded my wardrobe beyond anything I'd ever imagined for myself. No longer was I wearing the latest fashions from Target. Now I was in Prada, Gucci, Tom Ford, Manolos, and all kinds of other fashions I couldn't pronounce. I'd swapped my no name purse out for Hermes bags that had every woman eyeing me with envy. It hadn't gone to my head but I couldn't say I didn't enjoy being decked in the best of the best.

Still, even though I was easily wearing over ten grand in fashion at the moment, I was a nervous wreck about attending my job's Thanksgiving party tonight. The last couple weeks had been the worst of my professional life since the day I took my first job. And that's saying a lot because my very first job was at a clinic and involved cleaning bodily fluids and other things I never wanted to revisit ever again. This was worse than that.

Pelmington made sure that I got all the cases to work on that no one else even needed to come near. Easy stuff and misdemeanor crimes that could have been handled by someone who didn't graduate at the status that I did or the university I'd come from. But it wasn't just that—he treated me like shit. Or something worse than shit…whatever that was. He went out of his way to ignore me whenever we passed each other in the hallways and the occasional time that his eyes did land on me because I decided I wouldn't be ignored and chose to loudly greet him, he'd snarl at me before turning away.

My coworkers treated me like a leper. Because of the rumors swirling about how I'd fallen in love with 'the mark', no one wanted to associate with me. And the few who did still speak to me at least cordially only did it when no one was around. It was like I had a disease.

"Damn."

I heard Luke before I saw him. When I turned around, he was posted up on the frame of the door giving me a look that caused a flood between my thighs even in the midst of how nervous I was.

"You sure you don't want me to go with you to this shit?" he asked and I bit my lip before answering. He laughed.

"I'm just joking, Nell. Lighten up…damn."

Luke pushed away from the door and walked over to me, his eyes sliding up and down my thin frame before he pulled me into his arms and smashed his lips into mine. The connection was electric.

"Everyone knows we're together already. There is no more hiding but…I'm sure this party is probably the last place you'd want to be," I told him with a smile and he nodded his head.

"You damn right. Have fun but don't be entertainin' no niggas."

I rolled my eyes. Such a typical thing for him to say. Entertaining anyone was the last thing on my mind. I just wanted the night to be over, and I wasn't sure I really should have been attending. However, I was determined to not let anyone's treatment get me down. If they didn't want to talk to me at work, that was fine. But I was going to interact with everyone at the party like I normally would and show them that I was the same ole Janelle from before.

"I got your car out front. I'll be here for a few hours and then I'm heading to Brooklyn to meet with my fam. I'll see you when you get back tonight."

For a brief second, I wanted to tell him not to go. I wanted to tell him that I needed him to go to the party with me. Needed him by my side, the place where he always needed to be. But then he walked over and kissed me right on my hairline and walked out the room to let me finish getting dressed, and I came back to my senses. Luke's presence had a way of doing that...making me lose all of my common sense.

"Oh my God! I thought you said you had *my* car pulled up outside!" I exclaimed once I walked outside of the building and saw a chauffeur standing outside of an all-white Maybach and looking right at me. Luke ran his tongue over his teeth and tried to hide the smirk that was dancing its way up the corner of his mouth, but I saw it anyways.

"It ain't nothin'. Just figured you should ride in style to a party," he replied like it was nothing and ran his hand over the top of his braids.

Grabbing him by the sides of his face, I pulled him to me and kissed him deeply, pressing my body against his.

"You better stop that shit before you get somethin' started," he mumbled against my lips in between kisses. It set my entire body on fire.

The ride to the party was smooth, but my nerves were still frayed. The closer we got to the building where the party was to take place, the more I felt like I wanted to throw up. Tonight wasn't just a party for my coworkers and people I saw every day. The 'who's who' of the legal world would be there. Judges and other attorneys who I'd been looking up to my entire life, politicians—they would all be in the same room as me. Tonight, I could make all the right connections to get out of the current rut I was in.

The main person I was excited about meeting was Griselda Brown, mainly because she was everything I wanted to be in about thirty more years. She had an illustrious career as a high level district attorney and had fought more high profile cases than I could name in one sitting. She was a household name for anyone studying law but, on top of everything, she was a black woman just like me. And during the time she'd come about, things were much harder for sistas like us than they were now. However, she'd fought through it all and still made a name for herself. Now she was pretty much retired, didn't take many cases unless she was called specifically to handle something that only she could, and she was receiving major pressure to run to become a judge. I wanted to be just. like. her.

"I'll be here all night, ma'am," the chauffeur said as he helped me out.

All eyes were on me but I didn't let it shake me because I knew it was more about the car than anything else. The party took place in the grand ballroom of the Ritz Carlton hotel, and there was no expense spared. My daddy had been invited to plenty of these parties when I was younger, and I was left home wishing and dreaming for the day when I would be able to attend one. And here I was, but it was nothing like I'd expected it to be.

I walked in with my head high and my hand clutching a brand new Hermes bag that Luke had left on the bed for me to use specifically for this night. He was flashy, and I could tell he'd picked the bag out for me himself because it had all the bells and whistles. I didn't even want to look up how much it had cost for fear that I would faint and never want to take it out in public again.

"Hello Ms..."

"Ms. Pickney. Janelle Pickney," I finished for the door attendant who glanced at my attire approvingly before looking down the list of names in her hand.

"I see your name on the list so you're good to go on in!" she exclaimed and then her eyes fell to my bag. "And that bag is *everything*. How did you get it? It's not even in stores yet!"

That was news to me.

"My boyfriend bought it for me," I told her, bashfully. It was still strange to me to refer to Luke as my boyfriend.

"Damn, girl! He's a keeper for real. He had to pull some serious strings to get you that bag!" she added, still eyeing it so greedily that I wouldn't have been surprised to see her licking her lips. Luke didn't even know it but I was loving him even harder in that moment. I had no idea that he had gotten me an Hermes bag before it had even hit the stores. How in the world did he manage something like that?

Walking into the venue slowly, my eyes raked the crowd and I saw enough familiar faces to make my entire life. Crowds full of people I'd studied or followed all while I was in college and now I was actually invited to a party with them. I almost fainted and nearly stumbled over my own heels when my eyes finally sought out the object of nearly all of my career infatuations.

Griselda Brown. In the flesh.

She was talking to Pelmington, but there was no way that was going to stop me from getting to her as soon as she got alone. After busying myself with stuffing my mouth full of hors d'oeuvres and sipping on wine to give myself a little more courage, I finally saw my chance when Griselda seemed to be excusing herself to go to the ladies room. Perfect timing. I wiped the crumbs off my face and took off after her. Yes, it was a little bit creepy to confront someone while they were trying to pee, but I wasn't about to let her get by me without making a connection.

When I walked in the bathroom, Griselda was standing in the mirror checking herself out, reapplying her lipstick and fixing her already perfect hair. I walked next to her and started to wash my hands because I literally had no other idea of what to do. When I looked up from rinsing the soap from my fingers, I found myself looking right into her eyes through the mirror.

"Janelle Pickney?"

I nearly died. Griselda Brown knew *my* name! How?!

"Um...yes, and you're Ms. Brown, of course. I'm—I'm so happy to meet you in person, you've only been the one person I've wanted to be exactly like since I started my first year of law school!"

I held out my hand to shake hers and realized it was dripping wet when she ducked her eyes down to stare at it without moving.

"Oh, sorry," I mumbled and grabbed a few paper towels to dry the water from my hands.

"I find it funny that you would say that…that you wanted to be just like me," she stated and my ears twitched. How was that funny? I would imagine that any black woman in the law field wanted to be like Griselda. She was a legend. She was the goal.

"Of course I do! I mean, my love for the law field came from my father but when it comes to women in the field, you're the one who has given me the most motivation to work hard and continue on… whether you know it or not."

Griselda pushed her lips together, crossed her arms in front of her chest and then sighed. Not exactly the response I was looking for.

"But you're in a relationship with one of the Murray brothers, correct? Luke 'Outlaw' Murray?"

Her words nearly stole the breath from my body, and I know my devastation showed in my face. How did she know that? Had my reputation actually traveled this far? And was my love for Luke really going to haunt me all throughout my career, destroying the professional relationships I craved for before they even had a chance to happen?

"I—I just…"

My mouth clamped shut because I didn't know what to say. I furrowed my brows and looked down at my hands for the answer but it wasn't there. There was no answer for this. I'd chosen the man I wanted to be with, and now I was finding out that, regardless of what people said, there are consequences to love. Even a perfect love.

"Your law career is over," Griselda said, turning back to the mirror as she commenced to applying her lipstick. "I really don't know why you came here tonight. Everyone knows about your terrible decision to involve yourself with the smut of the universe, one of the Murrays. You've made an enemy out of anyone who is anybody, and we all know not to trust you. The only reason you're even being tolerated is because of your father. But…sad to say, I'm sure this little scandal you've involved him in has affected his reputation too. You're an embarrassment to him, you're an embarrassment to black women in law…my dear, you're just an embarrassment to us all."

My eyes filled up with tears so fast they quickly blotted out the image of Griselda, my idol, totally breaking me down until I felt nonexistent. I stood there, frozen in place for so long that it felt like time slowed down. Griselda finished up and walked away, leaving me alone, but I was still there. The tears of disbelief, anger, and hurt were in my eyes, and my insides felt like they had been torn out of me, leaving me a shell of the person I was. But still, even in that moment, all I really wanted was Luke.

The door opened again and this time in walked Tatiana, fresh-faced and beautiful, with a malicious smile on her lips and her eyes aimed right at me. Almost like she knew I would be in here.

"Griselda told me you were hiding out in here. Well…what she said was that she needed my help taking out the trash." Tatiana chuckled and I flinched, feeling like I'd been stabbed. "Why are you even here anyways, Janelle? Haven't we all made it clear that we don't want you? If it wasn't for your father—"

"*Shut up!*" I snarled. I was so tired of people bringing up my father as the only reason I was here. I was here because I worked my ass off and graduated at the top of my class. I was here because I deserved to be here, and not because of anyone else.

"Shut the fuck up, you two-faced, snobby, big-nosed bitch!"

Before I knew it, I was in Tatiana's face with my hand reared back. I slapped the shit out of her, hitting her so hard that I'd left a red mark on the side of her face. Her eyes bulged, and her mouth formed the letter 'o' as her brain tried to catch up to what had just happened. Hell, my brain was trying to catch up to what just happened...had I really just hit her? Like actually put my hands on another lawyer?

Janelle

"*Y*ou're going to regret that!" Tatiana spat, holding her face. "And don't think I have forgotten about Chris. I know your new boyfriend probably had something to do with it!"

She stormed out of the bathroom, and I ran over and locked the door. I needed some privacy. With my back on the wall, I sunk to my knees and dropped my head in my hands. I believed her. I knew she would tell anyone who would listen that I'd assaulted her, and now I actually had a reason to be fired and blacklisted from the law community. She was right I would regret it. Shit, I already did.

"What's goin' on, bae?"

I'd called Luke to talk to him and explain what was going on, but something about hearing his voice on the other line broke me down into a little ass child and all I could do was wail on the phone, occasionally sputtering out words through my cries. I told him about everything that had happened—all the things I'd been keeping from him, starting with Tatiana threatening me at the movies, telling Pelmington about the relationship I had with him, the 'demotion' I'd received at work, Griselda making me feel like shit, and I ended it with how I slapped Tatiana.

"Shit, bae!" Luke chuckled in spite of my misery. "You really slapped that bitch? A lawyer? That's gangsta as fuck!"

"I don't wanna be a gangstaaaa," I cried, tears still running down my face. I sounded pitiful as hell, even to myself.

"Aye, stay where you are. Give me about thirty minutes, okay?"

I agreed and then hung up the phone. It wasn't like I had nerve to show my face outside the door anyways.

So I waited.

There were knocks at the door but I ignored them, refusing to open up for anyone as I continued to cry until the tears would no longer come. I knew that Luke always had me. I knew that I didn't have to deal with the typical worries that people who lost their jobs had to deal with…I wouldn't lose my home or be put out on the street. But still, women like me didn't depend on a man for shit! I wanted to do my own thing, make my own money and have my own career. Luke and I had just made it official and now I was in a position where I'd ruined myself, and I'd have to depend on him. Just thinking about it made me want to break down all over again, but I was out of tears.

Knock, knock, knock!

I looked up but didn't even move to open the door. I wasn't letting anyone in unless they decided to break in and drag me out of here. I'd suffered enough embarrassment this night. A little more couldn't hurt.

"Nell… open up this damn door, ma."

It was Luke.

I jumped up and ran to the door, unlocking it quickly. I don't think there was ever a moment in life that my legs moved faster. Once the door was open and I saw him, I paused, taking a minute to just take him in. He was *drop dead gorgeous.*

Wearing an all-white custom-made suit that fit his athletic build perfectly, Luke was the picture of perfection. He had on a simple white t-shirt under his suit jacket, a gold chain, and designer shoes. His hair was pulled back into a neat, braided style and his goatee was edged to perfection. He was easily the sexiest man I'd ever seen in my life.

"You ready?" He held out his hand and I curled my brows before placing my hand in his.

"For what?" I asked him, cautiously. There was no telling what Luke had in mind. He was fearless, cocky, and arrogant. It was a deadly combination. And it usually meant anything goes.

"To cause a fuckin' scene, of course."

Before I could object, he pulled me out of the doorway of the restroom and pushed his lips against mine, kissing me with full-on tongue until I felt dizzy and drunk in his love.

Damn.

With my hand in his, he led me back into the ballroom that was packed with all the professional people of law and politics that I'd been nearly drooling to get to know earlier. Right now, I didn't give a damn about any of them. However, all of them had their eyes on me.

"Is that the Outlaw?"

"It looks like him…oh my God!"

Whispers of disbelief swarmed around us, but instead of hiding from them, I kept my head high, clutched Luke's hand as he stood by my side and walked through the crowd. Soon a red-faced Pelmington walked in front of us, stopping us from moving through the room.

"*You* can't be here!"

He said 'you' like the word repulsed him just to say it. There was so much hatred and disgust in his tone that I almost retreated, and I would have ran away if it wasn't for Luke holding me firmly to his side. With his eyes tight and focused on Pelmington's face, Luke stood tall and fearlessly, to the point that even Pelmington stirred a little under his stare. No matter who you were, you had to respect Luke's gangsta. My heart swelled.

"Why can't I? I heard you been lookin' for me." A forced chuckled escaped Luke's lips even though it was obvious he found nothing funny.

"My God, this is insane!" an older white lady said under her breath, I recognized her as a judge.

"It is, isn't Marigold?" Luke said, addressing her even though his eyes were on Pelmington still. "I know I was supposed to meet up with you last week, but I was handlin' some business. Let your husband, John, know our next poker game is scheduled for next Friday though. Yolo will have that package ready for him."

Luke finally brought his eyes to Judge Clemons, whom he'd referred to as Marigold, and rubbed at his nose suggestively as he mentioned the package that Yolo would have for her husband. The poor lady's face got so red, she resembled a ripe tomato and stumbled back a few paces like she was about to faint. Every face turned to her with wide eyes, unbelieving that one of the top judges in New York actually had personal dealings with Outlaw.

"And don't be quiet now, Gina," Luke said addressing another woman. I turned to look at her and immediately recognized her as the woman he was with in a restaurant a while ago. The same restaurant where he'd dicked me down in the bathroom after seeing me with Chris. At the mention of Luke saying her name, she nearly choked on her own spit.

"It wasn't too long ago that you were begging me for the dick… promising me that you would give it all up for a nigga. Remember that?"

Like Marigold, Gina nearly keeled over. The murmuring in the room continued. People were buzzing with the type of excitement that you could only get from good gossip.

"Judge Herald!" Luke called out to a man who was desperately running to the door, trying to escape. "You still need my brothers and I to help out with that little problem you got? I bet your uppity ass friends in here don't know about your gambling habit, huh? They know how many times the Murray boys had to bail you out?"

The Judge didn't stop. Actually, he nearly sped up into a run, trying to exit the building as fast as he could.

"And Ms. Griselda Brown…" Luke started and I nearly peed in my pants. There was no way the woman who had just shamed me to tears about being in a relationship with Luke had any ties with him. There was no way. My eyes locked on hers as I waited for Luke to finish his statement. I was dying to know what secrets Griselda had.

"Ezekiel Murray, also known as Luke Ezekiel Murray, Sr.—my father. Remember him? Yeah, you know him," Luke affirmed after she shook her head. "You want to shame Janelle here for being with me.

But I bet no one knows that you had an affair with, and got pregnant from, the biggest kingpin Miami had ever known before he decided to retire. You helped him get off a few times, huh?"

Griselda's chocolate brown skin nearly turned white.

"You got a problem with Janelle dating a Murray because she's a lawyer, but you're the originator of that shit, huh? And in case anyone is wondering, Griselda was with him during the time he was the king of Miami…while he was married to my mother. The only reason they aren't still together is because he broke it off to stay with his family. Now, Ms. Brown…tell me I'm lying so I can show this wonderful group around us some proof."

Griselda dropped her head and my mouth dropped along with it. I looked around the room and realized that the people I wanted so badly to rub shoulders with, and be accepted by, were nothing but a bunch of fakes and liars. No, I didn't want to be like them. I clutched Luke's arm proudly. I was exactly where I wanted to be.

"Let's go, Janelle. These muthafuckas out here ain't even worthy of you," Luke said and I nodded my head. I felt the exact same way. They weren't. At least I was true about the person I was and who I wanted to be with. They were nothing but cowards.

"I can't believe we did that," I laughed to myself as Luke pulled out of the parking lot at top speed, making as big of an exit as he had an entrance. "That was *insane!* Why didn't you tell me you had dealings with all of those people?"

Luke lifted one brow at me. "Because shit like that you don't tell. The only reason I exposed a few tonight was because I wanted to make a point."

"A few?" I repeated, completely confounded. "So there were more in the room that you could have exposed."

He shot me a lop-sided smile. "Ma, there is a lot you don't know about them muthafuckas you think uphold the law. They all crooked as hell."

I let my mind marinate on that for a moment. This was crazy. Absolutely crazy.

"Well, safe to say I no longer have a job. I'm not sad about that though."

Leaning back in my seat, I looked out the window as Luke drove and thought about my future. Or lack thereof. I guess this would be the time to figure out if there was anything else I was good at. But I already knew the answer to that...I wasn't! The only thing I'd ever wanted to do in my life was be a lawyer so it was the only thing I'd ever spent my time perfecting. What in the world would I do now?

Luke pulled up in front of a building and I recognized it as the place he'd purchased for me. I gazed at it with curious eyes, noting that it looked considerably different from the last time he'd brought me to see it.

"Let's get out the car. I wanna show you something," Luke said, and I obeyed quietly.

When he opened the door, I nearly gasped at all the changes he'd made inside of the building. The wood floors, glass walls, beautiful expensive oak furniture. It was the type of office space that I had dreamed of having once I made it. I looked at the wooden letters on the back wall: Pickney & Associates. I could barely believe it.

"What did you do?"

Luke walked up next to me, smiling with his arms tucked behind his back. He was so damn sexy and so full of surprises. I couldn't believe how lucky I was to have someone like him in love with someone like me.

"This is yours," he told me. "I know that you wanted to prosecute under Pelmington, but I don't think that's your style. You don't fit in with that fake ass group we just left. They didn't believe in you when they should have...so I think you should have your revenge. In the courtroom."

My eyes widened as I thought about what he was saying. "So you think I should be a defense attorney...battle them out in the courtroom? Me verses them."

Luke nodded his head. "You can do it. Ain't shit they can do that you can't do better. Use their reputation against them. If they pursue high profile cases, you defend the niggas they are after and build your own rep up. They don't wanna make you into the powerful woman you deserve to be by working with you, so you'll do it by working against them."

He was genius. Luke was a fuckin' genius. But I knew that, right?

"Well, how do I get clients?"

Chuckling a little, Luke had a quick answer for that. "Let me worry about that. Plus, you already got one family of criminals on your payroll. And I guess I can say that because I want you to be my lawyer. You good with representing the Murrays?"

Now it was my time to almost faint.

"Of—of course," I said, trying to conceal how excited I was.

Jumping up into Luke's arms, I wrapped my legs around his waist and kissed him. He quickly deepened the kiss by placing his tongue in my mouth and gripping my ass. Before long, my clothes were off and so were his.

We properly christened every room in my new practice with our love.

***

Loving Luke was toxic.

There was so much I could say about how wrong it was but, at the end of the day, I really didn't care because it just felt right. Especially now. The way that his body was pressed up against mine, the feel of his rock hard staff pressed against my back, the ruggedness of his facial hair tickling the nape of my neck as he slept with his face hidden there, and his arms around my middle…it was perfection.

Still, I knew there was so much about loving a gangsta that I didn't know. So much that I wasn't prepared for. Even still, I wanted to be with him and only him.

"Stop thinkin' so loud. I can hear you," Luke whispered and I jump slightly, not realizing that he was awake.

"How am I thinking loud?" I rolled my eyes, figuring that he was still half asleep.

He wasn't completely wrong though, I definitely had something on my mind. Although I was no longer working with Pelmington,

Tatiana's threat still lingered in my thoughts. Everything concerning me and Luke was out, but I knew she still was adamant on searching for answers when it came to Chris. I couldn't underestimate her. If she was determined to find something to connect me and Chris on that last night anyone saw him, she would. God knows there were enough witnesses around to give her some answers: the jeweler and damn near everybody in Brooklyn who lived on my block. They'd all watched what transpired between Chris and the Murray brothers.

"I can tell," he said and pulled away from me, instantly making my body cold from the sudden distance between us.

He stood up, pushing the thin sheet from his body and then walked over to the nightstand to check his phone. I watched him, admiring the cuts in his back and his arms. His long wavy hair was braided, going straight down his back, blending in with his multiple tattoos that I'd once saw as disgusting but was now intrigued by. Luke had told me that each one had a meaning behind it and, although he'd yet to explain them all, the ones he told me about showed me that, like an onion, there were many layers to the man the city knew as the Outlaw.

"Are you regretting your decision?" were the words that came out of his mouth once he finally put his phone down. He kept his back to me but lifted his head, and I knew he was on edge, waiting for me to answer.

"My decision...to be with you?" I further clarified, and he nodded his head. "No, I'm not. Why would I? You've handled my problems at work. There is nothing else I could ask for."

Luke went silent for a while but the way his shoulders remained tense told me that he was still thinking on something. I just didn't yet know what it was. And then he said it and reminded me that there was still something missing from my life. Or, actually, someone.

"But you miss your father. You won't be able to happily live the rest of your life with me without him being in it, right?"

I didn't answer because he already knew what I would say. Rekindling my relationship with my father was on the list I gave him. I didn't know if it would ever work the way I had it planned out in my mind, but he'd asked me to list everything in the world that I wanted and I did. My family was important to me. My father was on the top of that list.

"You're off for the rest of the week, right?"

I nodded my head. The Thanksgiving holiday was upon us much faster than I'd expected it. In fact, I'd been so caught up in everything that I didn't realize it until I'd left work the day before after enjoying a small Thanksgiving lunch at the office. I still wasn't able to enjoy it, thanks to Tatiana being all up in my face.

"Pack up your things. We're going for a drive. A long drive," Luke said in a way that didn't leave room for any questions or refusals. I was used to it; that was the way he did everything.

"We're going now?" I asked him and he nodded his head before pecking a few more things into his phone. "When is the last time you spoke to your sister?"

I screwed my face up. It was too early in the morning for him to be switching gears like this. We'd gotten home from my new office well after midnight and only slept a few hours before he woke me up with his head between my legs. My mind wasn't ready to perform the necessary functions required to keep up.

"Carmella?"

"Yeah…call her and tell her to pack her things too. She's coming with us."

I scrunched my nose even higher on my face, watching him walk out of the room and into the master bathroom as if he hadn't said anything strange. I wanted to ask more questions, but I knew from the way he'd dismissed me by walking away, he wasn't in the mood to answer them. His mind was made up, and he'd said everything he planned to say. With a sigh, I got up and began to do as he asked.

Carmella

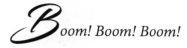*oom! Boom! Boom!*

"Who da hell...?"

First I rubbed the slob off the side of my face and then I rubbed at my eyes before standing up to answer the door. After crying loud enough for the entire hall to hear, I'd only just closed my eyes for some sleep about thirty minutes ago, and here someone was trying to break down my damn door. My heart fluttered a little as I got closer to the door, wondering if Cree had come to see me and apologize for kicking me out. But that thought was dashed to shit as soon as I looked through the peephole.

"Open up the damn door! I hear you breathin' and shit on the other side!"

I rolled my eyes, clutching the top of my robe together to make sure that my breasts weren't showing through the top before I opened the door.

"What are you doing—hey!"

Before I could officially invite him in, Outlaw strode into my place uninvited and began walking around like he owned it with his hands tucked behind his back in prison stance, inspecting my living room.

"What are you doing here and why are you looking around my

place like that?"

Frowning, I slammed the door closed and followed behind him as he walked down the hallway and straight into my room, opening drawers and shit like my stuff belonged to him.

"I'm makin' sure you ain't had no other nigga up in this bitch," he said finally, and then turned around to look at me, right in the eyes. "You serious 'bout my brother, right? I don't wanna have to fuck no nigga up because—"

"No," I said a little too fast, mainly because I wanted him to get to the reason why he was here so that he could hurry up and leave. After asking around, I had a nice sample of coke that I'd scored from someone one of the girls at my job knew, and I was itching to get high now that I'd been awakened.

"And even if I was, it doesn't matter. Your brother broke up with me...he didn't tell you?" I squinted my eyes and scrutinized Outlaw's reaction. But from the surprise on his face, it was obvious that he was hearing what I was telling him for the first time.

"No...he ain't tell me shit. Damn, why that happened?"

I paused, my thoughts merged and I shifted between my feet while hoping and praying that Cree hadn't said anything to Outlaw. At least, not yet. I still hadn't figured out how I would tell Janelle without her going crazy on me. I didn't have a problem, but I knew her ass would be convinced that I needed to be in somebody's rehab.

"He ain't tell me shit 'bout y'all stupid lover problems," Outlaw scoffed, as if he wasn't trying to put himself right in the middle of them only a few seconds ago. "Janelle and I are 'bout to ride out and I need you to come with us. Pack some shit to last you until Monday."

"I—I can't go. I have to work." It was a lie and from the look on Outlaw's face, he knew it.

"They got you takin' yo' clothes off and shit over Thanksgiving weekend?"

Instead of lying again, I just nodded my head because I knew Outlaw would be able to tell if I lied again.

"Where are you takin' my sister?" I asked, shifting gears.

"To your dad's." He exhaled heavily and sat down on my couch. I was just happy that he was no longer looking at me in the way that he had been only a few seconds ago. He seemed to be no longer worried about what was going on in my life and more focused on his upcoming trip. Actually, once he told me where he was going, I was more concerned about that as well.

"My dad's? You think that's a good idea?"

"No," he answered honestly, before looking upward and pinning his eyes on the ceiling. Then he lowered them and pinned them on me. "It's stupid as hell but I gotta do it. I have to do anything I can to get her back in good with that nigga because she's going to be miserable without him. I can give her everything in the world but, at some point, she'll be back thinking about him. We can't move on or get better with this shit still lingering."

I sat on the arm of the chair behind me and looked down, thinking hard about what he said. He was right. I knew my sister and, one thing about her, family was more important than anything. Although her heart picked Outlaw, some of it still ached because she couldn't have the other man that she had loved since birth in her life. At some point, I feared that she might blame Outlaw for the distance between them. I wondered if Outlaw felt that way too.

"You have any tips for a nigga?" He chuckled a little when he asked me, but I knew he wasn't joking. He really wanted to know.

"This why you really came over, huh?"

"Yeah, I figured you wouldn't want to go," he replied with a smirk and I shook my head. This dude was crazy. Perfect for Janelle but crazy as hell.

"Janelle is just like my father. Both of them like to move on their own and in their own time. My advice would be to not even go. He doesn't take well to people forcing him to do anything…" I looked into Outlaw's face and saw the stubbornness I was used to seeing there. He wasn't hearing anything I had to say if it concerned him not doing what he already planned to do.

"But if you're determined to go…just be aware that things may not go as planned, and be ready to change gears in case it doesn't," I added with a sigh before rubbing my nose. Damn, I needed to get his ass out so I could get high. I was about five seconds away from my teeth grinding together.

"Damn, you ain't really help worth shit," Outlaw joked, laughing a little as he stood up. "But I 'preciate it anyways, sis."

"I do what I can," I told him, anxious to get him to leave.

I didn't even realize that my leg was jumping until I saw Outlaw's eyes go to it. Biting my bottom lip, I stopped the movement abruptly and started fidgeting, feeling nervous about him watching me. Not to mention…damn, I needed a hit! My nerves were bad as hell.

"You good?" he asked me but his eyes said that he already had an answer of his own. I nodded my head and tucked a strand of hair behind my ear. Instead of moving, he stared at me for a few seconds longer, and I couldn't help squirming under his watchful eye. I even felt beads of sweat sprout up on my forehead. It was only a few seconds, but it seemed like an eternity.

"We need to talk sometime. You might be my sister-in-law so when I get back, let's catch up," was the last thing Outlaw said before he walked out the door.

I felt worried about his words for about three seconds…the three seconds it took for the door to pop him on the ass as he was on the way out. As soon as it closed behind him, I jumped up and ran to my bedroom, ready to enjoy another round of my at home party of one.

***

Fuck…I overdid it.

I was so high that I was almost numb. Usually, I was hyper as hell when I got high, but this new shit I'd been given had me tweaking. Not only was I agitated but I could barely feel my face, and my head felt heavy as hell. I felt like I was going in and out of consciousness.

"What da fuck is she doin'?" Zeke snapped, walking into the room just as I laid down right on the floor in the showroom. With the help of the other girls in the dressing room, I was looking right, wearing what I needed to wear, and pretty as hell from the makeup job given to me by the crew, but I felt like shit.

"I'on really know," Jake replied, scratching at the scraggly hairs on his jaw. "She been like this all morning."

"We ain't got one good fuckin' pic yet. What da hell?!" Zeke walked over to me; I couldn't see him but I could hear him. "Get the fuck up!"

Leaning over, he snatched me up by my arm so hard that it hurt. Straight up, fuckin' disrespectful…that's what he was.

"Get off of me!" I screamed at him, twisting out of his grip.

"She's high as hell…fuck!" Zeke grabbed at me again, and this time I didn't bother fighting back because I was slightly embarrassed by him screaming out that I was high in front of everybody. I looked up and saw that people were starting to gather by the door, everyone eager to see what was happening in the room with Zeke. He placed me roughly into a chair, and I rubbed at my nose and tried to cross my legs and look as sober as I could, but from the look in Zeke's eyes, he wasn't convinced and neither was anyone else around him.

"Carmella, get da fuck up and take your high ass home. Fuckin' cokehead," he added under his breath.

Hearing him say that stung, my cheeks literally singed from embarrassment. All I saw was red, I got angry so fast and it went from zero straight to one hundred. I sincerely wanted to kill him for how he was acting towards me. It only took me about five seconds to jump out of the chair and lunge at Zeke. I grabbed him, clipping him right under his neck in a sleeper hold and pulled back until we both fell onto the floor. He started fighting me off of him but I was ready for him and commenced to swinging and flinging my arms, attacking whatever part of his body that I could connect with. After I'd gotten more than a few licks in, I felt hands on me pulling me back, but I kicked out my legs as hard as I could trying to get more hits in before I was dragged away. When Zeke stood to his feet, with Jake's assistance, I was happy to see that he had a cut on his lip that was dripping blood.

"You only tryin' to play me because I wouldn't fuck you!" I screamed, trying to air Zeke out the same way he aired me. "I ain't wanna give you this pussy, and you caught feelings, huh nigga?! You wanna play me like this just because you couldn't smell this, huh?"

As Zeke watched, I wiggled out of the hands of the three women who were holding me and turned around, booting my ass up at him before twerking it in his face while laughing hard. It wasn't in me to act like this normally, but I'd be lying if I didn't say that it felt good to see the look on everyone's face as they laughed at my antics. When I turned around back to Zeke, I noticed the look of disgust on his and Jake's face and rolled my eyes. Salty ass niggas.

"Stank ass hoe," Zeke said, fanning his hand at me before turning around. "You're done... fuck you and the contract we had. Tear that shit up, it's a wrap. Somebody get her ass out of here. Now!"

"Ohhhh, his feelings hurt!" I sang loudly in between laughing and twerking my ass in the direction that Zeke was walking. I was on one for real. The worst of my high had passed, and now I was experiencing the top of my high and having fun with it, too!

But then suddenly, two big pairs of hands grabbed me by the shoulders and the waist. In less than a second, I was hoisted up over some large shoulders and being carried out of the building.

"Put me the FUCK down!"

I screamed and started lashing out, kicking and punching at the big beefy man that was holding me. He put his hands on both of my sides and squeezed hard as hell. So hard that I almost passed straight out, I couldn't breathe, he literally pushed all of the air out of my lungs and held me that way until we were outside of the front doors where he picked me up and lowered me down right onto the cement ground.

"Hey!" I wheezed and then started into a fit of coughs because I didn't have enough air to get anything else out.

I wanted to remind him that my purse and other things were still inside in my locker but I didn't even have enough air to speak. Luckily, about two minutes later, while I was still hacking my lungs out, Taylor, one of the high paid porn stars from Zeke's newest series and the one who had given me the hook-up with her dealer, came out with my things in my hand.

"Girl, you was doing the most today, huh?" she asked me, and I looked up at her, biting on my lip so I wouldn't snap. I wasn't stupid and I didn't want no problems with my newfound connection I'd gotten through her.

"Zeke ain't have to do me like that just because I wouldn't give him no pussy."

Taylor cocked her head at me. "You think this was because of pussy?" I nodded and she began to laugh, shaking her head. "Zeke don't give a shit about your pussy. He's fucked damn near every bitch up in there already. You weren't nothing special, of course he would try you, and he's not hurting because you turned him down either."

Pressing my lips together, I looked Taylor up and down and stopped myself from spitting her some hard truth and letting her know that just because she served her pussy up for him on a platter, didn't mean I had to. And, besides, if he'd fucked everything in there but me then I was special!

"This is about his money. He has a hard and fast rule about the talent using. He don't care if you use a little to get yourself in the mood every now and then, but when it starts to fuck with your performance, you get the boot. That's one rule he does not break, and I've seen him put it into effect time and time again. You coming in here today like that…you fucked yourself up."

Rolling my eyes, I stood up on shaky legs and shrugged my shoulders before bending down to grab my clothes from Taylor's hands so I could get dressed. Zeke's building was right on the busy streets of Manhattan, and Taylor and I were getting more than a few stares for sitting on the sidewalk just about naked. It was strange, even for New York standards.

"Fuck him and fuck that job," I told her, waving her away. "I didn't want it anyways so he can have that shit."

Searching through my purse for my keys, I screwed up my face when I noticed they were inside. I looked around about three more times before checking the pockets of my Bebe sweatpants and jacket.

"Where the hell are my keys?" I said, more to myself than to Taylor who was still standing in front of me.

"You mean the keys to the car and the apartment that belong to Zeke? His men took it before I could get your purse to you. When he said you were fired, he meant that. Baby, you lost it all."

Giving me a look that screamed of fake sympathy, Taylor turned

183

around and walked back into the building just like the fake ass friend she was, leaving me out in the middle of the street by myself with nowhere to go and no one to call on since Janelle was out of town.

"This is some bullshit!" I screamed, wanting to cry.

This shit was blowing my high. Grabbing my phone, I scrolled through the numbers of people I hadn't spoken to in a long time but I knew would help me. Or… at least I hoped they would.

Janelle

*W*hen Luke pulled up to the home that I grew up in, I couldn't even contain the emotions that I started to feel. My first thought was that I missed being home, and I could feel myself getting excited about that fact, but then I remembered the last time I saw my father and the look in his eyes when he told me that he was washing his hands of me because of the man I chose to love and be with.

"You're ready for this shit?"

Typical Luke.

"You have such tact with how you put things, you know that?"

Luke looked at me, weighing my question for a second before shrugging and then adjusting his chain. Although I felt like I wanted to throw up, Luke was cool as a fan. I watched as he flipped the mirror down and checked out his appearance to make sure that he was on point. Of course he was, but Luke had to check anyways. If my stomach wasn't so messed up by what I was about to do, I would have rolled my eyes at him.

"You gon' stay in the car forever, yo?" Luke asked me.

It was at that moment that I realized he was no longer sitting next to me but was out of the car and holding my door open, waiting for me to step out of the passenger side of his car. To be honest, no…I wasn't ready. I wanted to see my father again and wanted him to welcome me home with open arms, but I had a feeling this wasn't going to go the way I wanted it. Like me, he was stubborn and worked through things in his own time. I was pushing him to accept something he promised he wouldn't.

"I don't wanna do it. Let's just leave," I told him. My eyes darted from Luke's face to the house and then back to his face. He was shaking his head. I dropped my head down and looked at the palm of my hands, which were red and blotchy.

"We can't do that. If you don't go up there and at least try, you'll regret this shit, and I can't let you do that to yourself. Let's go."

I didn't budge.

"You want me to go first?" he asked, and I lifted my head to look at him once again. It didn't matter how strong of a woman you are, there is nothing like having a stronger man by your side prepared to fearlessly fight your battles for you if you needed him to. And that's exactly what I had in Luke. When I was weak, he was always strong, and he was always ready to set shit straight for me just like I needed him to. He was always there for me.

"Yes."

Before I could get the word fully off my lips, Luke turned and began walking towards the grand estate that I'd grown up in.

"Big ass muthafuckin' house," I thought I heard him say under his breath as he walked away, but I couldn't even bring myself to reply.

The house I'd grown up in was fairly large to the normal person, boasting well over 8,000 square feet, but to me it was home, and the only thing I wanted was to be welcomed back into it. Licking my lips,

I turned and watched Luke walk to the door. My belly flopped and flipped and rumbled the entire way until I saw him press the doorbell and then knock on the door. Then my entire body seemed to freeze in place as I waited.

The door opened and I sucked in a breath, waiting to see who it was that would step out. A second later, a head appeared and my lips curled into a smile when my eyes landed on my sister, TreVonia. Can you believe as soon as this heffa saw Luke, she leaned against the door frame, smiling hard while pushing her breasts up in the air? She was such a damn hoe when she wanted to be! Then Outlaw must have told her that I was in the car because she looked in my direction and took off running.

"Janelle!"

Jumping out the car, I held my arms out to my sister and ran to meet her halfway. We collapsed into each other, hugging tightly and laughing hard. It seemed like forever since I'd seen her, and looking at my sister reminded me just how much I missed her.

"Jani!" another voice yelled and when I pulled away from TreVonia, my eyes fell right on Mixie. Like TreVonia, she ran into our direction and grabbed me into a tight hug as if she hadn't seen me in years.

"What are you doin' here?" Mixie asked.

"No, more importantly...what are you doin' here with his fine ass?" TreVonia added, cutting her eyes to Luke who was still standing near the closed door, watching us with a half-smile on his face. Seeing us watching him, he leaned back on the cobblestone wall beside the door and crossed his arms in front of him. I knew his ass could tell he was the topic of conversation, but he was used to it so it was okay in his book, and he took it with ease.

"He is cute, Jani," Mixie added, to my surprise. She was even more of a nerd than I was and here she was with her thick ass glasses propped on her nose as she looked back and forth from me to Luke.

"He really doesn't seem like your type though."

"No, he really doesn't. He's more *my* type."

"Vonia, calm your hot ass down! You so damn fast!" Mixie was forever the mother of us all.

"But really, Jani, how in the world did you get mixed up with somebody like that?" Mixie added and then glanced one more time at Luke and I could've sworn I saw her lick her lips. "Damn, he got a brother?"

"Yes, he does. Five but one is dead. And *all* of them are fine as hell," TreVonia added before I could butt in, and I gave her a cock-eyed look. "What?! I read about them as soon as you told me that Daddy was tripping about you messin' with somebody named Luke Murray."

Two minutes into seeing my sisters again and I was already feeling like telling the both of them off.

"I don't know... it just happened."

"I bet he got good dick. He got good dick?"

"VONIA! I didn't come here to talk about his... *Anyways*, we came here to speak to Daddy and see if—"

"What—what the hell is going on here?!"

My mouth dropped to my toes, and I looked up just in time to see my daddy pelt out of the front door, his eyes glued on me, TreVonia, and Mixie. His eyes narrowed into slits as he thought out the scene before him, and then I watched in horror as he slowly turned and looked at the man standing to his side. Luke stood confidently next to him, unflinching and unmoving, as if he had a right to be standing right where he was. As if he'd been invited. And from the look on my daddy's face, he was *obviously* not invited.

"What the *fuck* are you doing on my property?"

I flinched. Like nearly jumped out of my skin. I could count on one hand how many times I'd heard my daddy curse and still come up short. It just wasn't the type of person he was. In fact, the last time I'd seen him he was acting unlike the type of person he was. Me being with Luke completely changed the nature of our relationship. Now, the least aggressive man I'd ever seen was looking right at the one I wished to spend my life with and had his hands balled into fists and fury in his eyes. I knew I shouldn't have come here. I *knew* this wouldn't end well.

"I thought you would like to see your daughter for the holidays," Luke explained, not at all put off by my father's anger and aggression.

"You've got five seconds to remove yourself from my fuckin' property before I call the cops. I know all about you and your brothers. You're not welcome here. For you to have the *audacity* to show your face at my home when—"

"Listen, I came to you man to man because you have a daughter that you made feel like shit when you decided to disown her based on your opinion about her life. Believe me, if it wasn't for her, I wouldn't

189

be here."

I could see that Luke was trying his hardest to keep his cool, but the way my father was reacting to his presence was definitely testing him. When I saw my father move a little closer to Luke in order to respond, Luke's fingers twitched, and he situated his hand to his side. Horror filled my body. I just knew he was going to go for his gun.

"Jani, you gotta get in there," Mixie urged me, but by then I was already running towards the two men in the world that I loved the most, hoping that I could stop a tragedy from happening.

"You're not a fuckin' man, you're a criminal!" my daddy barked, his finger pointing right in between Luke's eyes. "You destroy the Black community...the type of community I grew up in, and that's why I've vowed my whole life to putting scum like you away!"

"What da fuck you know about the Black community, livin' out here among all these white muthafuckas," Luke gritted through his teeth, still speaking in a low tone with as much restraint as he could muster up. "When the last time you even took a ride through the community you claim to be protectin'? My hood still loves me. Do they even know you? You can't even protect your own daughter, don't even want to see her. But that's okay because that's my damn job now."

"You fuckin'—"

"DADDY!" I screamed, jumping at him just as he lunged at Luke with his fist up. The blow connected with the side of my jaw, and I dropped straight to the ground, seeing stars.

"Oh shit, Janelle!" I heard my daddy's voice, but I felt like I was going in and out of consciousness. Couldn't see a thing. Then there was a blurry face hovering above my face.

"Oh my God, Jani! Are you okay?"

It was Mixie, but before I could answer her, the next thing I heard was TreVonia screaming.

"Nooooo! Don't shoot him…Daddyyyyy!"

And then there was Luke…the Outlaw.

"I should blow yo' muthafuckin' brains out right now."

His tone was low, but only because he was talking through his teeth. Blinking a few times, I sat up as much as I could and focused my eyes on the large figures above me and gasped. Luke had my daddy pinned up on the wall with a gold-plated gun to his neck, with his finger on the trigger, threatening to shoot. TreVonia was on her knees, sobbing silently into her hands, and Mixie was frozen into place, but I knew that, like me, her mind was racing with options on how we could handle this situation.

"Luke! Put the gun down!" I screamed.

"It was an accident…I would never put my hands on her. An accident…"

My father wasn't even looking at Luke or seemed to be conscious of the fact that he had a gun to his throat. His eyes were pointed upward like he was talking to himself. A single tear fell down his cheek, and it tugged at my heart.

"Daddy," I whispered. "It's okay, I know you didn't mean to. Luke…please."

With his jaw still clenched, Luke finally released him and stepped back, pushing his gun back behind his spine. I took a few steps forward to console my daddy, but he held his hand up to stop me. And Luke was on him again.

"You wanna push her away because of me. But who's the fuckin' monster now? Me or you?" Luke paused, glaring at my father who had tears in his eyes. His shoulders were slumped and he dropped his head down, hearing what Luke was saying but still not wanting to be near me.

"I just want what's best for you. And he's—"

"I'm not best for her? I guess you liked Chris for her because he was a lawyer. He's the same nigga who wanted to destroy her career and threatened her, but he's better for her, huh? Or I guess you would have rather she be with her ex the one from out here, your golfing buddy who used to put his hands on her and cheated on her every chance he got?"

I sucked in a breath, feeling like a hot iron singed me right in the chest. How did Luke know about that? How did he know so much about me without me knowing as much about him?

"I—I just want what's best…" My father shook his head, and the words flew away. I knew he was still trying to come to terms with the fact that he'd just punched his own daughter, even if it wasn't on purpose.

"I'm what's best for her. I'll never hurt Janelle, and I'll work my ass off to provide her with everything thing she needs…everything she wants." Our eyes connected when he said that last statement, and I was floating on clouds. He broke our connection to look back at my father.

"I know you think I'm not the type of nigga you would have wanted your daughter to be with and, normally I wouldn't care, but she loves you and she wants you in her life. So that's the only reason I'm here. And it's he only reason you're still alive. Thank your daughter for that...Janelle, let's go."

Luke reached his hand out to me, and I grabbed it without a second of hesitation. He pulled me to his side, and I felt our connection strengthen. My love grew.

"Jani, I love you," Mixie said before giving me a tight hug. TreVonia came up behind her.

"Yeah, I wish you could have stayed," TreVonia added, still rubbing away her tears. Then she cut her eyes at my daddy. "It would have been nice to at least have you home for the holidays."

I shrugged, wiped a tear from my cheeks, and hugged my sisters one more time. I didn't know when the next time would be that I saw the two of them. My mind was made up that if I wasn't welcome home, I wouldn't be back here. It hurt, but I knew in my heart that Luke was the one I wanted to spend my life with and, in the end, I chose him.

Luke helped me into the car, and I realized just how drained I was: emotionally, physically, and mentally. I was spent. My eyes closed, and I fell asleep thinking about how much I enjoyed the touch of his hand on my thigh as we drove away. No matter what, this was going to be the perfect holiday.

Sidney

I was completely lost on how I was supposed to break this news to Yolo but I had to figure out a way. And it had to happen tonight.

Finally, I was seeing LaTrese for the type of person she was. She wasn't just a bitch. She was crazy… like mentally ill. The things that she did were horrific and yes, I believed that she should be dealt with but I didn't want Yolo to kill her. She needed help. She had a family history of mental illness and there was a difference between a mentally ill person and someone who intended to do harm. And if I didn't come at Yolo correctly, he would be the latter. He would intentionally aim to hurt her. I couldn't have that on my conscience. I couldn't be responsible for him ending her life no matter how much I didn't like her.

"What's got you lookin' like that?" Yolo asked me as he got dressed. I looked at the clock. I wasn't the type to tell him what to do but it was damn near midnight and he was headed somewhere.

"Just got a lot on my mind. Where you goin'?"

He gave me a strange look from under one raised brow. "Gotta handle some business."

The way he said it made my heart drop.

"Business? Like…" my eyes darted towards the door that was between where we were and where LaTrese was in the other room. "You mean something dealing with LaTrese?" He nodded his head. "I thought you said this weekend for that?"

"This Thanksgiving weekend," he informed me nonchalantly as if gangstas really took a break over the holidays. I guess the Murrays did. "Plus my boys got him here early. I can get this shit done so you and I can go back to normal."

My lips moved and my eyes darted around the room but no words came out. LaTrese was right in the other room. I didn't want to tell him everything I knew with her so close by. I'd intended on waiting until we were somewhere alone but now I was running out of time.

"Yolo, you can't kill him."

Sighing, Yolo sat down in a chair near his bed and started lacing up his black Timb boots. I licked my dry lips and tried to stop the slamming of my heart against my chest. I was caught up in a corner.

"Sid, we already went over this shit," he repeated with an annoyed tone while staring at me from under his bedroom eyes. "Just stay the fuck out of it. That's why I didn't want to tell you."

"No... Yolo, you can't kill him because he's innocent. Please, just listen to me! I have proof!"

Before Yolo could object, I ran to him and sat between his knees. Through tears in my eyes, I told him everything I knew. Revealing it all from the beginning when I saw the pills in LaTrese's place and ending with the call where Calvin had revealed everything. Even though I initially had refused to read it, I eventually had read over the reports from LaTrese's psychiatric visits that made it into her court files. I told Yolo what I'd read there, about how she'd confessed to using medication to abort multiple pregnancies, resulting in stillbirths. I left out Faviola,

195

Carmella and Janelle's involvement for fear that it would bring some unnecessary shit on them that they didn't need.

By the time I finished, Yolo's face was tight and his eyes were cold and narrowed into slits but he wasn't moving. Barely seemed to be breathing. I'd seen Yolo angry on rare occasions but it was never like this. It was like heat was radiating from off of his body. I could feel it in my soul… like the devil's fury. And it was at that moment that I knew, no matter what, I wouldn't be able to control it or him. Whatever was about to happen was out of my control and that single thought scared the shit out of me.

"Move out the way, Sid."

I opened my mouth but only air came out. Still I didn't move, I couldn't let him murder LaTrese for the things she'd done. She wasn't in her right mind.

"Move out the fuckin' way." His voice was calm but his tone was deadly.

"Please don't hurt her, Yolo. She didn't—"

Yolo picked me up by my shoulders, clear off my knees, and flung me back like I weighed nothing at all. I landed on the top of the bed and before I could collect my bearings, he was out the door.

"Yolo, stop! Please!" I screamed and ran towards him. He slammed the door behind him and it nearly knocked me right in the face.

Grabbing the handle, I twisted and ripped it open but by the time I got into the living room, it was too late. Yolo had LaTrese's neck in his hand and was squeezing the life out of her. He was only about half a foot taller than she was but his strength was enough to be able to lift her clear in the air, only the tips of her toes touching the carpet as she dangled high, her eyes bugging out of her skull as she looked back at him, pleading for her life. The sight of it all froze me in place. I clasped my hand over my mouth as tears ran down my cheeks.

"You killed my seed! My son!" Yolo spoke through his teeth, squeezing even harder. I saw LaTrese's eyes bug nearly out of her skull and her face began to change colors, from brown to a purplish color. She was grasping at his hand, fighting for her life but her efforts were no match for his strength.

"Yolo, stop! Pleaaase!" I whined, crying harder than I ever had in all my life. I dropped down to my knees and continued to plead with him right as LaTrese's body fell into convulsions. I looked away, unable to stomach the sight of her losing her life. My stomach retched and I turned to the side, dry-heaving out my guts onto the floor.

And then the shuffling of her feet stopped. The silence that echoed through the apartment seemed deafening loud. I knew LaTrese was dead. It was all over. I knew she was gone. Still, I looked up, afraid of what I might see. I heard a loud noise and by the time I looked up, Yolo had released LaTrese's dead body onto the sofa that he'd pulled her up from. Then he reached in his pocket and pulled out his cell phone, pecking at the keys with ease. As if he hadn't just murdered someone before my very eyes.

"Aye, I need you down here. My apartment. Yeah," was all he said before hanging up the line.

He walked by me like I wasn't even standing there and went back into the room, leaving me alone in the same room as LaTrese's body.

I was devastated but more than that, I was terrified. Never had I seen Yolo like that and I was genuinely afraid of him. How could he murder someone and just walk away like it was nothing? He'd been with LaTrese a long time and, according to him, he had a connection to her that made him feel responsible for her. But then, he just ended her life like she meant nothing to him. In a matter of minutes, she'd gone from being a pain in my ass to being dead. If he did that to her… what would he do to me if one day I fucked up and got on his bad side?

"I'll be back," he said from behind me and I turned around, tears still in my eyes as I stood up on wobbly knees to face him.

"You're leaving me here? I can't… Yolo, I can't be here alone, please."

He gave me a look but it was so cold and distant that I started to shiver. It was probably more from fear than anything else. I'd grown up my whole life knowing that the Murray brothers were from the streets and I'd heard stories about the things they'd done. Things that would make anyone want to distance themselves. But there was something about seeing that shit in action that changed the script up for a bitch like me. I felt like I didn't even know Yolo. *Who the hell had I fallen in love with?*

"Get your stuff together and I'll drop you off at your place. I've got shit to do and this had thrown me off my timeline."

"Wait… you can't be serious. Calvin's free to go, right? I told you he's innocent, You gotta let him go now."

Yolo lifted his head and crinkled his brows at me in a way that made me feel like I truly understood nothing about the ways of the streets. Being close to him and his brothers for my whole life, I thought I did but it was becoming obvious how clueless I really was.

"Ain't shit changed, Sid. The nigga knows too much so he gotta go. No loose ends."

After saying that last part he looked at me peculiarly and I wondered if, in that moment, he was considering whether I was a loose end that needed to be dealt with. I felt like I wanted to cry.

"I never wanted you to be apart of this shit, Sid. I'm sorry I pulled you in but now we gotta go."

Without saying another word, I went into the room and grabbed a few things that I knew I couldn't do without and walked out, following behind him and careful not to turn anywhere near LaTrese. We got in the car and I looked out the window the entire way back to my place.

For the first time in my life, I felt like Yolo, the one person I'd loved my entire life, was not anything like the man I thought I knew him to be.

Carmella

"*B*aby girl, I don't wanna be the first to tell you this but… you look like shit," Bryan said, eyeing me as I stood in front of his door.

"You ain't funny."

Rolling my eyes, I pushed my shades higher on my face and rushed inside, cradling my suitcase in my hand. Luckily, Zeke had been so gracious as to let me collect a few of my things while he had the locks getting changed, but no matter how many tears fell from my eyes, he still put me out on my ass. Muthafucka didn't even give me money to grab a Lyft across town to Bryan's spot.

"This is a nice place," I said, looking around at his condo. For the first time, I wondered what it was that Bryan did because his place was *laid*. It was a modern style condo that was definitely a total bachelor's pad, but almost every single thing was white. He was for sure a neat freak.

"Yes, it is. And you're welcome to stay, but just don't fuck my shit up," he added, and gave me a look that said he was serious.

"I'm not gonna be here long," I assured him. "I just need to get my shit together, find a new job or something so I can have money to return to Cali, and get back into school. I lost my scholarships… no need to even go back unless I can pay my tuition."

I huffed out a heavy breath and flung myself into one of Bryan's white leather sofas, halfway expecting it not to be comfortable, but it was. Before I could lean my head all the way back, Bryan ran and placed a towel under my head. I turned and looked at his ass like he was crazy.

"Unt uhn…black girls put grease in their hair, and that shit will fuck up my couch. You're free to lay down and lay back, but keep the towel with you."

Bryan laughed and I rolled my eyes at him. He was worse than Janelle about his furniture, but it was a good thing because that meant that I would definitely be trying to get my ass up out of here.

"So tell me what happened."

Bryan sat across from me and tucked his legs up underneath his body as he waited for me to speak. I spilled out the entire story with ease, not skipping anything. Bryan was the type of person who didn't judge you because he'd been judged his whole life and that's what made me feel so comfortable to speak to him. Janelle was the exact opposite. She was so judgmental of every damn thing. If you weren't perfect, it was hard as hell to talk to her, and that's coming from me, her own damn sister.

"Shit, Carm! You know even I use a lil' candy from time-to-time." He nudged his nose suggestively. "But you gotta learn how to put a cap on that shit. There is a reason people get strung out on this shit, and I don't want you to be one of them."

Bryan continued preaching and I continued pretending to listen but really I wasn't trying to hear him. Everybody thought people had a problem with drugs once they heard they were using, but I wasn't one to be concerned with. I knew how to put a cap on it, and I knew how to stop if I wanted to. The problem was…I didn't want to! And with all the bullshit happening in my life, why should I? It was my only way of escaping and having fun. I was tired of people trying to ruin that for me.

"Okay, well…can you show me to the bedroom? I'm kinda tired, and I wanna lay it down for the night," I said once Bryan seemed to be done with his lecture.

He stared at me with eyes wide and then curled one to the ceiling before stroking the top of his perfectly defined mustache.

"Lay it down? It's only like seven o'clock in the evening, Carm."

"Yes, and I've had a long ass day full of getting fired, packing up my shit, and getting tossed out my apartment. Not to mention I no longer have a car, so I been calling cabs and shit just to get where I need to be. I'm fuckin' tired!"

I knew I was being a little rude, but I was agitated as fuck. Although I was craving some coke, I told myself I wouldn't take a hit tonight because I wanted to prove to myself that what everyone thought about me wasn't true. I wasn't addicted, and I could stop whenever I wanted to. But even after all the pep talking and convincing I was doing in my mind, I still took a small hit to help me get to sleep.

The next day, I woke up around noon, and Bryan was already off to work. He left a note on the fridge reminding me not to fuck up his apartment, and it actually made me giggle when I saw it. The pleasure was short-lived because, instantly, my mind went to Cree. Both of us were stubborn as hell, and because of that I wasn't planning on calling him, and I knew he wouldn't call me. Still, I missed the hell out of him, and I was beginning to think that having pride was fucked up. What was the point of hanging on to it when it just made me miserable inside?

Grabbing my phone, I dialed Cree's number. but it only rung twice before going to voicemail. He was obviously ignoring my calls. If I ever thought in the past that he didn't give a shit about me, I may have been wrong then, but it was definitely a fact now. Blinking back tears, I thought about the look in his eyes when he told me he was done with me and that I should leave. His face was void of all emotion; almost as if he'd been able to rid himself of his love for me just that quickly. I didn't know how it was so easy for him because my body still begged to be close to him at night. That's why I needed a little something to put me to sleep.

I rubbed my nose with my forearm and then pinched it tight. Deep down, there was a voice telling me that I was a little too addicted to coke and that I needed to lay off of it. The voice told me that I needed to try to go one full day without using so that I could get myself on track, get my life together, and get my man back. But the loudest voice in my head told me that I would feel a lot better about my situation and think even clearer if I only took a small hit. My eyes darted back towards the room where I had my stash, and then I shook my head. I'd only been awake for a couple minutes and hadn't even had breakfast yet, but I was fiending.

A couple hours later, I found myself dressed, sober, and on my way to Cree's place wearing a short bodycon dress that hugged all the curves that he proclaimed to love and some five-inch stiletto Louboutin heels that made my silky legs look even more toned than they were. I was taking a big risk by coming back here unannounced, but I was positive that he didn't have another woman in there with him. Not this soon anyways…Cree didn't seem like the type to move on so quickly.

"I'll show myself up, Barry," I said to the building doorman, gliding by quickly while also praying that Cree hadn't told them I wasn't allowed in the building. "Cree's here, right?"

"Sure thing, Ms. Carmella. And yes, he is here." Barry replied, and I thanked my lucky stars that he was letting me through without a problem. "Should I call up to let Mr. Cree know you're on your way?"

"No! I mean…no," I corrected my tone and then gave him a sexy smile to smooth out the alarmed expression in his face. "I'm trying to surprise him by coming over and…doing a few things. You know us women have to always stay on our toes to please our men."

I winked at Barry, and his cheeks went red when he thought on what I was saying. Barry had to be almost forty years old, but I was convinced his ass was still a virgin.

"Oh, sure thing, Ms. Carmella. I'll leave you to it."

And then I was up the elevator and confronted by another situation. Now what if Cree turned me away? What if he refused to answer the door? Shaking my head, I pushed away those thoughts and swallowed hard, mustering up all the courage I could to do what I needed to do. I was here to get my man back and I was going to do just that.

"What are you doing here?" Cree muttered after opening the door.

Not the response I was looking for. But at least he opened the damn door.

I looked at him as he put his hand behind his head and rubbed the back of his neck while glaring at me. He was wearing a pair of soft gray sweatpants and a white wife-beater, body looking sick as hell and muscles popping like he'd just got done working out before I knocked. My pussy throbbed in between my thighs, and every emotion that I felt for the man in front of me came to the surface. I wanted to drop down on my knees and beg him to take me back, to tell him I was sorry and that I would never use again. After all, the only thing I really accepted that I was addicted to was him.

"I'm here because I want to talk...I think *we* need to talk," I further clarified, and then licked my lips, trying hard to keep my eyes pinned on his and not on his body.

"We don't need to talk, Mel," he said with a sigh. "We've done enough talkin'. We can't do this shit any longer and I'm sorry."

His words devastated me, but I tried to take that shit like a champ and swallow it down along with my tears. I wouldn't cry in front of him right now. I needed to remain strong about this and show him that he and I needed to be together. Shit...what was all that stuff Outlaw said when he was trying to get back with Janelle?

"Cree, I'm not an addict, and I don't have a habit. I just use every now and then, mainly when I'm working or going out. Is that really so bad?"

My voice cracked at the end of my sentence, and my heart clenched tight in my chest. This whole thing was killing me. We were standing in the damn hall having a conversation that meant my entire life to me at the moment. Cree wouldn't even let me into his place. I was losing my nerve when it came to him. Why didn't he love me anymore?

"Mel, it is that bad because this shit isn't as simple as you may think. I've been watching you for a while. You've been using for a while. This ain't no 'party type shit' either. You got a fuckin' problem, and I can't let myself deal with chicks like you," he finished, delivering the final stab into my heart.

Chicks like me?

"I want you to leave. Now," he said, looking me right into my eyes to let me know he meant it. I dropped my head and shook it gently, ready to take the rest of my pride—the little bit I had left—and go back over to Bryan's place. That is…until I heard a woman's voice.

"Cree! Can you help me—"

I was about a second away from jumping on Cree's ass when I saw Teema walk up behind him, holding Kenya in her arms. What her ass was doing in Cree's place instead of Kane's, which was right down the hall, was a mystery to me. I never thought that she had a thing for Cree but, then again, she wasn't with Kane the last I heard, but would she really move on to one of his damn brothers?

"Oh hey, Carmella," she greeted me with a smile once her eyes fell on me standing at the door, but I didn't even attempt to return one back to her.

"What are you doin' here? Shouldn't you be at your baby daddy Kane's house?"

Teema's head jerked back as if I slapped her. She frowned at me while clutching her baby in her arms, and I frowned right back at her ass.

"Oh so you think..." She looked from me to Cree and then chuckled incredulously, shaking her head. "Baby girl, I don't want your man. The only reason I'm over here is because I can't stand to see Kane's ass at the moment."

Now I felt stupid, but I played it off by nodding my head and throwing my hands up, stepping back a little to give her some room to say whatever she needed to say to Cree.

"Cree, I need to take a shower and was wondering if you could help me by watching Kenya for a minute."

Before waiting for him to respond, she pushed Kenya into Cree's arms and twirled away, down the hall. I watched her leave and still couldn't help but feel jealous that she was welcome into Cree's place and I wasn't.

"Can I come in?"

"What?! No, Mel. Listen...you need to leave," Cree's brows crunched together, and he held up one hand, signaling for me not to come any closer. Kenya smiled and leaned out with her arms open, beckoning for me to hold her. She seemed to be the only one who wanted me around.

"But Cree, it's not what you think...I don't have a problem and if you'll just let me explain—"

"I don't want to hear no fuckin' explanations," he said under his breath but in a tone rugged and rough enough to send chills down my spine.

He meant what he was saying, and I was beginning to understand that I was not going to get to him this way. I was beginning to understand that I'd lost the man that I loved. We all had our things that our boyfriend or girlfriend could do to make us totally shut down on them. Mine was if a man ever put his hands on me and, obviously, Cree's was if he ever found out his woman was using drugs. But shit...I wasn't a damn junkie. Was it really that bad?

"Go and have a good life," he said, backing away so he could close the door between us. "Don't come back here. I mean it."

The air around me felt chilly and cold as he delivered that last warning. I knew Cree, and I knew better than to test him. I wouldn't be back. I finally accepted that it was over.

Teema

"*H*ere you go. I put a few of her favorite things in this bag, but I didn't bother packing any clothes or diapers because you should have all that here and—"

"Teema, stop," Kane cut in, stopping me mid-rant from rattling off all the basic information he'd need for his time with Kenya over the weekend. I really didn't need to tell him anything because I knew he'd have everything under control. He'd turned into a great father, even if he was a pain in the ass baby daddy.

"What, Kane? I mean…I know you don't need the rundown but I feel better sayin' it because—"

"Teema, this isn't about Kenya. Come in…please."

Pushing my brows in the air, I looked into Kane's face, noting the seriousness of his stare but also the softness in his eyes. He licked his lips and ran his hand over the top of the curls on his head, and I had to blink away from looking at him so that I could stop my body from reacting to him.

Damn it, Teema! You can't go here again. Not with him.

But the more I told myself that shit, the less it worked.

"What do you want, Kane?" I huffed out as I walked by him, trying to be hard.

I sat on the sofa and watched him walk across the room with Kenya in his arms and place her in the playpen in the living room before coming over to me. He glanced in her direction to make sure that she was playing with her toys before sitting down across from me.

"I don't wanna fight with you, Teema," he started, keeping his voice low. He had a hard rule about not arguing in front of Kenya.

"I ain't gon' lie though, I'm not feelin' you datin' other niggas."

Opening my mouth to remind him for the umpteenth time that he *wasn't* my man, Kane stopped me with a single look, and my mouth clamped back shut. Although I was sassy and headstrong, I still knew the boundaries I shouldn't cross when it came to him.

"The reason I'm not cool with that is because I'm not over you," he revealed, nearly taking the breath out of my lungs. "What we got going on here...I want this shit. I want you and I want Kenya. I want all of us to be a family together. I guess, with you guys staying here, I got used to the family thing, and then you popped up entertaining another nigga."

He blew out hot air and ran his hand over the top of his head again. I watched him, nearly not blinking. My mind hadn't caught up with my heart, and I was nearly floating on his words, not even thinking about the practical side of things. What did he want? A relationship or just a live-in? Was he asking me to be his girl?

"So...you want me to be your girlfriend? I'm—I'm just not getting this." I pressed my lips together, thinking about how I'd already been Kane's girlfriend for over five years before becoming his baby mama. Now to be his girlfriend again and be living with him and our child...I don't know, it felt kind of backwards.

"We're far beyond the girlfriend stage, ma," Kane said and stood up, shoving his hand in his pocket. I clasped my hand over my mouth when he walked over to where I sat and then suddenly dropped to one knee. Before I could even remind myself that I needed to breathe before I passed out, he pulled out a small box from his pocket and held it up in front of my face, pausing and blowing out a breath before opening it.

"Look—we ain't gotta rush into this, but I can't have you be just my girlfriend anymore. What we are building together, with Kenya, it's more than that play-play shit, and I ain't getting' no younger. To be honest, neither are you."

I sucked my teeth and rolled my eyes at that last part, but he only laughed. It felt good to hear Kane laugh. His serious ass acted like it was a crime to do so half the time. I almost smiled myself, but then he opened up the box and all the shits and giggles came to an end. It was the most beautiful diamond ring I'd ever seen, emerald cut, just like I loved.

"Teema Joy Ellison, will you marry me?"

I couldn't bring myself to utter a single word so I simply nodded my head, smiling so hard that my cheeks hurt as tears streamed down my cheeks. Coming over here, I thought a lot was going to happen between Kane and I, but the last thing I'd ever expected was that we would be married.

"Kiss me," I told him and he gave me a sideways look.

"You know I ain't into all that mushy shit," he joked, but then leaned up and kissed me right on the lips before pulling away only to place the ring on my finger.

Looking at it brought fresh tears to my eyes. I couldn't wait to call Cyndy and Miyani because I knew both of them bitches were about to be all kinds of jealous of this shit right here. Well, they would be happy for me, but I knew they would also be low-key jealous, too! For a second my thoughts went to my mama and what she was up to. I was living the life that I'd always wanted, and I couldn't even have her here with me.

"You good?" Kane asked, kissing me again on the lips, and I nodded my head. Smiling, I tried to push the thoughts of my mother away, reminding myself that she was grown and had chosen her own path when she decided to steal food from out of my baby's mouth and the roof from over her head.

"Yes, I'm more than good. I'm happy as hell."

"Well, we should be celebrating," he replied, pinching me on the cheek.

The space between my thighs nearly dripped like a faucet, and I cut my eyes at him before glancing over at Kenya. I didn't even have to say anything for Kane to read my mind.

"Don't mind her. Turn on Smurfs and her ass stays quiet for hours."

Grabbing the remote, he flipped to the pre-programmed shows, and in a matter of seconds, Kenya was singing loudly in baby-talk to the theme song. Kane grabbed my hand and led me down the hall as I eyed my ring, feeling crazy inside about the sudden change my life had made. I'd always dreamed about one day being Mrs. Kane Murray but I had no idea it would happen like this and after all of the shit Kane and I had been through.

"You nervous?"

My back was to Kane and I was clutching the white towel he'd wrapped around me, after bathing me and himself in the shower, so tightly that it was probably making indentations in my skin. I shouldn't be nervous. Kane had seen my body more times than I could count. Matter of fact, he'd just seen it again in the shower. But still, I caught myself second-guessing what I was about to do, even though I knew I wanted to do it. I was much thicker than the last time I'd been with him, being pregnant with Kenya had made sure of that. My stomach wasn't flat, my hips were wider, legs flabbier, tits not as perky as they were before breastfeeding. What would he think?

"Take that towel off."

One look into Kane's face and I knew he'd read everything going through my mind. It was crazy how well he knew me, sometimes I loved it and, times like these, I hated it. I didn't have to say a word...he just understood and could read my innermost thoughts. I didn't want him to think I was some chick with low self-esteem, even if that was how I felt right now.

"C—can you turn off the light?" I asked him, feeling like it was the hardest thing to say.

"Listen, love, you're beautiful." Kane cupped my chin in his hand and pulled my face up to look into his eyes. "I don't want to miss any part of you because I'm trying to squint through the dark. There is no reason for you to hide from me…don't you know that?"

Aw, shit!

Kane's words sounded nice but it didn't hide the fact that I was used to model-looking chicks being on his arm or in his face, and here I was with a few rolls more than I wanted on my stomach, stretch marks that I wished I could rub off, and some jiggles here and there that I couldn't get rid of. When I put on clothes, I still was a little thicker than I liked to be, but I'd learned over time how to hold everything in. I couldn't hold shit in with all my clothes on the floor!

Kane must have seen the apprehension on my face because he chuckled lightly and shook his head before backing away a little and then running his hand over his smooth waves. I took a deep breath and sat on the bed, watching him and waiting.

"I don't know how shit got fucked up like this," he said under his breath, and then lifted his eyes to mine. "You remember when I met you, right? You were dirty as hell, hungry as shit, and… you ain't smell, in fact you smelled good as hell, but you damn sure looked like you did."

I almost took offense to that statement, but I smirked and ducked my head because it was true. I tried to do the best I could with rewashing my clothes back in the day but after a couple years of hand-washing the same shit out of your clothes each day, at some point the shit just doesn't come off.

"But even with all of that, I didn't give a shit about the bitches *you* thought I should've been with. You thought I should have wanted the ones with the long hair, nice clothes, long nails and shit…I didn't want that shit. I wanted you and I still do."

By the time Kane finished what he was saying, there were tears in my eyes. Tears because I remembered that moment he was talking about. I'd broken down in tears after he asked to take me to a date and came to find me not dressed and not ready to go because I was panicking over the fact I had nothing nice to wear. I felt so stressed over the fact that I couldn't dress like the women I was used to seeing swarm around him, but in the end he didn't even care about that shit. He just wanted to date me.

Reaching out, Kane dropped to his knees and pulled my chin up again so that I was looking right at him. Into him.

"That being said. We keepin' these muthafuckin' lights on so I don't miss a fuckin' thing."

I giggled at his crazy ass all the way until he lightly pushed me back onto the bed and spread my legs apart. I closed my eyes when I felt him pull at my panties and slip them down my thighs. My breathing came fast but steady as I waited in anticipation for what was about to happen.

"Relax," he breathed against my thighs and I did everything but… until his fingers slipped through the lace material of my panties.

"Oh!"

I tensed up around his finger. I was so damn tense, I could have broken it off.

"Relax!" he persisted, and I tried again just as he slipped another in.

Kane kissed against my thighs as his fingers probed my insides, and in less than a minute I'd gone from wincing and pulling from him to moaning and winding my hips against him. I felt like a virgin again. It had been so long since I'd felt a man inside of me but my body was familiar with Kane's so I fell right into place, just like I had many times before.

He was a gentle lover, careful with me like I was fragile. Or I guess more like he was a man in love, appreciating every part of my body. When it was all over, I felt like I was floating on clouds. Breathing lightly, I lay in the bed with my eyes closed and the covers pulled over the top of me, more satisfied than I'd probably ever been in my life. I was safe, didn't have a care in the word, and I was finally able to admit that Kane was the man I loved. Still loved and would forever love.

"I'm gonna go check on Kenya. Rest up a little and then get yourself together. We're spending Thanksgiving with my moms. Pack because in the morning we gotta get down to the airport."

"Thanksgiving? In Miami?" I frowned but I was actually already looking forward to the trip.

I'd met Mrs. Murray a few times and loved being around her. And I damn sure could use her cooking. Plus… now I had a little bit of good news to share with her. A ring as well as introducing her to her granddaughter.

"I'll be more than ready," I replied and pulled my hand up to look at my ring.

It was crazy how quickly life changed. Never in life would I have imagined this being my reality, but it was. And, truthfully, I couldn't wait to be Mrs. Kane Murray.

Outlaw

"*N*igga, how da fuck you stopped yourself from shootin' every fuckin' thing around?"

"Bruh, I don't even know," I answered honestly as I walked around the convenience store picking up some snacks and drinks for the long road ahead of us. Janelle was in the car sleeping like a baby, not even knowing how close she was to not having a daddy alive on this side of the Earth. After leaving her dad's spot, we checked into a hotel for the night but now we were on the road again. This time, I had another destination in mind.

"You done grown up, lil' bruh. Shit…I didn't think I'd ever see the day," Kane said, chuckling a little after he said it.

He was right. It was bad enough that I'd gone to Janelle's dad's house on some 'let me make amends with the daddy type shit'—that was something I didn't do. Make amends with niggas when I knew I wasn't in the wrong? That wasn't an Outlaw move. But this love shit had me doing some things I never thought I'd even think of attempting before. Including not putting a hot one in her pops for putting his hands on her. I knew it was an accident but, to be honest, I didn't give a shit because initially that fist was aimed at me. Either way, it was a death wish.

"On some real shit though, I'm on my grown man shit," I said into the phone as I threw everything I was buying onto the counter. The broad posted behind the register was trying her hardest to catch my eye, and I knew it but I wasn't feeling it. There was only one woman on my mind and dealing with her was a handful.

"Word?"

"Yeah, her pops had her living in some big ass estate type shit," I told him, thinking back to the big ass crib that Janelle grew up in. "I gotta buy a new spot because I'd be damned if I let that nigga outdo me."

The shit Janelle had lived in took up damn near the whole block in Brooklyn that I grew up on. In order to get into her spot, there was a big ass gate and, had it been closed, you would have to enter a code just to get in. The lawn was perfectly landscaped, and I could've sworn I saw some horse stables and shit out back. She grew up like a damn princess and I wanted to make her the queen of her own castle. I couldn't keep her holed up in my condo for much longer. My spot was fly as hell for me but what she was used to was shitting on everything I had going on.

"Damn, you really are switchin' stuff up for this one. Proud of you though. Where y'all headed now?" Kane asked, and I only paused for a second before I answered.

"I'm headed to Miami. I'm takin' her to meet moms," I told him, looking at Janelle through the window. She was still sleeping peacefully. I wanted to keep her as content as she looked for the rest of her life.

"*What, nigga?!* You takin' her to…aye, Cree! Outlaw takin' his ole lady to see our ole girl!"

"*What, nigga?!*" I heard Cree yell in the background, and I laughed a little knowing that they knew a nigga was really caught up now. No one met my peoples. Matter of fact, the only one of us who had let a chick meet our folks was Kane when he was dating Teema back in the day.

"Good luck with that shit, nigga. You know moms got a soft spot for her baby boy. She don't wanna think about another woman getting in her way," Kane joked.

"All that damn talkin' you doin', you need to be bringin' yo' ass down too so moms can meet Kenya."

"We getting' ready to head to the airport now. Cree, too. We'll get there before you, nigga! Yolo said he couldn't make it but Tank and his greedy ass kids should already be there though. Eating up all the shit before moms can cook it."

Getting in the car, I laughed at what Kane was saying because I knew the shit was true. I loved all my nieces and nephews, but they was some greedy muthafuckas.

"He brought his new chick with him?" I asked, thinking that it would be crazy as hell seeing my moms meet that crazy ass broad that Tank was now chilling with.

"Naw, she ain't here but I ain't ask why and he ain't say. But I gotta go get ready to catch this flight. Anyways, I'm proud of you. You doin' yo' thing," he said.

I didn't reply, simply hung up the line, but I knew he knew it meant a lot to me to hear him say that shit. Kane was my big brother who always gave me a hard ass time, but I didn't fault him for that. Now I can see that the shit I was on months ago wasn't worth a damn.

What I was doing now was worth a damn. And who I was with now was worth everything. The stupid shit I was doing before I met Janelle could have landed me in the pen for life and ruined all my chances of being with her. Kane's ways were fucked up most of the time, but I'm happy he did what he did.

Janelle slept the whole way and didn't wake up until I got off I-95. She stirred awake, yawning loudly and wiping the slob from off her cheek. I chuckled but tried to keep my eyes forward because I knew she'd have a fit if she knew I'd seen her drooling. Damn the fact that her ass was snoring like a trucker the whole way there. I swear she slept like a grown ass man.

"Wh—where are we?" she asked, leaning up to look around the car.

"Miami. We're goin' to my folks' house since we couldn't stay at yours."

"WHAT?!"

I almost laughed out loud seeing her pull down the mirror and start straightening up her hair. She looked perfect in my book but her uptight ass was trying to give herself a complete makeover from the passenger seat.

"You don't need that shit," I told her when she opened her makeup case.

"My skin is breaking out a little so I just want to get myself together. I can't believe you didn't tell me what you were planning! I can't meet your parents looking like this! I have bumps and shit on my face from drinking too much soda and—"

"Too bad I respect you enough not to nut on you like I used to do these hoes out here. A nigga like me comes packed with a lot of protein that could clear that shit up from off yo' face," I joked. Janelle didn't find it funny at all.

"Luke, I don't wanna hear about that nasty shit!"

I shrugged. It was true though. A little bit of nut on the face kept the pimples away.

By the time we got to my folks' house, Janelle looked like damn near a whole 'nother person after putting all that extra shit on her face. She looked good with it, but she was even better without it, but I was down with whatever made her happy and helped her calm her ass down.

"Oh my God…this is where they live? Such a nice house! Wait, what's your mother's name? No…I should say Mrs. Murray. Shit! We should have stopped by the store so I could grab some cake or cookies or something. I can't go in there empty-handed! Turn around!"

"Hell naw, I ain't turning around! I'm sick of drivin'!"

She hit me on my arm hard as hell.

"Janelle! It's not that damn serious! I already told my moms that you didn't know you were coming. You good, ma. Damn!" Twisting up my face, I rubbed my arm and then shut off the car. She was tripping. I should have dicked her down before we pulled in. That would have calmed her ass down.

We walked to the door with Janelle by my side giving off crazy anxious vibes. I grabbed her hand and pulled her close to me, kissing the top of her head and hoping that would make her feel more at ease.

She leaned into me, and I felt her relax a little. Before I could open the door, Tank opened it, chewing on a chicken bone that was in his mouth.

"Damn nigga, anything left on that bone?" I laughed, reaching out to dap Tank up and pull him into a half hug.

"Nigga, this all the damn kids done left for me to eat. What's up, Janelle?" He hugged Janelle and she greeted him back before reaching out to grab my hand once again. I squeezed it tightly, trying to urge her to relax a little.

"Where Favi? She okay?"

"Yeah she just wasn't feelin' up to the trip. But I really think she afraid of my mama," he replied with a light chuckle.

I was surprised Tank was actually gonna bring her ass to begin with. Guess you couldn't choose who the hell you fell in love with.

"Luke! Is that you?"

The sound of my mom's voice instantly brought a smile to my lips. I walked forward past Tank and pulled Janelle along with me. My moms emerged from around the corner looking just like her look-a-like, Angela Bassett. She was beautiful, the first woman to have my heart.

"Hey baby," she said, cupping my cheeks before kissing me on my forehead. Then she turned to the woman by my side whose hand was still in mine. "And you must be Janelle."

"Yes, ma—"

Before Janelle could finish her sentence, moms had pulled her into a tight hug, kissing her on the cheek like she was one of the family. The fact that I'd brought her here let everyone know she was. I'd always vowed that I wasn't ever bringing a chick here unless I wanted her to be mine for life. At the time that I'd made that declaration, I'd never thought a chick would get that far with me. But here I was…Crazy shit.

"You can call me Kathy, no need to be so formal," she told her, smiling brightly and holding her hand. "You're so beautiful…" Her eyes washed over Janelle's face and then the rest of her as she took her in as only a mother could.

"Let's go in the kitchen. You can wash up and help me with these greens. Teema and my new grandbaby are already in there. Time for some girl time so that I can get to know you."

She tugged Janelle away from me, but I tugged back slightly, giving Janelle a kiss on the cheek before she could walk away. I saw my mama's eyes sparkle at our simple display of affection, but I didn't do it for her. I did it to put Janelle at ease and let her know everything would be fine. She smiled, and I could see it in her eyes that she was just fine.

"Luke Ezekiel Murray, Jr."

The bass of my pop's voice rung through the house long before I saw him. He appeared from around the same corner my mom's had come from and was looking straight at me. Everyone said I was the spitting image of my pops, and I was. We stood at nearly the same height, had the same build, damn near the same everything except that I was about thirty-something years younger. Even though I had five other brothers ahead of me, I was the one he'd chosen to give his name. And like Kane, he was hardest on me than any of the other ones. It didn't matter what the hell I did, I could never seem to get my pop's approval on shit.

"What's up, pops?" I greeted him with a straight face, tucking my arms behind me, in prison stance.

"That's any way to greet your father now? With that street lingo?"

I felt my jaw twitch, but I clamped it closed, trying my hardest to control my temper. Cree and Kane walked in behind him and I saw their eyes go from me to my pops, knowing that sparks were about to fly, like they always did when I came home. Tank stood behind me, still gnawing on that dead ass chicken bone. I tried to avoid this nigga as much as I could because he was always on my ass about something. Like I said, he was like Kane in that way but he was worse. At least Kane had practically raised me. Where had this nigga been at? Working too hard and shit to be a fuckin' father but he always wanted to be on my case about how I lived my life. I guess both me and Janelle had father issues.

"At least you look better than you normally do…coming in here with all that jewelry and gang-related paraphernalia. Nice to see you finally looking like a young man who wants to do something with his life—"

"I have done somethin' with my life. Or that degree that you got hangin' up in your office don't mean nothin' no more?"

He twisted up his nose at my words. It wasn't what I said but how I said it. He was one of them niggas who got an education and forgot they were from the hood. I vowed not to be like him. Even though I went the college route, I never forgot where I came from or acted like

I was too high up on the totem pole to talk to the niggas on the corner that I used to chill with.

"Obviously English wasn't a subject you embraced while you were getting that degree. And let's talk about that…the degree that you no longer use. Well, not for anything that we can openly discuss, correct?"

I had just about had enough of his ass, but I saw movement to my left and looked towards it, seeing Janelle standing, her eyes moving back and forth between me and my pops with a crazy ass look on her face. I didn't know how long she'd been there, but it was obvious it was long enough for her to understand that shit wasn't all sweet in the Murray household.

"I—I just needed to get my phone out of the car. I think I left it." She ducked her head slightly and started to walk towards me. Then she stopped and looked up.

"Um…hello, sir," she said, greeting my pops, and I waited with my arms crossed for him to say any kind of disrespectful shit so I could set it off like Christmas in this bitch. It was Thanksgiving, but I didn't mind shifting things a little if I felt the need to, and I was sure Kane, Cree, Tank, and my pops could all see that from the look on my face.

"Hello, you must be Janelle. You're very beautiful. A lawyer, huh?" He looked at her and smiled which immediately seemed to put Janelle at ease.

"Yes, sir. I'm…" She glanced over at me. "Starting my own practice. Very soon."

"That's admirable."

I glanced at my pops wondering why he was on the corny shit.

You would think he was a college professor instead of the retired kingpin he really was.

"Thank you," Janelle beamed and then looked back to me. "I'll be back. Just going to get my things."

I nodded my head and the room went silent until we heard the door close behind her.

"A lawyer, huh?"

Pushing my lips together, I fought the urge to do as the old Outlaw would have done and take the opportunity to deliver a jab, reminding him of his old flame Griselda Brown who was also an attorney. It seemed like I was following in his footsteps, but the difference was that I was making an honest woman out of Janelle. I wasn't cheating on my wife or ducking around with my sidechick. As much as he liked to be a pain in my ass about my life decisions, I was a better man than he was.

"I'm proud of you, son. In spite of everything, it looks like you're finally on your shit. For real." Walking over, he pulled me into a hug, patting me hard on the back before turning to walk away.

Kane, Cree, and Tank all stared at me with wide eyes, sharing the same feelings that I had. That probably was the first time that my pops had ever said he was proud of shit that I did.

"Damn, I'mma play the lotto tonight," Cree joked, and Tank snickered along with him.

Thanksgiving dinner went smoothly just as I knew it would. My moms threw down in the muthafuckin' kitchen, cooking all the shit that had niggas like me stuck in the damn gym trying to work it all off. Still, I couldn't stop stuffing my face full of food. Kane and Teema announced that they were getting married, and I couldn't believe that shit. Only a few weeks ago, Kane ain't even want to let her ass in his house, and now he was popping the question. Crazy shit. What was even crazier was that during their announcement, I looked over and caught Janelle giving me the googly eyes like my ass should've been kneeling down and popping the question next.

In due time, I wanted to tell her, but I kept my mouth shut. Whenever I chose to do that, it would be a surprise, and I wasn't giving her no hints about when or if it was coming. The last thing on Janelle's list was that she wanted to be married and have her first child by the age of twenty-eight. She'd put a timeline on a nigga but that's all the hints she would get about when I'd make her dreams come true.

"You helped cook this shit?" I asked Janelle, my mouth full of food. She knocked me on my knee and reminded me not to speak with my mouth full before nodding her head.

"You need to cook like this at the crib," I told her before popping a turkey leg into my mouth and following it up with some mac and cheese. She rolled her eyes and glanced over at my mama who was watching us with a big ole smile on her face.

"You didn't have to tell her I don't cook!" Janelle whispered at me, punching me on the knee as soon as my moms looked away.

"She don't care about that shit. If you don't cook, it'll keep my ass comin' home!"

Janelle punched me again, and I couldn't help but laugh. She was so on edge trying to make a good impression. It was cute, but her ass really needed to chill.

After dinner was over, my pops called me into his office, and I glanced at my other brothers to see if any of them knew what it was about. They all shrugged. Before following behind him, I checked on Janelle who was sitting with Teema, holding Kenya on her lap, and watching cartoons with my other nieces and nephews in the living room. She seemed at home, even though I knew she felt some type of way about my moms refusing to let her help clean up the kitchen. Janelle was so old school like that, but I loved it.

"Sit down, son," my pops said as soon as I walked in his office, and I did as he asked.

Like my brothers and I, Luke Murray, Sr. had that street swag about him no matter how much he tried to hide it by pretending that he was just another green ass nigga living on the rich side of Miami. Back in the day, he was the man and made millions off of running drugs in all over the southern part of Florida but, after he cheated on my moms and lost the baby that Griselda was carrying for him, he put an end to everything and became a family man. Still, even knowing his past, he was always in my ass about how I chose to live my life. Just me. Not Kane, Cree, Yolo or Tank, even though we all did the same thing. Just me. He never even gave a shit about what Tone was doing with his life.

"Griselda called me. She told me about what happened at the Thanksgiving ball for Janelle's job."

He paused and I didn't say a word, wondering if he expected me to apologize for the issues I caused for his little sidepiece. If so, he could wait for hell to freeze over twice and pigs to fly out of my ass. There was no way I was going to apologize for shit, especially when it came to the woman who tried to ruin my mom's life.

"When she told me what happened and why…I realized how much you've grown. In your line of work, it's important to make friends of the type of people in that room. People who are in high places with the power to get you out of shit when you need them to. What you did showed me that you finally have decided to value and care for someone other than yourself. Even to the point that you sacrificed yourself."

Pausing again, he turned around and pulled out two glasses and then a large bottle of Hennessey. He poured both of us a glass and pushed one towards me before taking a sip of his.

"The reason I've always been so hard on you is because you're a lot like me. The selfish parts of me that I've hated and had to learn to get rid of. When I was in the streets, all I cared about was myself. I hurt your mother, I hurt my family…I hurt all of you. But out of all of your brothers, you were the one who always seemed to want to be just like me. You watched everything I did, and you inherited a lot of my ways…Naturally, but also through watching me. I think this Janelle young lady is good for you. I think she's helping you see that it's not always about you and that you can't walk through life with the motto 'fuck everyone else'. I'm glad that you've finally realized how to be a better man for the people in your life, than I could be for the ones in mine."

"I appreciate that," I replied like it was nothing. But it was everything to finally get his approval that I was doing something right. Especially since it had to do with Janelle.

He raised his glass and I followed suit, clinking my glass against his before draining the liquid. With a nod of his head, he dismissed me, and I stood up to walk out.

"Before you go," he started, and I stopped short of the door but didn't turn around. "Don't worry about any bridges you may have burned that night at the Thanksgiving ball. I still have a lot of strings to pull and I've done that to make sure that you and your brothers will remain protected."

Turning slightly, I looked at my pops with awe, and he winked his right eye at me before sipping from his glass. A part of me had always wondered if he still had his hands in the streets. Now I got my answer. I guess you can take a thug out the streets but can't ever take the streets out a thug. My ole man was still a goon. That's some G shit.

That night, Janelle refused to sleep in my old room and instead opted for the guest room in order to be respectful to my moms and her house. I didn't object because I knew that as soon as everyone went to bed, I'd be creeping my ass right in there and under the covers with her. And that's exactly what I did.

"Luuuuke, stop!" she moaned as I sucked on her neck while wrapping my arms around her body. "Not in your mama's house. That's so disrespectful. Ohhh…"

She couldn't say shit once I pushed her legs apart and dove two fingers into her wetness. With my other hand, I pinched her nipple, and she started twerking her ass back, rubbing it against my dick. I knew she couldn't deny me once I had my hands on her. What I wanted, I got, and there was nothing else to say about it. Fuck her objections. I wanted her pussy and I was about to get it.

"Stoooop," she groaned.

"Shut that shit up, Janelle. You know you want this dick. Now tell me you don't."

Smirking, I bit my bottom lip and waited for her to object. She knew better, and so did I. It was all an act. She wanted this as bad as I did.

"Plus, my mama don't give a shit 'bout us fuckin' here. She cool like that."

Pushing her knees apart, I dove on top of her and slipped my mans out of the flap of my boxers, diving right into her. I wanted to do a little more foreplay and shit but I was lying about my moms not giving a shit about what we were doing. Truth is, my moms didn't play. If she knew I was in here dicking Janelle down, she would whoop my ass like I was a kid again. She let it be known that this was 'a Godly house and wouldn't be no fuckin'"—her words, not mine.

I slipped into Janelle's velvety insides and nearly lost my mind. She felt so damn good. Every single time felt like the first time.

"Mmmm…" she began to moan like her ass forgot all about not wanting to have sex under my mama's roof.

"Shit…you gon' get us found out," I muttered, and then closed my eyes as I dove deep into her.

"What?! You told me she didn't care!"

"Shhhh!"

Gritting my teeth, I pumped in and out of Janelle as we both tried not to make too much noise. All it did was make shit feel that much better. Then she lifted her hips and wrapped her legs around my waist, and I almost lost my shit and said 'fuck it'. It felt too damn good to be on the hush-hush shit. Janelle held me tight, pulling me to her face and started kissing me sweetly while I rocked into her and it wasn't long before we were both cumming, her legs trembling as she held me tight, pulling me further into her.

I busted hard, filling her up to the brim with my liquid, not giving a damn that I was supposed to pull out. We'd deal with that shit later. Plus, she was officially mine. Whatever happened, we would deal with it together. And yeah, I know that's some crazy shit coming from a nigga who had a baby-phobia, but that was just how crazy I was about her.

Carmella

"*How* do I look?"

I posed in front of Bryan's floor-length mirror once again, twisting and turning so I could get a good look at my ass. To me, I looked pretty good, but I felt like I needed a little something more. It was the Saturday night after Thanksgiving and we were going out. It had been a while since I'd hit the club, not counting those lil' mini appearances I'd gone to at the Brooklyn spot that the Murray brothers practically owned. This was a real deal party night for me to get loose with Bryan and let all my worries go, at least for the night.

"You look...no lie, you sexy as hell, Carm. If I was straight, I'd definitely be tryin' to take your sexy ass home tonight," Bryan replied, putting me somewhat at ease.

"I still feel like I'm missing something." I continued to look at myself in the mirror and Bryan joined me with his arms crossed in front of his chest.

"Bitch, you just want to dust off that nose. That's what you think you're missing because this might be the sexiest I've ever seen you look. If you're tryin' to get attention, then that's what you'll be getting."

Looking down at the short, black and white Prada skirt and the white crop top that I paired it with, along with my Chanel bag and Louboutin heels, I knew I was the shit. But Bryan was right, my mood wasn't on point, and it had nothing to do with my outfit. I looked up into Bryan's face and saw that his lips were puckered and he was shaking his head softly from side-to-side.

"I knew it, bitch. Just do a little bit to get the edge off and then that's it, we gotta go. And this is only because we goin' out. You need to get a handle on this shit."

I smiled deeply, feeling excited just because I knew what was coming next. Licking my lips, I watched Bryan cut up the lines that led the way to my next good time.

The club was thick and the music was thumping. Before I even walked inside, I saw about five ballin' ass niggas who had their eyes on me while standing outside. Bryan cut his eyes at me, giving me a gloating look, and I had to laugh, silently admitting that he was right about my outfit tonight and the effect that it had. I was getting looks from both men and women, and most of them looked like they would have loved the opportunity to take me home tonight.

"Shit, that man over there looks like Cree."

"Oh no!" Bryan cut in, grabbing me by my upperarm as we stood near the entrance of the club. "Tonight is not about Cree. The purpose of the night is to say 'fuck Cree!' and move on with your life."

I swallowed the bulge in my throat and nodded my head.

"You're right. Fuck Cree!"

A half hour later, I had about three drinks in me, and I was turning up on the dance floor. Bryan had tried to keep up with me, but after the third song, he found something that caught his eye and left me dancing with a sexy ass man who had sponsored my last drink. I didn't know his name, didn't really care, but I knew that he looked good, smelled good, and was paid, judging from the ice in his ear, around his neck and on his wrist. A lot of New York niggas could fake ball, but I knew that wasn't his style. My eyes were trained to dissect a man down to the basics in a matter of minutes, and everything about him screamed authenticity.

"You want another drink?" he whispered in my ear, and I smiled coyly at him.

"You trying to get me drunk?"

Chuckling, he licked his juicy lips, and I felt my panties get moist. That chocolate brown skin of his did something to me. He had a Caesar haircut under his fitted NY cap, but what turned me on the most was his smile. His teeth were pure white except for four teeth at the bottom center of his mouth which were full gold. His aura screamed thug, and lately that's what I had an attraction to: sexy ass thugs just like him. I didn't want nothing serious with Cree still in my heart, but there wasn't a thing wrong with having fun and maybe grabbing a sponsor.

"Nah, I ain't tryin' to get you drunk, ma," he said, his southern accent thick…so thick and sexy that I damn near fell in love with his voice. He smiled and my eyes went back to them damn golds at the bottom of his mouth, instantly making my thong wet. This nigga was fine, but there was only one problem: I still had Cree in the back of my mind.

"Give me a second," I told him, realizing what I needed. "I need to powder my nose right quick.

He nodded his head and turned away to walk to the bar. I could tell he was the type that didn't chase behind women, or worry them about coming back to him, because he was too sexy for that kind of shit. If I didn't come back, the hoes were flocking and ready to take my place. But I was definitely coming back. I just needed to get Cree off the brain.

I came back out floating on clouds and ran right into Bryan on my way out the door.

"You havin' fun?"

"Fun ain't the word, bitch. I think I found one for the night," he replied and turned his head. I followed his eyes and saw a sexy ass light-skinned nigga who was looking in our direction and then winked. He was obviously gay but so sexy that he had both men and women gazing at his ass.

"Why don't you go ahead and handle your business. I'll be alright," I told him, not wanting to stop his fun. Plus, I was planning on getting into a little fun of my own.

"You sure?" Bryan's brows shot straight up in the air. "I don't know if I feel comfortable doing that."

I raised my hand and placed it on Bryan's chest, both to assure him and to get myself together; the drink and the drugs were getting to me, and my ass was about to start leaning.

"I'm fine, Bry. Have fun…I might have some fun of my own."

My eyes darted over to the bar, and this time it was Bryan who followed my eyes. He turned back to me and winked his approval before wishing me luck and walking away to his flame of the night. I smiled, pressed my hair down to make sure my edges were laid and tried my best to walk sexily over to the bar.

"Now about that drink," I said, as soon as I sat down to the fine chunk of chocolate that I'd spent the better half of my night with. He laughed and I shifted, trying to stop my kitty from popping.

"I'm already ahead of you, ma," he told me and pushed a glass in my direction.

An hour later, I was gone. Like totally *through*. I felt good as fuck, but I couldn't tell my ass from my forehead, which was a dumb place to be being that I was in the club alone.

Janelle would have been smarter than this. Janelle wouldn't have gotten drunk as fuck and high as hell while out on her own.

I don't know why every time I was in a fucked up situation, I thought about what my sister would do. I should have thought about her *before* I did stupid shit but it was always after.

"Let me get you home, ma. What's your address?"

The guy, who told me to call him Renegade—what the hell kinda name is that—had a nice ass ride, but I couldn't even fully appreciate it because I felt like I was about to throw up all in it. I mumbled the address to Bryan's place and laid my head down on the door, hoping that it would steady my spinning head.

"You fucked up, ma. I'm just gonna take you home and dip out, a'ight? I ain't tryin' to fuck. Just wanna let you know that off rip."

For some reason that kind of disappointed me even though I knew I wouldn't have slept with his ass anyways. I got loose sometimes, but I was no hoe. I wanted to have fun with him, but I'd played myself thinking that snorting a line would get Cree off my mind. I missed his ass and no matter what I did, I couldn't get rid of the pain of him being gone.

We got to Bryan's place but I was too gone to even get out of the car by myself. Renegade jumped out and pulled me out of the car, allowing me to lean on him in order to steady myself. Not too long after taking my first few steps, I nearly collapsed so he picked me up in his arms and carried me to the door. I handed him my key, and he opened the door, walked inside and placed me on the couch.

"I'm—uh, I'm gonna leave. Nice meeting you."

I snuggled up into the couch and didn't even respond. A few seconds later, I heard the door slam shut and I drifted off to sleep.

About a half hour later, I was up again and couldn't get back to sleep. Grabbing my phone from my purse, I looked at it and rolled my eyes when I saw the many texts from Bryan asking me if I was okay. I replied back to let him know I was home and told him to have a good night before standing up to walk to my room. But then another message came through as soon as I sat the phone on the nightstand. I grabbed it, thinking it was Bryan.

But it wasn't.

Aye, I'm in the city...got some shit I'm tryin' to get rid of. You in?

It was the guy who Taylor had hooked me up with. He was texting me late as hell, but it was still right on time because my supplies were getting low. So was my money but I'd worry about that later. I bit my lip, thinking briefly on whether or not I should go through with this, and then closed my eyes, took a deep breath and then texted him the address all while promising myself that this would be my last time.

Be there in like 10. Meet me outside.

Ten minutes later, I was downstairs in front of the group of apartments that Bryan lived in, waiting for Taylor's guy to roll up. I looked down at the screen on my phone. He was late as hell, and it was chilly outside. If I didn't want what he had to give me so bad, I would have taken my ass upstairs and cursed him out for wasting my time.

"Aye, nigga, look at this fine muthafucka right here."

Hearing some movement from somewhere behind me, I turned just in time to see a group of guys walking up. I'd never seen them around the building so I didn't know if they lived there or not, but I could tell they were drunk as fuck. And if I couldn't tell it from looking at them, I could definitely smell it.

"Damn, you from 'round here?" another one asked, shooting off his lame line. I snorted and folded my arms across my chest before turning my back to them. I should've changed out of the little ass dress I had on before coming outside because I definitely looked like a hoe working the corner and, from the look in their eyes, that's just what they thought I was.

"Come here. I got money," another one said, so close to me that I could feel his hot breath on my neck.

"Fuck off!" I told him and turned around to push him away. His friends began to laugh at me dissing him, but he looked pissed off.

"You out here sellin' the shit but you don't want my money?" he shot back, getting all up in my face. "What you think yo' used up pussy too good for me?"

He snatched at the hem of my skirt, pulling it up to expose my thong and I gasped, attempting to knock his hand away.

"Yo, Meke, leave that bitch alone."

"Hell naw," Meke replied back. "I need to teach this bitch a lesson."

Before I could run away from him, he grabbed me tight, pushing me back into the shadows around the side of the building. His friends around him started to snicker and laugh as he roughed me up, not finding anything wrong with the fact that their homeboy was about to rape me on the side of the building.

"Yo, nigga, we goin' inside. Live it up," one of his boys said as the crew started to walk away.

I started fighting against him, but he was too strong and I was still a little out of it from everything that I'd taken at the club. He was dodging my hits like a dodgeball champ, and I wasn't sure that I could stop him even if I did hit him.

Bam!

Punching me in the side of the neck, I nearly saw stars and it paralyzed me for a few seconds as I tried to get my bearings.

"Be fuckin' still or I'll kill your ass," he threatened me, the stench from his breath making me nauseated.

He snatched at my dress, pushing it up with one hand as he held me with the other and then snatched at my panties, trying to rip them off of me. Tears streamed down my eyes as I felt him fumbling with his jeans, and the only thing I could think about was the fact that I was bout to be raped because my ass was standing outside waiting for some coke. I squeezed my eyes closed and waited for the worst of it all to pass.

Click!

"Step da fuck back."

The man in front of me froze, but so did I. My eyes whipped open because I recognized the voice instantly.

"I said *step da fuck back*."

The venom in his voice was unmistakable, and I knew him well enough to know that the man in front of me needed to obey immediately or he'd find himself with two hot ones in his chest. Cree was standing behind him, dressed in all black with a hoodie over his head and his gun drawn and aimed right at the man in front of me. With wide eyes, the whites of them so bright they seemed to glow in the dark, he stepped back and placed his hands in the air.

"Aye, nigga, she was askin' for the shit. She a hoe… standin' on the corner sellin' her shit. I bought it fair and—"

Crack!

Cree knocked him so hard against the top of his head that he dropped like a sack of bricks, straight to the ground. Breathing heavily, I straightened up my clothes and wiped the tears from my eyes. I'd never in my life been so happy to see Cree. Lifting my arms up, I started forward to hug him but he blocked me, waving my arms away as he stared at me in disgust.

"The fuck were you doin' out here—"

"Aye!"

Turning around, I locked eyes with the last person I wanted to see right then. He couldn't have come at a worse time.

"Shit, I walked all around this building lookin' for your ass. I thought I told you to meet me out front!"

I looked at my supplier and then back to Cree who was eyeing him with suspicion at first and then recognition. I didn't know if he knew the man personally, but it was obvious that he knew what he was there for. The guy looked over at Cree, as if trying to figure out whether or not it was cool to complete the transaction in front of him. Luckily, it was too dark in the shadows for him to see the man who was blacked out in the grass, but that still did nothing to help the shitty situation I was in.

"Oh, I know what this is," Cree said under his breath, chuckling incredulously like he couldn't believe it. He looked at me, and I felt like my heart was crumbling into pieces all over again.

"This how you do it now, Mel?"

"Aye, I'm just gonna bounce outta this shit," the guy said and stepped off hurriedly.

Great, now after Cree dragged my ass, I wouldn't even have anything to help me get through the depression that would surely follow.

"This is how you do?" he repeated and this time the hurt in his voice and on his face made my eyes instantly tear up. "You better than this shit! I thought if—I thought if I gave you some time, you would come to your fuckin' senses. But here you are waiting outside like a fuckin' junkie for a nigga to serve you. You almost fuckin' got raped! If

I wasn't here—"

He paused, and it was then that I noticed the tears flowing down my cheeks. It took Cree putting my actions into words to make me realize how far I'd fallen. He didn't even know about the stranger who had taken me home. I'd gotten lucky because I could have gotten raped then too…or worse. I didn't know Renegade from a can of paint. I'd even gotten pissy drunk at the club while I was out by myself. I wasn't the same Cree from months before. In fact…if I knew a woman who was acting like me, I'd say she was dumb as hell.

"You're fucked up, Mel. Get your things out of there. I'm taking you home."

Frowning, I watched as he kicked at the guy on the ground who was still out cold.

"Home? You're taking me to your house?" I asked him and felt disappointment sting in my chest when he shook his head no.

"Naw, I'm puttin' his ass in the trunk so I can deal with him later. And then…I'm takin' you home. To Atlanta."

Janelle

*T*hanksgiving at Luke's parent's house was amazing, but now we were back home, and Luke was hitting me with bad news. He had to leave. Something about work but he wouldn't tell me what it was.

"If I'm supposed to be your lawyer now, why can't I know what's going on? Why can't I be with you?"

I was fully aware that I was whining and sounded more than a little annoying, but I couldn't help it. After having the best Thanksgiving holiday with Luke and his family, the last thing I wanted was to be left alone. The fact that Teema and Kane were engaged had me feeling some kind of way. Not because I wanted Luke to ask me to marry him… it was much too soon for that. But I still felt the need to be around my man. I just wanted the security of being around him and being wrapped in his arms. I didn't want him to leave, and he wouldn't even tell me how long he would be gone.

"Nell, even as my lawyer, there is some shit that you don't need to know. It's easy for you to represent me if you only know certain things. Okay?"

I didn't get it, and I wasn't buying it so I didn't reply.

"I really don't want you to leave though. I don't want to be alone. And now that I don't have a job…"

He lifted one of his brows and looked at me. I could almost read his mind. Yes, I was laying the guilt trip on him hard. It wasn't his fault that I didn't have a job but....then again, it kinda was.

"I'll stay in the hotel or something while you do what you have to do. I don't want to mess anything up for you, I just don't want to be by myself. That's all."

Luke gave me a deep look, and I could tell that he was considering my words. Finally, he crossed his arms in front of his chest and nodded his head.

"Fine," was his only response, but it was more than enough for me. I jumped up, screaming, and pounced right into his arms, kissing him all over his face.

"Why I feel like I'mma regret this shit?" he chuckled as I continued to kiss him. I didn't know why he felt that way, but it wasn't necessary. Having me by his side was always better than anything else.

***

I could easily get used to being with Luke. If vacations and shipping was what came with dating someone of his status, then I felt like I could easily turn a blind eye to whatever shit he had going on and just enjoy our life. As long as he always came home at night and I didn't have to know the details of what it was that he did, I could handle being a thug's girlfriend. Or better yet... a thug's wife.

We didn't pack a single bag of clothes, only a small carry-on full of things that we couldn't leave without. Luke told me that he wanted me to do all my shopping once we landed and, even though I wasn't the shopping type, the clerk in the store had my back.

"Try this on!" she handed me a beautiful multi-colored maxi

245

dress and I checked the tag first to decide whether or not it was cheap enough for me to fall in love with it.

"$245?! Oh no, that's okay. I don't need to try this on." I pushed the dress back at her and she frowned deeply, giving me a crazy look like she didn't understand what I was talking about.

"You no like?" she asked, holding up the dress.

"No, honey, I no like the price," I clarified for her and Luke's ass started laughing.

"Try the shit on, Nell. Stop clowning. I wanna see you in it," he said and I twisted around towards where he sat, leaning back on the seat with his arms sprawled out like he was Tony Montana or something.

"Luke, that one dress is $245—"

"I didn't ask you for the price, ma. Try it on," he said again and I huffed out a breath, knowing that he would continue on until I did.

By the time we left out of that store, the clerk had definitely done her damn job. Noticing that I wasn't the one she should have been catering to, she focused all her attention on Luke and began bringing him outfit after outfit, complete with the matching shoes, for me to try on. I was on my way to a million dollar wardrobe and, had we been there any longer, I'm sure should would have made sure of it before I left out of there.

"Loosen up, Nell. It's just money," Luke laughed but I didn't see a damn thing funny. I didn't like feeling like I had to depend on him to buy things for me. And shelling out that much cash at one time was definitely something I was uncomfortable with.

"That was way too much money that we spent in there. I'm not a materialistic woman and I'm not with you for your money."

"I know it. And that's why I don't mind breaking bread on ya," he shot back with a shrug. "You're the one I love, Nell. You need to get used to being spoiled. You need to get used to having all the shit that you desire because, if I can make it happen I will." He placed both of the bags he was holding into one hand and then draped his arm around my shoulder, pulling me close.

As we walked, I saw nearly every woman on the street turn her head to get a look of Luke but he didn't seem the least bit interested in any of them. His attention and all of his focus was on me.

"You making quite a scene out here, huh?"

"Naw, that's all you," he replied back, not missing a beat. "I don't know 'bout everybody else but all I see is you." I smiled hard, probably showing all of my teeth.

Yeah, I could get used to this.

Outlaw

$\mathcal{M}$y brothers were gonna fuck me up.

It was finally time for us to complete the job that I'd been planning for a while now. Another bank heist. This one in Los Angeles. I'd received a tip that some billionaire from some Arabic nation was arranging for a pick up from the safe deposit box that he had at a major bank there. The bank had to develop a protocol outside the norm just to allow for him to pick up some gold bricks, jewelry, and money all worth over $30 million. Any deviation from the norm was a perfect opportunity for the Murray brothers because, most times, the people in charge weren't really on their shit but we always were. If everything went how it should, we would be $30 million richer.

The only problem was, I had Janelle with me and that was against the rules. Kane had a hard and fast rule that we never brought civilians along for jobs. No one extra was allowed, it didn't matter who it was. But I was weak for Janelle. Before her, I didn't have a weak spot. But now I had her and I discovered she was my weak spot. Whatever she wanted, I had to make it happen.

"WHAT DA FUCK?!" Kane bellowed as soon as I told him that Janelle was in the hotel. "Luke, what about the fuckin' rules don't you understand?! Nobody is allowed when we do shit. Fuck…we can't do this job."

"Can't do this job?! Da fuck you mean, bruh? I been plannin' this shit for over a month!"

"Well, you should've thought 'bout that shit before you brought 'bae' along!" Kane retorted, slamming his fist against the table we were all sitting at. "What if I had brought Teema and Kenya along?"

"Difference is, Janelle is our attorney. She's a part of this shit now."

"He's right," Cree added, taking my side as usual. "Janelle has shown that she's down for the team, Kane. Even lost her job because of it. Her loyalty is with us."

"I agree," Yolo said, nodding his head, and Tank did the same.

Kane's stony eyes concentrated on me for a while as he thought everything over, and then finally he nodded his head.

"Ain't shit I can say about it now because she's here," he said finally. "But if this shit goes wrong…it's on you."

I nodded my head. I could take that responsibility because wasn't nothing about to go wrong. Everything was set for the job in the morning, and I'd already briefed Janelle on what to do and what not to do while we were there. She was good.

"Now let's get down to business going over the details. When are Benny and Jamal coming in?"

"They are due in tonight," I replied back, referring to our cousins who would help us with this hit.

I knew that Kane was superstitious, and that was cool because I was too. But having Janelle around has always been good for me, and I didn't see the problem with her being in town with me during this hit.

If anything, it would be nice to have her put my mind at ease before shit had to get serious.

***

When I got back to the hotel, I found Janelle sitting at the bar enjoying herself, exactly where she'd texted me that she would be. The only problem was that sitting next to her was this big goofy ass nigga, all up in her face, looking like he was trying to fuck something that night. Janelle was engaged in conversation with him and that was cool with me because I wasn't the jealous type but, also, the nigga looked like a lame. He wasn't someone I had a reason to be threatened about.

"Yeah, I've always thought I would have like three kids," the guy was saying as I crept up on them.

"Really?" Janelle exclaimed, her eyes wide. "I think I would like around that many, too." Then she looked down, the light from her eyes dimming a little. "I'm not sure that my boyfriend would go for that though...he's not really the family type."

Frowning, I stopped in place so I could listen to more of their conversation.

"Well, if he doesn't want kids and you do, I don't think that's the type of relationship that will work," the lame nigga replied.

"Well, fuck you, and fuck what the fuck you think!"

His ass nearly jumped straight up in the air as I stepped forward, pushing myself in between the two of them but keeping my eyes on the dude.

"I'm sorry, who are—"

"I'm the nigga whose shoe is gonna be up your ass if you don't move the fuck outta my face," I snarled, and in seconds he was gone. Left his freshly made drink and all. Fuckin' lame ass nigga.

"Scary ass dude. That dumb ass Chris nigga had more guts than him," I chuckled before sitting down in his seat. Looking at Janelle, I saw her eyes were narrowed at me.

"You didn't have to do that. We were only talking. He was helping to waste time before you got here." She rolled her pretty brown eyes.

"And I'm here now so ain't no reason for his ass to be here," I replied. "And what the hell you talkin' to that clown ass nigga about kids and shit for anyways?"

Pressing her lips together, she turned away from me and sipped on her drink instead of responding. I waved my hand in front of her face.

"I know your ass heard me. What it is for real, Nell?"

"You've always told me you didn't want kids...I was just being honest."

"How many more niggas you plan on being honest to?" I asked her, and she rolled her eyes again.

"I thought you weren't jealous, Luke, but that's exactly how you're acting right now."

"Maybe because you and that nigga was talkin' about fuckin'!"

She gasped, her eyes growing wide. "We were *not!*"

"Y'all were talkin' 'bout kids. You gotta fuck to get 'em. Same difference." I shrugged, and she punched me on the shoulder.

"It's not the same, but it doesn't matter. I would have to be married before I even think about having kids."

Here she was dropping the 'm' bomb. Janelle had my mind fucked up. She always said that it was too early for us to be discussing marriage or anything serious like that, and I felt the same way. But then there would be times like this where she made it obvious that marriage was what she had on the brain. She wanted to be Mrs. Murray, I didn't care how many times she denied it.

"What about practicin'? You gotta be married to practice havin' a baby?" I asked her, and she started to giggle. I didn't care what anyone said, I had the prettiest girl in the world. And ain't shit on her was fake. She was a natural beauty, and she was all mine.

"Nooo, nothing is wrong with practicing…"

"Good."

And with that, I grabbed her drink out of her hand and placed it on the table before scooping her up in my arms. She screamed for me to put her down, and I knew it was because we were causing a scene. Janelle hated to be the center of attention, but she needed to understand that if she was rolling with me, all eyes would always be on her.

That's just how it was being with Outlaw.

Janelle

"Don't leave out the hotel," Luke told me, and I rolled my eyes. Here he was with the rules again.

"I'm serious, Nell. You got massages, food and all kinds of shit you can order in this hotel. Don't leave out until I get back."

"Yeeeeesss, sirrrrrr," I droned, rolling over in the bed.

I was sore as hell. Especially between my legs. It was the next morning, and Luke and I had spent most of the night before 'practicing for babies' as he called it. Thank God I was on the pill or I would be pregnant with triplets. Luke's sexual appetite was always on one hundred, and it was hard for me to keep up sometimes because he literally seemed to rub my insides raw. But then I remembered all the nasty bitches who would love to take my place and got my act together.

Today was the day that Luke and his brothers did whatever the hell they were in town to do—of which I still had no details. Maybe it was the lawyer in me but I was dying to know what was going on, however, Luke knew how to keep a secret and wouldn't let a single thing slip. So I just left it alone.

"Remember when you put things on the room, don't sign in your name. We aren't here... according to the hotel, your name is Joyce Robertson."

"You could've gave us some better names, James Robertson," I told him, using his fake name with a roll of my eyes.

"Whatever. Just enjoy bein' my Mrs." He kissed me on my forehead and started towards the door with a bag in his hand.

My heart fluttered at him saying that I was his Mrs....even if he was being facetious. My emotions were crazy because I kept telling myself that it wasn't time to be pressing Luke for a ring. I hadn't even thought about wanting a ring until Teema and Kane became engaged. But now, ever since they announced they were getting married, it was all that was on my mind. I'd been stung by the marriage bug.

"Don't forget what I said, Janelle," Luke warned me one last time before leaving the room.

"Yeah, yeah, yeah," I told him and waved him away.

After he left, I rolled over to get a little more sleep since I hadn't slept much at all the night before but was awakened about an hour later to my phone blaring in my ear.

"Hello?"

"Jani, do you know what's going on with Carm?" It was Mixie and she sounded way too worried for this early in the morning.

"No, I haven't talked to her in about a week or so. Why? What's going on?"

"Well...she's home."

That got my attention. Blinking a few times, I sat up in the bed and gripped the phone even closer to my ear.

"What do you mean she's home? Daddy let her come back?"

"Yeah...she's living back home now. She spoke to daddy but

they've been all top secret about what happened and why she's here."

I grabbed my owl necklace and squeezed tightly on it, not knowing why my heart was throbbing in my chest. I guess because I missed my daddy so much, but he still didn't care to see me but had seemingly welcomed Carmella with open arms.

"Has daddy called you at all?" Mixie asking that question only made the throbbing pain in my chest even stronger and more painful.

"No."

"Have you tried to call him?"

"Yes." That admission brought tears to my eyes.

"He'll come around, Janelle. I promise he will. He loves you."

A few tears rolled down my cheeks, and I wiped them away. Mixie and I shared a few words of small talk, but I knew that she was only trying to make me feel better about being daddy's only daughter that he refused to see, and then we hung up the phone. I laid in the bed crying for what felt like hours before I decided that I needed a pick-me-up. I needed to get to the spa and get my relaxation on. Reaching over to the nightstand, I picked up the spa card and nearly fainted when I saw the price list of activities. Thankfully, I had a man with a black card who had given me full access so I was free to do everything I could dream of.

"Hello, how may I help you?" the spa clerk answered the phone with a French accent that made me wonder if it was authentic or fake.

"Hi, I would like to order a few spa treatments for the day," I started before rattling down everything I wanted to try out and then some extra for good measure.

The clerk happily repeated everything that I wanted, as if she would be getting paid a percentage of the cost just for taking the order, and then told me to head on down in an hour. I was there fifteen minutes early. So much had happened in my life within the past few weeks, and I needed this.

Four hours later, I was a new woman. Rose petal baths, warm pumpkin and aloe facials, and a deep tissue massage could do that type of thing to you. I was floating on cloud nine all the way until I got to the register.

"I'm sorry, we are going to need an ID for us to charge the card on file," the spa clerk stated.

Blinking a few times, I frowned and stared right back at her. "Why? I haven't needed to show my ID for anything else that I've charged to the room."

"It's because of the price. Our hotel has a policy that anything over $2,000 requires proper ID," she replied, and I could've sworn I heard her lil' fake ass accent falter a bit. She was a fake.

"Well, I don't have my ID," I told her, knowing damn well that no driver's license I had said 'Joyce Robertson'. Can I just have my husband come settle this when he gets back? He should have cash."

The bitch gave me a look that said everything her mouth didn't say. I knew she was calling me all kinds of 'niggas' and 'bitches' right then.

"We require payment as soon as the services are rendered. We have an ATM on the first floor that you are free to use to get the money…if you have it."

I wanted to slap the shit out of her. So there it was she felt like I was as much of a fraud as she was with her fake ass accent.

"I *do* have the money, but I'm pretty sure that I can't deduct $2,000 out of the damn ATM," I said, waving my debit card in the air angrily.

With a straight face, she offered me another alternative.

"That bank that matches your card is two blocks away. Any of our courtesy drivers can take you there. I apologize but without proper ID, we can't run the card on file. It's a security protocol the hotel uses to keep *our patrons* safe."

The way she said it pissed me off. Like I was an imposter that didn't belong in the building. The only thing stopping me from slapping the shit out of her was because I didn't want to cause a scene that would have Luke cussing me out later after he bailed me out of jail.

"Fine, I'll go to the bank."

"Mercedes will lead you to the courtesy driver," the clerk added, and I rolled my eyes. The only reason Mercedes was leading me anywhere was not because she was being nice, but to make sure I didn't run off somewhere without paying. This was some bullshit. The whole reason for the massage was to relax and as soon as I got out, these assholes were stressing me out.

I stomped into the bank mad as hell. Not only was I being made to withdraw money out of my account when I shouldn't have had to, I had to ride the entire way to the bank with the stank ass courtesy driver who smelled like old cheese grits. I swear I felt like I was going to vomit the entire way to the bank, it was so disgusting.

"Welcome, how can I help you?"

"Hi," I began, huffing as I lay on the counter. "I need to withdraw $2,356 from my checking account. Big bills are fine for the two grand."

I read off the exact amount of the spa bill without adding any for tip. They could miss me on that because I'd be damned if I paid them anything extra. My tip would be to tell their ass to get their shit together so that high paying customers like me didn't have to take a fuckin' stank ass car two blocks to the bank to pay a bill.

"Here you go, Ms. Pickney. Let me count this out for you. One, two, three, four—"

"Everybody get on the fuckin' floor! Hug the fuckin' floor right now!"

Pow! Pow! Pow!

Absolute chaos erupted around me and, without even thinking, I obeyed the orders that were given and hugged the ground. People were screaming, some were praying and others were crying but my only thought was that I had to think.

"Get on the fuckin' ground! And keep your eyes down!" the robotic voice said again.

My head was too close to the ground to see anything, but I could hear a collection of feet running about, demanding different things from the bank tellers and staff.

"Grab one of them muthafuckas and bring 'em in the back," another one said, speaking through whatever instrument they were all using to disguise their voices.

Squeezing my eyes closed, I prayed to the Lord that whoever they chose to grab wouldn't be me, but the reality was, I'd already had a fucked up day, and me being the one they chose to make a hostage would only be icing on the cake. Sure enough, while I had my face pressed to the ground, praying to Jesus to shed a little grace on me, I felt my body being plucked off the floor by my arms.

"Get da fuck up. Keep your head down!"

Tears burned in my eyes, but I did as I was told. When I worked at the clinic, we were often drilled on the proper procedures to take if we were robbed. Since we had a little bit of change and were in the pit of the ghetto, it was a risk of working there, but it never happened while I was employed. Now here I was trying to drudge up the memories of what I'd been told to do. The only rule I could remember vividly was to always comply with the robber's demands. Never play the hero. Shit, I couldn't play the hero if I tried. I was scared to death. I felt like I was about to piss my pants.

"I got the hostage. We good to go, fam," the man holding on to me said as he roughly pulled me into a room. His fingers were pressed so hard into my arm that it hurt, and I winced in pain.

"Move another fuckin' muscle and I'll fuckin' put a hot one in your brain, bitch!"

The next thing I felt was metal to my head, and tears began to stream down my eyes. I was gonna die.

Oh God, please! Don't let me die like this. God, please! I screamed within my mind.

Although my head was down, I heard movement in the room and

I knew that there were many other people there. One was a woman and she was crying pretty hard. I assumed she was a hostage just like me.

"Stop all that fuckin' cryin' and open the fuckin' safe up. Now before I blow your fuckin' brains out!"

"Or do you want us to blow her brains out and let you watch?" the man holding me asked with a teasing tone that could be heard through the robotic voice disguise. I let out a loud sob, unable to play the strong one anymore.

"Right...actually, I think that's a good idea," another one said. "If you don't get your shit together and open this shit in the next few seconds, we'll blast a hole in...OH SHIT!"

The room went silent except for the woman's sobs, and the hairs rose up on my arm as I got the crazy feeling that all eyes were on me.

"Get that fuckin' gun from her head, yo," one of them said.

"Huh?" the man holding me asked, gripping me even harder. "What da fuck you—"

"I said put da fuckin' gun down now!"

Instantly, the gun was pulled from my head and I let out a deep breath. Then there was silence in the room.

Something seemed off.

Against my better judgment, I looked up even though I knew that was a rule that I was breaking. You were never supposed to look them in their eyes or look at them at all for fear that you would make yourself a witness to their identity and cost your life. But there was something about this situation that seemed peculiar to me and I found myself breaking the rules. When I lifted my head, my eyes fell first on the one who had yelled for my captor to move the gun from my head and I froze.

He was covered from head to toe in army fatigue as well as a mask on his face and I couldn't see any of his skin… nothing but the white of his eyes. But that was enough. I knew the man I loved when I saw him.

"Luke!"

He lifted his hand but I could tell I'd done something wrong by the way the tallest one in the room stiffened up. Luke's eyes went to him and I saw him let out a breath. His shoulders slumped and I tried to realize what I'd done wrong. It only took a few seconds of racking my brain before I got it.

Fuck! I said his name!

"Shit," another one said. I didn't recognize who it was and his voice was disguised.

"It's open," the woman who had been working on the safe said with a shaky voice and one of the other men pulled her aggressively away from the opening as another one filed in. My eyes were still on Luke. The man I thought I knew better than I knew myself. I was learning that there was more to learn. And I was about to get my first lesson.

"Y'all four go get everything so we can get out of this bitch. Luke… you responsible for this fuck up so I'll leave you to handle it."

He walked away and I backed into a corner, wondering what was meant by that statement.

"Nell, turn around," he said and my knees started knocking.

Oh God... he wasn't going to kill me, was he? I didn't know the rules of the street or what happened when things like this happened. Was I the fuck up that needed to be handled?

"I'm sorry, I—"

"Turn around!" he ordered with force and I did as I was told. I wanted to cry but I was afraid beyond tears. Squeezing my eyes closed, I waited for death to come.

"Please... please, no!"

Zip! Zip!

The sound of something heavy dropping to the ground was the next sound I heard. With my knees still knocking against each other and my bottom lip quivering, I turned around slowly. The first thing I saw was the bank employee sprawled out on the ground with a perfectly round hole in her head and another in her chest. I felt weak and I nearly fell onto the floor, using only a metal beam on the wall to steady myself from hitting the floor.

Tears fell but they didn't block out the image of Luke walking towards me. I couldn't see his face but I didn't need to in order to feel his anger. And there was no mistaking it. All of it was aimed at me.

"I said this one time and I'm goin' to say the shit again... hopefully for the last muthafuckin' time," Luke gritted through his teeth. "Let this be the last fuckin' time you don't listen to me."

I sunk to the ground and dropped my head in my hands, sobbing uncontrollably.

"FUCK!" Luke yelled, making me jump. "Let's get da fuck out of here. We got 30 seconds to leave."

"We need to get her?" someone asked.

"No," Like replied back. Even though he still had on the voice disguise, I could still hear the fury in his tone. "Leave her there. Let's go."

And I stayed there… right where he'd left me. I was still sitting in that same spot, long after the footsteps were gone and even when I began to hear the sirens approaching. My heart was so tight in my chest that I felt like I was going to have a heart attack. I was scared out of my mind, in the room with the woman Luke had murdered because of my own stupidity and, worst of all, Luke had abandoned me.

If this was what it meant to be in love with an outlaw, I wasn't sure if it was what I really wanted.

TO BE CONTINUED!

…The wait won't be long!

NOTE FROM PORSCHA STERLING

Thank you for reading!

Yes, there will be a 4th book! There is more that I want to happen with the crew—lots of things that need to come out and I couldn't rush through it by squeezing it into this book. They aren't done just yet and I hope you're okay with that! One thing for sure, I'm trying to get it out very soon. I've already started so stay tuned! I want to thank everyone who waited for me to get this book out. I'm expecting a little one soon and also getting married in only a few days so it's a busy time for me and my family. I appreciate you all for being so patient, supportive and uplifting!

Part 4 will be out soon but in the meantime, join my Facebook group (Porscha Sterling's VIP Reading Group) so you can get some exclusives and interact with me. I love to hear what you all have to say! I love to interact with my readers because I APPRECIATE ALL OF YOU! Hit me up!

Check out my website to get an overview of the characters mentioned in this installment of the series. I pulled some visuals so you'll know what they kind of look like to me when I'm writing about them. Hope you like what you see! Visit www.porschasterling.com to check them out!

Please make sure to leave a review! I love reading them!

I would love it if you reach out to me on Facebook, Instagram or Twitter!

If you haven't already, text PORSCHA to 25827 to join my text list. Text ROYALTY to 42828 to join our email list and read excerpts and learn about giveaways.

Peace, love & blessings to everyone. I love allllll of you!

MAKE SURE TO LEAVE A REVIEW!

Text PORSCHA to 25827
to keep up with Porscha's latest releases!

To find out more about her, visit www.porschasterling.com

Join our mailing list to get a notification when Leo Sullivan Presents has another release! Text **LEOSULLIVAN** to **22828** to join!

To submit a manuscript for our review, email us at <u>leosullivanpresents@gmail.com</u>

Get LiT!

Download the LiT app today and enjoy exclusive content, free books, and more!

CPSIA information can be obtained
at www.ICGtesting.com
Printed in the USA
LVHW040016010319
609156LV00003B/204

9 781946 789068